THE BRIDES OF WOODMYST

The Brides of Woodmyst

THE WOODMYST CHRONICLES BOOK VII

Robert E Kreig

WHITEKEEP BOOKS

For Fred and Rita.

The Realm

THE FROZEN WASTE

THE CORE LANDS

BLACKROCK HAVEN

WINTERMARSH

IRONFIELDS

ERIMOOR

WHITEKEEP

BLACKSHORE

THE CANYONS OF TERKITH

REDLOCH

MALLOWHILL

STRONGHOLDT

LIGHTHOUSE

THE
SEA
OF
SOLACE

MELAMWED

THE PILLARS OF MOHAA

HAVENCREST

KALIBARD

CLEARFOO

THE SHADOW FAR

BROOKNESS

WINTERSPRING

OAKBEACH

THE
FOREST
OF
RHUN

MEADOWMOOR

WOODMYST

NEWHOLT

OSTFORD

DELLMOOR

OLDCASTLE

THE

GRASSBEACH

BELBURN

PRYHOLT

GREYROSE

LUNKHUL
FOREST

THE WESTERN SEA

THE EASTERN SEA

DWEAGAN

BARROWFIELD

THE SEA OF LUNKHUL

REDEDGE

LINPORT

N
W   E
S

BUTTEREDOE

BYVIEW

ROSEFORD

FREYMOOR

BELMORE

Prologue

Orange, yellow, and red adorned the path before her. It was leaf litter, discarded by the long branches that stretched over the road to the west.

She shuffled her feet through the mess, rustling and crunching the dried foliage as she dawdled along. She folded her arms tightly across her chest, her eyes moving around to soak in her surroundings.

Parts of the wild had reclaimed the trail here and there. She couldn't remember the last time a wagon, or a team of horsemen, had used the road.

At least, not since the aftermath of the Mirikin.

Birds chattered and fluttered from branch to branch. Some of them eyed her cautiously as she drew near to them before zipping away through the trees or into the undergrowth to hide.

She understood why Alice had spent so much time out here.

It teemed with life.

In a small clearing, a short distance from the road, a brace of deer pawed the leaf litter to get to the grass roots beneath. She startled a few of them, causing them to look at her. This alarmed the others in the group, distracting them from their feast.

Several snorts and nostril flares attracted the attention of a large buck.

His majestic form appeared in the clearing, moving between his harem and the young woman on the road.

Her heart skipped a beat as she stared at his immense antlers. Spread out wide over his head, the intimidating growth could easily cause her irreparable damage.

They had her to stay inside the walls. Her aunt had specifically warned her she would be safer in Woodmyst. There was imminent danger from outside now that the Maji had ascended.

"I just need time to be alone," she had replied. "I need to find a place to reflect."

"Try the ruins," Joanne urged. "There is power and strength there."

"That's for you and the coven."

"It's for all of us, Catherine."

"I don't think so." She shook her head. "I need to find a place for me."

"There's nothing you can do for them," Joanne told her, perceiving her thoughts. "Your mother and sister are lost to us. They will never yield to our cause."

"I still need time to be alone," she replied.

And so it was. She had set out to find that place to think and reflect. To meditate.

After leaving the confines of Woodmyst and moving along the western road, she felt more and more at peace. The farther she walked, and the less that she could see the walls, the more at ease she became.

Until now.

Facing off with a monstrous stag made her fearful, on edge and increasingly nervous.

It padded the ground, flared its nostrils and lowered its head.

I should have stayed inside the walls.

She turned her head slightly, trying not to move too much, too suddenly. The wall was beyond her view and screaming would only aggravate the beast.

Running wouldn't be of any use as the creature was larger, faster and would have her in an instant.

It lunged.

Her heart throbbed in her ears.

The stag raced towards her, its antlers angled for her body.

She instinctively lifted her hands in defence.

A tiny part of her brain seemed to trigger.

A dark place awakened.

Something that she hadn't touched before.

Her lips moved.

Her voice was distant, unemotional.

There was no fear.

There was no care.

She felt nothing.

"Absorb."

The stag toppled over and over, flipping onto its back.

It kicked violently, trying to lift itself back to its feet. Instead, it could only cry out as a deepening agony swept over its body.

Pale, twisting vaporous forms seeped from the beast's eyes, stretching through the air towards the young woman.

With a thud, the stag's legs dropped to the ground as it rolled onto its side.

More cloud-like forms permeated through the creature's skin surrounding its sockets, spreading wider and wider until its entire body seemed to be covered with a white, shimmering haze.

Twisting and folding together, the misty form soaked into her fingertips.

It filled her.

Renewed her strength.

Crammed her with vigour.

A wide smile beamed upon her face as the stag breathed its last.

She had taken everything it was and absorbed it.

She felt strong.

She felt powerful.

She felt alive.

She scanned the trees for the rest of the herd.

The woods were empty.

The deer had run away.

Even the birds had vanished.

A tiny element of disappointment swept over her as she peered at her hands.

The energy flowing through her veins, her muscles, her spirit was beyond anything she had ever experienced.

Beyond anything that she had thought possible.

But it wasn't enough.

This is my awakening.

This is my ascension.

A hunger had developed.

She wanted more.

She needed more.

One

Emily ran the brush through her daughter's hair. Alice sat on a wooden stool in her bedroom, staring at the looking glass on the dresser, still getting used to the appearance of the girl staring back at her. White had replaced her dark hair and piercing blue eyes watched her where once a deep brown pigment had been.

It wasn't just her external features that were different.

Deep inside, she understood her full potential. She knew what she was capable of. Once the darkness inside of her was expelled, the light exposed to her the extensiveness of who and what she was.

Alice wanted so much to share this with her mother, but the auburn woman wasn't ready for such an overflow of information. She had just found out that her own sister and elder daughter were partakers of an unforgivable crime.

The murder of innocents.

Even Alice, who now had a deeper understanding of many things, felt shocked that her own family could be capable of such a thing.

She saw the faces of little Antony and Holly flash through her mind. It took a great deal of energy to fight back the urge to cry again.

Not in front of Mama, she told herself.

Alice looked over her mother's attire. She dressed in her warrior garb, all cleaned and polished. She strapped her leather breastplate to her chest, vambraces wrapped over her forearms and greaves stretched from her knees to her ankles. She wore a narrow, slightly curved sword on her hip, sheathed on a belt fastened to her waist.

"How do you want it?" the auburn woman asked.

"Tail," Alice replied. "High up."

Emily took a dark ribbon from the dresser and tied the girl's hair up. "Do you want me to braid it?"

"No." Alice shook her head slightly.

"Hold still." Her mother placed her hand on top of her daughter's head to steady it.

Alice sighed.

She was the leader of people, the Kayl'sro of the Agrodien, a formidable sorceress, and her mother still had the irritating ability to overpower her.

"Don't huff at me," Emily chided.

"Sorry, Mama."

"Now," the auburn woman said, placing her hands on the girl's shoulders, "all done. What are you going to wear?"

"My armour," Alice told her matter-of-factly. "The bearskin and the iron claws."

Emily moved to a wardrobe positioned against the wall to the side of the room and opened the doors.

"I also need my cloak." Alice pointed to the right side of the closet, where a long leather garment hung. "The one given to me by the Agrodien females."

She rose and started lacing up her trousers.

"You don't want to wear a dress, or something nice?"

"Can you see a dress in there, Mama?" the girl asked as she reached for her boots by the foot of the bed.

"You should get one," Emily said as she lifted the cloak from the wardrobe.

"I'm the Kayl'sro," Alice reminded her mother. "A dress is not good apparel for a warrior."

"You're meeting your new sisters," the other replied, draping the leather garment over the bed. "One of them just happens to be the queen of Newholt. It's a special occasion, Alice. We should get one for you just in case you are required to attend more special occasions."

"When this is all over," Alice said, wishing the conversation would change topic, "I'll consider it."

She slid her boots on and started strapping her greaves over her shins. Emily took her daughter's breastplate from the floor and handed it over.

"We should let them stay here," she said, sounding concerned.

"Why?"

"She's a queen."

"We've fitted out two caverns nearby as best we could in such a short time," Alice informed her mother as she slid the armour over her chest. "We've given them bedding, blankets, and furniture. In some ways, the equipment in those two caverns is better than what we have here. They'll be fine, Mama."

"I don't know..." Emily shook her head as she helped her daughter fasten the breastplate. "Queen Amicia has a refined taste. Just look at that clock that she gave to Woodmyst."

"They'll be fine," Alice said again, placing a hand on the woman's cheek. "You worry too much, Mama."

"Says the girl with grey hair," Emily responded drily.

"I have reason to worry. I'm a leader of a great people," she replied. "All I seem to do is worry about them. And it's silver. Not grey."

***

Alice stepped upon the porch, her leather cloak draped over her shoulders, the cowl lowered so her hair could trail over her back. Her two swords sheathed and fastened to her hips, their hilts sticking out from beneath the shroud within easy grasp.

She looked over at all the others gathered near the hut. They were all dressed in their best, ready to receive the approaching guests. A small smile crept on her face as she noticed several children fidgeting and tugging at their clothing after having shirts tucked in tightly into their trousers. The little boys were the most annoyed by the ordeal, touching their neatly combed heads only to have their hands smacked by watchful mothers.

"Kayl'sro," Yuri said as he greeted the girl with a slight bow.

"Good morning," she replied, stepping off the porch and to his side.

The Agrodien towered above her as he gestured to a row of fourteen reptilian warriors standing tall and proud. They wore their armour well. She guessed they must have spent the most part of the night before cleaning their coverings and polishing their weapons.

"Very impressive," she said as she strolled along the line to inspect their appearance. She stopped before of the last warrior in the line. It was a young female of whom Alice had grown very fond. She placed a hand on the warrior's shoulder. "And how are you this morning, Nola'ee?"

"Scared, Kayl'sro," the other answered.

"Scared?" Alice frowned playfully. "Well, that's not good. I can't have my personal bodyguard being afraid."

"I'm sorry." Nola'ee lowered her head in shame.

"I'm joking," Alice said, lifting the warrior's head gently with a finger on the chin. "I'm a little nervous as well. It's to be expected."

Nola'ee nodded before Alice continued a little further. Yuri clasped a reassuring hand upon the female's shoulder before steering her in line to follow the girl.

"Remember your duty," he said to her in their tongue. "You are the first guard of the Kayl'sro. She chose you above all others."

The young warrior nodded again.

Alice locked eyes with her husband, who was standing a few yards away. He wore his finest trousers and shirt with a long dark coat that hung to his thighs, covering his frame. It reminded her of the attire that the bookkeepers wore in Woodmyst.

"You look handsome, Arthur," she said, straightening his collar with her fingers.

"And you look like a princess." He slid his hands around her waist and planted a kiss on her lips.

"Can't you two let up for a couple of hours, at least," David Gyfford grumbled. "I barely got a wink of sleep last night because of…"

"David," Emily snapped. "There are children present."

He looked at her sheepishly.

"Sorry," he said. "But honestly. I don't know how you put up with it. I'm sleeping way out the back and I can hear them. You're in the room right across the way."

"I stuff cotton in my ears," she informed him as she moved to his side.

"Does that work?"

"For the best part." She lowered her voice.

Both chuckled softly as the procession moved onto the open ground.

Alice held Arthur's arm as they walked over the pastureland. Her heart was beating quicker and quicker with each step. Soon, she would meet two others like herself. She could feel their approach.

In moments, they would be together.

To her right she could see Liana, her dragon, sleeping near the entrance to the large cave. She stretched upon the grass, soaking up the morning sun.

Walking parallel to her, somewhere between the dragon and the group, was Shadow the rukyul. His huge form seemed to glide through the long grass as he scanned the crowd.

His face turned towards the trees on the far side of the glade. Suddenly, he stopped moving and sniffed the air. His hackles raised as he bared his teeth.

"They're here," Alice announced.

She gestured for the rukyul to relax. It tilted its head curiously before resting its haunches on the grass.

One by one, a line of horsemen slowly made their way through the tree line on the north-eastern edge of the clearing. First, there were five, then ten. In the end, twenty-two riders and four pack horses made their way towards the small settlement.

"There they are," Richard pointed. He adjusted his legs as he placed his weight on his walking stick. Sure enough, they could see two women riding near the centre of the group.

"Good eyes," his wife Becka commented.

"Only the legs are weak, my dear."

"Just the knees," she riposted. "Everything above them works just fine for me."

"Not you two as well," David grumbled.

"Shhh," Yuri hissed as the horses drew nearer.

Alice lowered herself to a knee, bowing her head in reverence.

Her Agrodien warriors followed suit immediately. Only the younglings hesitated, but were quickly brought into place by their mothers tugging at their arms.

Several men dropped from their steeds and assisted the two women from their horses. Within moments, they moved past their entourage and stood before Alice.

"Your Majesty," the girl offered. "Welcome to my home."

"Please stand." The queen gestured for them to rise with her hand.

Alice did so, examining the women who stood before her. Their eyes appeared as hers with striking blue pigmentation. Snowy streaks extended from their temples.

The people of the glade lifted themselves from the ground. Those who remembered Amicia Elynbrigge looked on with amazement. The transformation was clearly apparent, just as it was with Alice.

Both women looked at the girl in awe.

The queen's chin quivered before she, and the other dropped to their knees.

"My Prime," they both said together before bursting into tears.

Alice didn't have words to respond with. She understood they had all experienced and shared something that no other could ever comprehend. So, she did the only thing that made sense.

She fell to her knees and wrapped her arms around both women.

"It's all right," she told them. "We're together now."

Two

Lor stabbed at the embers with a long stick, evoking the flames to life as he placed another chock of timber onto the hearth.

"They've been gone a while," Alan, his son, muttered as he peered over his shoulder at the cabin set into the rock.

"They have much to discuss," Lor told him, placing a pot of water onto a rectangular iron frame set over the fire.

"Why couldn't they talk here?" the boy asked.

"There are some things that boys and girls don't need to hear," Linet, his mother, answered.

"Alice and Arthur are only a year older than me," he argued.

Lor looked at his son sternly. "Alice is the Kayl'sro. She is our leader. She needs to be in there. Arthur is her husband, and as her husband, he needs to support his wife. One day, you'll understand."

Alan pouted and turned to the fire, resting his chin on his hands. He was sitting cross-legged by his mother's feet, growing more and more agitated by the minute.

They all were.

The three women had vanished into the cabin with a small entourage for a seemingly long time. Commander Brondt and Captain Thornton had accompanied the two sorceresses from the coast into Alice's hut. The Kayl'sro had requested that her husband be by her side. But she had also invited her mother and Yuri the Agrodien.

Four large reptilian warriors stood in a line on the ground by the porch, guarding the entrance to the dwelling. Their right hands rested upon the hilts of their curved swords, strapped to their waists.

Behind them, by the door, Nola'ee watched the glade vigilantly. Her eyes scanned the dark shadows beneath the trees to the eastern edge, straining to see any movement or sign of the dark creatures that had surrounded their homes previously.

Everyone else in the encampment had found a place to sit and wait.

The men from Newholt set up camp nearby, pitching tents and gathering wood for their fires.

A few of the visitors found themselves on edge as both Shadow and Liana approached them to investigate the strangers.

"Go on, get," David heard one man shout at the rukyul.

Shadow had crept up behind the soldier and had sniffed the bent over man as he picked firewood from the ground.

The creature instantly set his hackles on edge and his lips peeled open to bare giant, white, razor-sharp teeth.

"Oh shit," the soldier gasped, dropping the timber and reaching for his sword.

"I wouldn't do that," David called, racing from his place by the hearth towards the beast. "He's likely to have you for supper."

"Call him off," the man pleaded as the rukyul stepped forward, growling menacingly.

"He's not mine to master," the other told him. "Just take your hand away from your sword."

"I'll be dead if I do that."

"You'll be dead if you don't."

"Do what the big man says, Edmond," another man hollered.

The soldier raised his hands out to his sides.

"There," he said. His voice quivered and his body shook with fear. "Now what?"

"I don't know," David told him, moving slowly to the rukyul's side. He tried talking to the beast in the softest voice that he could muster. "Shadow, back down."

The creature closed his lips, concealing his fangs. Slowly, his hackles lowered as he sniffed at the man curiously. With a low grunt, Shadow turned and moved away towards the open ground of the clearing.

"Are you all right?" David asked.

"I think I shit my duds," the other replied as several others came running to his side.

"I thought you were a goner for sure, Edmond," a young man laughed. "That thing could have had you in two bites."

"That's not funny." Edmond held his hands before him, watching them shake furiously.

"You should sit down a bit," another told him, guiding him by the arm to the ground.

"I'm sorry, Lieutenant."

"No need to apologise." The officer smiled at him. "I think you handled that much better than I would have. Sit here and rest a bit."

"Yessir."

"I'm Hugh Brook." The lieutenant extended his hand to the large bald man from the glade.

"David Gyfford."

"This man that you helped is Edmond Cobham." Brook gestured to the other.

"Hello." Cobham gave a small wave. "And thank you."

"My men…" the lieutenant turned to the others gathered about. "Jendryng, Sparrow, Vawdrey, Cheyne and Bacon."

"I apologise," David said to them. "But I don't remember names all that well."

Brook turned his attention to the rukyul moving towards the livestock. "That creature can't be tamed. How is it you have one here?"

"Alice has a way with animals. Some kind of connection."

"It's never attacked any of you?"

"No. But I wouldn't want to be near it if she wasn't close by."

"And the dragon?" Brook glanced at the giant beast. It had moved towards the large cave and plonked itself onto the ground to sleep.

"A gift from the Haigok," David said. "We've discovered she's a gentle beast by nature."

"Didn't dragons destroy Woodmyst?" Sparrow asked.

"A long time ago," the large man acknowledged. "But that was under the instruction of the Haigok."

"And now you're allies?" Sparrow shook his head. "With your enemies?"

"We are," David agreed. "With time, things change. Enemies become friends."

"And friends can become enemies," Brook added. "Woodmyst, for example."

David frowned and peered towards the south, remembering his home.

"Indeed."

***

"Other people will be under threat," Alice warned the small gathering seated around the table. "The Maji has an instinctive desire to conquer all. It's his nature to take control."

"Why didn't we see it before?" Emily asked. "Takmel lived with us. He was part of us."

"I don't think he ever was, Mama," the girl answered. Her eyes filled with sadness as she peered at the others around the table. "I think Takmel knew that a part of him was never going to be satisfied with being a simple man living amongst us."

"It was his destiny," Amicia broke in. "His fate was to be raised amongst witches. The Sovereign, and indeed most of the Mirikin, believed the prophecy of the Maji to be fulfilled under the watchful eye of Yasmeen Svoboda. But that didn't come to fruition. I thought, when Sumaiyya fell on the battlefield, that the prophecy proved to be false right there and then. But, upon reflection, I can see it was still being unravelled and gradually reaching its fulfilment.

"He *was* raised amongst witches," she continued. "You. Your sister, Joanne. The Seven and the Erilian warrior women. Your daughters. All he needed to do was sow his seeds of influence over time. It would appear that his focus was upon the Seven all this time."

"And Catherine," Alice put in. "But I suspect she needed little coercion."

"Alice," Emily chided. "She's your sister."

"Something changed in her after Papa died," the girl replied. She reached across the table and placed her hand on her mother's. "I was too young to see until now. There was, and is, a deep hatred in her. Like a dark chasm. And it still grows."

"These other people that are under threat," Arthur said. "What can we do for them?"

"Nothing," Ursula answered. Her eyes glistened as tears built on her lashes. "We three must remain here. We need to spend this time to unify and build our connection to one another. We don't have the numbers to help anyone out there. And we don't have the strength to fight the Maji and the Seven."

"So?" Brondt looked at his wife curiously. "We just let people die?"

She inclined her head, frowning apologetically.

"The worst of it is that our home may come under attack while we remain here," she told him. "But we need to remain. I need you here with me."

He took her hand in his.

"I'll be right here," he assured her. "Newholt will still be there when we return. We left her in excellent hands. The generals and admirals are prepared to defend her and I trust them to do what they can to ensure that our people remain safe and sound."

"I know they will," she said, hiding her fears.

"We are not many," Yuri said, peering to the surface of the table. "We are no army. How we fight magic and army?"

"We will fight magic," Alice told him, gesturing to Amicia and Ursula. "Concerning Takmel's forces, I really don't know what to do. He doesn't just control the guards of Woodmyst. He also has an armada in Dweagan, left there after the defeat of the White Witch. The forces in Dweagan remain loyal to him also."

"Not to mention those dark creatures in the woods," Brondt reminded them.

Emily moved her gaze to the other soldier seated at the table.

"You seem rather quiet, Captain Thornton," she said. "Have you anything to add?"

He pursed his lips and nodded.

"You're forgetting the west coast," he told them. "There are loyalists to Sumaiyya Tarkin from Wintermarsh in the north to the Griralith Pass. Or, at least, what remains of it. If the word hasn't reached them already about the ascension of the Maji, it will soon enough. Not only will we be contending with soldiers and ships to our south, but we will be fucked in the arse by those buggers in the west at the same time. Begging your pardon, my ladies."

Alice placed her hand strategically over her mouth, pretending to scratch her lip to hide her grin.

"What we do, Kayl'sro?" Yuri sounded concerned.

"We bide our time," she told him. "We three need to build our strength and prepare. Perhaps some time connecting with one another may help with building a strategy for what we must face."

"Do you need a place?" Arthur asked. The others looked at him inquisitively. "A special location? The Seven have the tree in Woodmyst, for example."

"The glade will suffice," Alice replied, lacing her fingers with his.

"Do you know where this new power comes from?" Emily asked them. "It seems strange that you were all affected so similarly, and at the same moment."

The women shared a look, meeting each other's blue eyes momentarily.

"We are Three of the Four," Alice answered. "Or, at least, that's where our power is drawn from."

"Three of the Four?" Arthur furrowed his brow.

Emily shook her head. "The gods?" she glanced around the table to see that all others seemed to share her confusion. Her eyes landed on Alice. "But you don't believe in the gods."

"I still don't." She frowned. "But I cannot deny that my power is drawn from life. Just as Ursula draws hers from the sky and Queen Amicia draws hers from the earth."

"Three of the Four," Arthur said. "So, who is the fourth?"

"The Maji, of course," Brondt suggested. "Who else would take their power from death?"

The three women shot a quick glance at one another.

Yuri noticed the exchange and held his tongue.

Three

The auditorium of the assembly hall was dark and full of deep shadows. Only a few of the lanterns posted along the walls and the supporting beams had been lit.

Takmel leant back in his chair, slumping slightly as he placed his elbows on the armrests, pressing a finger to his brow. His mind was engaged in deep thought as he considered what his next move would be.

Newholt had held his army of creatures at bay. He needed to send a more formidable force to conquer the seaside city.

He could march his soldiers from Dweagan and sail his warships around the horn. A coordinated attack from the ocean and the land may be enough to see Queen Amicia's generals surrender, or die.

Either outcome would have the same result.

Newholt would be his.

But he also needed to send ships to the west. Wintermarsh and Ironfields needed to be roused. Soldiers loyal to the White Witch were still guarding his home, where he lived as an infant.

Or at least Vonavo, his once-loyal guardian, had told him so.

He had no reason to doubt the words of the Gomatha. And the Gomatha had no reason to distrust Takmel.

That was until the Maji stole the life force from the vaporous being and his kind.

"What troubles you, my love?" a soft voice called from the aisle that stretched through the centre of the hall. His mind snapped back to reality as he moved his eyes towards the speaker.

His first wife, Catherine, strolled towards him. Her hands were behind her back and her body swayed with a confident swagger.

"You look different," he said.

"How can you tell in this gloom?"

She waved a hand, sending ribbons of flame along the walls to ignite the unlit lanterns.

He sat up straight, alarmed by the action she had taken.

"You've been practising." He glanced at the lights.

"A little," she agreed, climbing the steps to the platform.

"I've never seen you do something like that before," he said, peering to her curiously. "It's more like something that your aunt would do."

She lowered herself onto his lap and kissed his lips.

"Let's not talk of her," Catherine whispered. "Or any of the others. Talk to me. What troubles you?"

He wrapped his arms around her and held her tightly.

"I think I will need to send a few of the others to be my representatives," he told her. "I can't be everywhere at once. But I can stay connected to them if they go in my place."

"You plan to break the Seven?"

"I believe I must." He sounded saddened by the idea.

She tilted her head to the side as she considered his face. He looked tortured.

A deep connection had taken place between Takmel and his nine wives on the night of his ascension.

They were one.

All of them.

To separate would be painful.

No wonder he appeared so wounded.

"I know you don't want to hear this," she began, "but the Sovereign took to a similar strategy, if you remember. She sent the others of the Mirikin to all corners of the realms to wait for the time to strike."

"That time never came," he replied. "Svoboda was killed by the Seven, if you recall."

"That's not my point, my beloved." She stroked his face gently with her hand. "She could keep a strong connection with them all the way from her palace in Blackrock Haven. You are much stronger than she ever was."

"So, you think I should break the Seven?"

"I think you should do what you think is right." Catherine placed her forehead against his shoulder.

"That doesn't make it any easier," he told her. "If I do decide to send any of them in my place, I need to consider who and to where. Should I send them alone or in twos?"

"Just remember one thing," she whispered.

"What is that?"

"Who your first love was," Catherine said, turning her face to lock onto his eyes. "Who it was that helped you from the beginning. Who it was that kept your secrets safe and sound. Who it is that will not leave your side. Ever."

He got the message.

"Don't worry yourself, my love," he assured. "I could never be apart from you."

She relaxed her posture and rested against his frame. He ran his hand over her waist and held onto her.

Some silence passed before Catherine spoke again.

"I think you should stop the supplies to the caverns."

"I gave my word," he replied. "Besides, they are family. We don't simply abandon our family."

She sighed.

"You disapprove of my decision?" Takmel asked.

"They are a threat to you and this city," Catherine explained. "We can't rely on them to keep peace with us."

"I don't believe they will," he replied.

"Why not?" She sat up and turned to face him.

"She meets with the queen of Newholt and another woman as we speak."

"You know this, how?"

"I have eyes on them."

"Your creatures from the north?"

"Yes."

She glared at him momentarily.

"I hope you don't keep watch of me when I am not in your presence."

"No need," he assured her with a tiny grin. "We are connected. We are as one, you and I."

She thought back to the look of surprise on his face when she had ignited the unlit lanterns only moments ago.

Not all that connected.

She lowered herself to him again and ran her fingers over the stubble growing on his face.

"I should shave," he said.

"Let it grow," she whispered. Her voice resonated around the empty room.

It frightened him a little.

"There is something different about you."

She giggled softly and kissed his chin.

"All is well, my love," she told him before nestling against his chest again.

Four

His good eye moved over her bare skin slowly, scrutinizing every curve and line from her forehead to her toes. Her soft breaths swept over his chest with every exhale she made. A calloused hand rested on his shoulder. Her thigh draped over his loins.

She was exhausted.

So was he.

But duty called.

He edged towards the side of the bed, causing her to stir awake.

"Where are you going?" she asked.

"I'm on night patrol, remember?" he answered.

"No," she groaned, lifting herself from him before slumping onto the mattress to his side. "I don't remember much at all. You got me drunk again."

"The only way to get you into bed, my dear captain!" He smirked.

"You play dirty, Landon." She chuckled softly as her eyes closed again.

He sat up and threw his legs over the side of the bed. His gaze fell upon her flesh again. This time, he ran his fingers gently down her spine. She reacted with a soft moan.

"Keep that up," she said, "and you'll be back in here, Lieutenant."

"I should go." He got to his feet and lifted his trousers from the floor. "Will you be all right?"

"I've sailed from one side of the ocean to the other," she reminded, turning over to face him. She flicked her long, dark hair from her face and peered at him in query. "I have twenty men under my command and you ask me if I will be all right."

"It feels strange leaving you here on your own," he told her as he tied the cords of his pants.

She winked playfully. "I'll be fine," she answered. "I plan to return to the *Gypsy* later. I should start thinking about another run to Dendadia before all my coin runs dry."

"How soon?" he asked. "For how long?"

She heard a hint of concern in his voice.

"I don't know." She sat up and wiped her eyes. "I don't plan to linger there. Perhaps a week if the weather holds."

"Oh." He sat on the edge of the bed to put his boots on.

She slid over to him and ran her hands over his back and shoulders.

"Come with me," she suggested. "I've got a bed on the ship big enough for the two of us. We could walk the streets of Dendadia and see the marble columns of the citadel together. We can listen to the melodious chimes in the Temple of Four and watch the sunset over the Bay of Dreams. Come with me, please. We could leave tomorrow."

He lowered his head, as if in pain.

"I have my duty," he grumbled. "I can't just simply leave. If I could, I would. I would go anywhere with you, Davine. To the ends of the Earth. But I can't. Not yet."

She rested her chin on his shoulder and let out a long, soft sigh.

***

Straightening his eye patch, Lieutenant Landon Wake quickened his pace as he started climbing the road to the palace gates. Several guards posted along the sides of the wide thoroughfare saluted him as he passed by.

This was a new and strange affair for him. He wasn't used to such formalities.

Being a lieutenant rarely required the men to pay him so much attention. He had walked this road many times before without having as much as a look in his direction from the other men.

After all, he was an officer of the auxiliary forces. A leader to the men, who, like him, had been wounded in battle or were not seen as being fit enough to fight in the regular army, or stand guard at the palace.

Men who were too fat to run. Men who were too scrawny to hold broad swords. Men who could not hit a target with a bow. Men who were missing parts.

Those were the men Wake worked with.

The docks, or the marketplace, were the sectors that they watched over. He and his squadron would mill about and watch for any trouble. They kept their eyes peeled for thieves, scallywags and disruptive drunks who threatened the peace.

Until recently, the worst that any of them had dealt with was old men pissing against the walls of the library as they made their way home from the tavern.

Then the dark creatures from the north came.

Everything changed after that.

Commander Brondt had given him a position at the palace. Overseer of Arms.

When he enquired what they expected of him with such a lofty title, the Commander had simply told him it was a very important role.

"Good morning, Sub-Commander," an older man dressed in navy regalia called from the gates.

"Vice-Admiral Morris," Wake said with a curious smile. "I'm not one to correct my superiors, sir. But if you care to look at my uniform, you will see that I am…"

"A lieutenant," the other said, and grinned. "Yes, yes. I can see your attire. Although, it is a little unkempt."

"It's old," the lieutenant replied. "Just like the one who wears it."

"Not anymore, Sub-Commander." The vice-admiral turned to face the palace as Wake drew alongside. "You've been promoted. The

Overseer of Arms is not a job for a mere lieutenant. So, Commander Brondt saw to it that we give you a rank that fits the bill."

Wake felt a knot tighten in his stomach.

"I don't understand." He stopped walking, coming to a halt at the base of the steps leading up to the palace's large doors. "How can I simply leap from lieutenant to sub—"

"Sub-Commander," Morris finished. "Commander Brondt is our commander. He can bloody well do what he bloody well wants to do. It's as simple as that."

"And here I was, thinking that the Overseer of Arms position was just some cushy position he came up with to keep me content until I retire."

"Sorry to disappoint you." The vice-admiral turned towards the doors again. "This way, sir."

"Sir?" Wake raised his brow as he followed the other.

"You outrank me, Sub-Commander," the older man chuckled.

"Oh my," Wake gasped. He swallowed hard and made his way up the steps. His legs felt wobbly, and the world seemed to spin.

"Commander Brondt must have seen something in you, sir," Morris assured him. "Otherwise, he wouldn't have made you second in command of Newholt's forces."

"Second in...?" Wake put a hand to his stomach. His heart raced. It felt as if it was about to burst from his chest. "I think I need to sit down."

"Here..." the vice-admiral took the other by the arm. "There are seats inside."

"He made a mistake," the younger man stated. "I'm not the man for this job."

"Yes, you are, sir," the other said, pulling him through the doors and steering him towards a chair positioned against the wall of the foyer. "All your men have claimed that you are the only one that they would willingly follow into battle. All the civilians you protected on the docks gave their support for your promotion. Captain Thornton, who has accompanied the queen and the commander on their trek, recommended you. There are others who have fought beside you at the battle of Woodmyst who gave their encouragement. Everyone who has ever met you has said as much. Landon Wake is the man for the job. So, here it is. Embrace it, son."

Wake took in some deep breaths as he rested on the seat. He looked up to the vice-admiral standing nearby. His eyes moved to the guards standing at attention about the room.

"All right," he said, feeling his heart settling down. He looked back at the older man. "So why are we here in the palace?"

"The commander has made an appointment for you to meet with the royal tailors," Vice-Admiral Morris replied. "It's time for that old uniform of yours to be replaced with something more fitting."

***

Wearing his damson cloak, Takmel strolled along the corridor of the storehouse with the master bookkeeper, Lewis Drayton, by his side. He scanned the countless barrels of cider and ale that rested on their sides in tall racks along the walls on either side of them.

"We should have a neat surplus of coin this season if we can transport this stock to Dweagan before the snow closes the road to the south," Drayton said.

"It'll be done," the young man replied. His voice was distant.

"There are rumours," the bookkeeper added, "that you intend to sail the warships into the Eastern Sea. Are we at war with someone, my lord?"

"Just a precaution," Takmel replied, continuing to peer at the barrels. "How many trips will this lot take? I'd like them in Dweagan sooner than later."

"We've ten teams of bullocks that aren't being used by the quarry, and another twenty teams of horses that could cart this away in say..." the older man looked back towards the way they had come from, mentally calculating the number of barrels lining each wall. "Perhaps three drives."

"Get it underway." Takmel peered towards the doorway at the end of the room and made his way towards it, hastening his pace a little.

"Forgive me, my lord..." the other bowed his head slightly. "But is everything all right? I don't mean to pry, but you seem distracted."

"Distracted?" The Maji turned his head to see the older man struggling to keep up.

"As if you are elsewhere."

Takmel immediately thought of Catherine and the way she had caused the lantern flame to shoot around the assembly hall earlier.

"Small things, Master Bookkeeper," he replied with a small grin. "Small things are on my mind. Nothing to be concerned with."

"Of course." The other grinned back.

"In the meantime, organise the transport of these barrels to Dendadia," Takmel instructed. "We need to maintain the trade agreements and keep the shipping routes open."

"Keep the shipping routes open?" Drayton stopped in his tracks. "I thought that was the responsibility of Newholt."

"I intend to control the shipping routes and all the ports," the younger man explained, turning to face his bookkeeper. "To do so, I must control Newholt."

Lewis Drayton felt a dribble of cold sweat run down his spine. "But Queen Amicia is an ally. Is she not?"

Takmel placed a hand on the other's shoulder and stared into the old man's eyes, pushing past the surface and deeper into the bookkeeper's being.

"You are a loyal servant of Woodmyst, Lewis. I don't think there are any more loyal than you. Please understand, Amicia Elynbrigge is not one who can be trusted. She is a traitor to her kind. She will turn her forces against those who she calls her allies and friends. She has done this before. She will do it again.

"We must take a pre-emptive approach. We must prepare to strike before we give her the opportunity to do so. And she will. But, we need to be assured that we have control of the trade routes of the Eastern Sea.

"Woodmyst must be the power that the lands near and far give homage to. Not Newholt. Not the traitorous Queen Amicia."

"She is a traitor," Drayton agreed. He understood. "We can't let her enact an embargo. We can't let her prevent supplies from getting through to the people."

"Precisely." Takmel felt the corners of his mouth rise. "Most of the warships will accompany our merchant vessels on this voyage. Once they pass the horn, the navy will sail north to Newholt and our cargo ships will continue east."

"Most of the warships?" Drayton furrowed his brow.

"Hmmm?"

"You said *most* of our warships will accompany the cargo ships. I don't understand."

"Three galleons and five frigates will remain," Takmel explained. "I've got other plans that require their use. But that is for another time."

"Of course, my lord." Drayton bowed. "If I have your leave, I will prepare the transport of these goods."

"Thank you, Master Drayton." Takmel took his hand from the bookkeeper's shoulder.

As the Maji watched the other walk away, back along the corridor of the storehouse, he churned his many thoughts around in his mind. Newholt. Amicia. The trade routes. The glade. Alice and her band of followers. Catherine and her growing abilities.

There was too much happening at once.

Too much to control by himself.

But he dared not show his concerns, especially around his nine wives.

They would see it as a weakness.

They would pounce like ravenous beasts and tear him to shreds if given the opportunity.

He had manipulated them, robbing them of their freedom. He had made them believe they served him of their own will. If they could see his doubts, his concerns, they would try to take back what was theirs.

He couldn't allow that.

Splitting the Seven was becoming more and more the only viable option.

Five

"I still can't get my head around it," Oliver Weston said as he shook his head. He stabbed at the embers with a long stick, sending orange glowing flecks into the air as the fire bit into the chock of timber he had just put in place. "Do the gods possess you now?"

"There are no gods," Alice replied. She nestled against Arthur as her eyes stared into the flames. "There is what there is."

"But you claim to draw your power from Gwendra," he said, peering across to hearth to meet her gaze.

"I draw my power from life," she replied. "Gwendra is the name that man gave to it."

Oliver furrowed his brow. She could see his confusion deepening.

"A cleansing has occurred in the three of us," Alice explained. "Darkness has been expelled, and the power of the three has been accepted. And yes, there have been some sacrifices." Alice ran her fingers over her snow-white braid.

"With this new gift came knowledge too," she continued. "Life, death, earth and sky were just that. Four things coexist alongside one another. It was man who gave them power when he gave them names.

"Those of the north prayed to one called Haan; a word from tongues of old that meant sky. Their understanding was that everything beneath the expanse above should be thankful for the stars, the moon, and the sun that travelled from the east to the west. All existence was beneath Haan. So, all should give Haan their respect."

The children seated about the fire leant forwards, soaking up the words of the young woman. A stillness filled the campsite as Alice continued to speak.

"Those of the south called upon Areang, believing that all owed their survival to that which produced crops to eat and grass for their herds. Tall trees with timber to build with grew from Areang. Rivers flow over her, and our feet are blessed to have the fortune to touch her. She is beneath us, but she loves us so much she provides for us.

"The men of the east bowed to Gwendra. As the sun rises, life renews each day. They saw it wasn't the sky or the Earth that we should thank, but that it was another who held the wellbeing of all in place. Life itself.

"The people of the west saw things from a different perspective. The sun sank into the sea and brought shadow to the land. Grolle was in control. Out of fear, they honoured their deity as insurance against death. Grolle held all in her clutches. In an instant, life could be taken away, just as easily as the sun could be taken from the sky each and every night.

"That's how the four got their power," Alice explained. "Through spoken words."

"Words?" Glaun tilted his head to the side.

"Words," Alice repeated. "Words are powerful. They can be influential. Words can break or ignite hearts. Words can command armies. Spells are conjured. Wars are started. We should not be careless with such power."

Glaun felt a quick, sharp pain in his chest as Alice directed her speech towards him. He was careless with his tongue, and he knew it. He watched her piercing blue gaze dart around to the children seated about before they locked back upon him.

Learn to control yourself, her voice whispered in his mind. *Your loose language will reach young ears no more.*

His chin quivered as tears welled in his eyes. He nodded, silently admitting his guilt to her and acknowledging her instruction.

"What's the matter?" Lilen, his wife, asked from his side.

"Nothing." He tried to hide his shame.

"But now and then," Alice continued, "one of the four believed themselves to be more powerful. More necessary than the others. They would rise and sway humanity to their will."

"Let me guess," Akasati said. "Grolle."

"Not always," the girl said with a smile. "They have each had their moments. Many wars have been fought over the gods. Some have even been written about in those books of yours, Arthur."

"Seems a silly thing to fight over," he replied, tightening his arm over his wife's shoulders. "It took one man to unify the people and get them to understand that the four gods work together and that everything happens because they work together. Doreven Grorewyth, I think his name was. He was the first priest of the Four. Officially, the idea of the four wasn't recognised as being legitimate for another seventy years after he died, but he started the religion that we take for granted today. There's a statue of him in the Temple of Four in Dendadia."

"It seems a bit of an act of desperation when you consider all the factors. Uniting the four, I mean. It was during such a war where the followers of Haan were attempting to gain control of the west. We also need to remember that this occurred in the lands far across the sea to our east. Grorewyth's home, at the time, was Dendadia. So, in an attempt to save his home, he started talking to soldiers on both sides, influencing them with *his* words." He looked at Alice, and then the children, quite pleased with his ability to link his rhetoric with his wife's explanation about the power of speech. Expecting to see engaged faces, he saw bored stares and yawning mouths.

"Well," he said as he lowered his head slightly. "In the end, the people listened, and almost everyone accepted the idea."

Alice tilted her face up to his and kissed his cheek.

"I love you," she whispered.

"So, the gods are real," Oliver remarked.

"They're not gods," Ursula replied. "They exist as beings because of us. Humankind gave them that gift. Without us, they would not be."

"But we would not be without them," David added. "The sky, the earth, life and death are all around us. They surround us and keep us."

"And that would continue to happen even if we did not give them names," Ursula explained. "The sun would continue to rise and set. The rain would fall and the rivers would flow. Crops would grow. Creatures would breed. Life and death would continue their cycle.

"But now they have names," she continued. "Now they are aware. And sometimes, they want more for themselves than they should require."

"And this has happened, I suppose?" Jeremy Schoenbach asked. "I mean, you wouldn't be granted this power from three of the four if it hadn't."

"You are correct," Amicia Elynbrigge replied, nodding to the other. "Something transpired back when the Sovereign first started stretching her fingers across the land. When she first enlisted the others of the Mirikin.

"Grolle was drawn to the energy that was birthed then. There was something familiar in Svoboda that attracted the power of death. But Grolle did not share herself with the Sovereign. Instead, she observed."

"It's unclear whether Grolle enjoyed what she saw," Alice interjected, "or whether she simply felt compelled to watch. You must understand, the four are not malevolent. Nor do they show favour with any people. They are curious. At other times, they are greedy. In any circumstance, it is power that attracts them."

"In this case, Yasmeen Svoboda drew Grolle's attention," Amicia added. "Eventually, her focus fell upon Sumaiyya Tarkin."

"More correctly," Ursula interjected, "the unborn child she carried."

"Takmel," Emily muttered.

"After he was born," explained Amicia, "Grolle continued to watch, spending most of her attention on the happenings of the white witch. By then, death had pulled away from the other three. The balance was askew.

"The advance of the Mirikin followed. The three attempted to counter Grolle's separation as best as they could, influencing some here and there to act against the odds and rise against the tide." She looked across the hearth to Ruttger Harrow, the once commander to the armies of the Lilac Mistress. He sat in a chair with Courtney on his lap.

"The boy is the power that Grolle was drawn to," Amicia continued. "Although, he is not the one that Grolle has chosen."

"Then who?" David asked.

"It's Catherine," Alice told them.

Emily's jaw dropped. Linet, her sister-in-law, was quick to her side, wrapping her arms around the auburn woman.

"I cannot say whether this is a good or bad thing," Alice admitted. "The four have done nothing like this before. One thing is for certain. The four have never been at war with each other. Men have fought over the gods. But the four have never been at war.

"What death has done is incomparable. Why she chose Catherine is something we find confusing.

"However…" Alice peered around the fire to every face. They were all listening intently, hanging on her every word. "You must know this. We three were given this power before she was. The three saw the need to intervene first. Grolle may have been acting out of desperation and offered herself to the first available sorceress. There is no way of knowing for certain."

"Who do we turn to if we can't rely on the gods?" David asked as he scratched his beard.

"Rely on yourself," Arthur told him before moving his gaze over all seated nearby. "Rely on each other. We're strong together. We're a power more intimidating than the Mirikin. We don't need the gods."

"My father said there are no gods," Alice said.

"There are no gods," Arthur called triumphantly.

"There are no gods." David lifted his mug of tea in a mock toast and sculled the contents.

Before long, everyone chorused the words together.

"There are no gods."

***

Dark eyes watched the encampment from the shadows of the trees. Soft clicking sounds emitted from the creature as it slunk through the undergrowth at the edge of the clearing.

It clawed at the moist foliage beneath it as it turned its attention to the ridge to its rear. Many others waited in the blackness. They skulked in the shadows patiently.

Watching, the creature observed those gathered by the fire separating and moving away from the hearth. Its eyes flicked from face to face, always returning to the silver-haired girl.

The master was deeply interested in this one.

She kissed the auburn woman on the cheek and hugged the large, bald man before wrapping an arm around the waist of the boy beside whom she had sat. The two of them, the girl and the boy, headed towards the cabin set into the rock.

The creature's eyes fell upon another dark beast lying on the porch of the cabin.

It lifted its massive head as the young couple approached. Its jaws opened in a wide yawn, revealing its large, pointed teeth. As it closed its mouth, the boy reached his hand out and rubbed the beast on the head.

The creature observed the auburn woman and the bald man following the white-haired girl and the boy into the hut. The large beast on the veranda stood up and stepped down on the ground, moving closer to the campfire as the others moved away to their dwellings.

The beast sniffed the ground near the fire. Its long tongue lapped at some discarded food left behind before it turned its nose to other interesting scents.

It sniffed the dirt by the fire's edge before moving past the light of the flames and onto the grass between the encampment and the trees where the watcher lurked.

Raising its head, the rukyul sniffed the air, turning its face slowly to the left, then to the right. Before long, he was facing directly towards the hidden creatures.

He raised his hackles and bared his teeth.

A deep growl rumbled towards the shadows beneath the trees.

The hidden creatures clicked and crackled their messages to one another.

The master had seen enough.

Like a dark flash, the creatures darted through the forest, fleeing away from the camp.

The beast gave chase, racing into the woods with immense speed.

The watcher turned to see the monstrous shape of the pursuer getting closer and closer. It tried to increase its speed to catch up to its own kind. But they were too far ahead to see.

Only the sounds of their calling whistles and screeches drew it on.

The heavy breaths of the horror giving chase were getting louder and louder.

The dark creature's eyes darted this way and that, searching frantically for an escape.

It realised that running on the ground was not benefiting it.

Seeing a large tree just to the left of its path, it turned and started up the broad trunk.

A quick glance over its shoulder as it climbed revealed the rapid approach of an immense black shadow.

Large white teeth filled its view as it clung to the trunk of the tree.

The beast snapped its jaws shut around the creature's leg and tore it from the tree with a twist of its neck. The creature scraped its claws deep into the bark, leaving long marks behind.

It flung onto the ground with immense force, landing on its chest. It wheezed and coughed as it tried to suck air back into its lungs.

But the rukyul wouldn't let it.

Shadow applied his weight as he pressed his paw against the creature's back.

Loud, wet crunching sounds exploded from deep inside the creature as its ribs broke.

Thick, dark blood spurted from the creature's mouth and nose as its limbs flailed wildly.

The rukyul reached down and picked the creature up in its mouth.

With a violent shake of its head, more bones broke before Shadow dropped the creature back to the ground.

There was no more movement.

There was no more life.

Distant clicks and hoots echoed through the trees.

The rukyul turned its face to the sounds and snorted.

It turned its attention back to the kill and sniffed the carcass.

After a moment, it opened its jaws and fed.

Six

Sub-Commander Landon Wake stood upon the parapet of the palace. He gazed at the horizon out to sea. The definitive line between water and sky was hard to see in the darkness. His only guides were several lights from ships moving upon the ocean.

A cold breeze swept down from the mountains behind him and over his neck. He shivered slightly as the wind penetrated his thick clothes.

"Do you wish to go back inside, sir?" asked a soldier standing beside him.

"Of course I do," Wake answered. "But I'm not ready yet."

He pulled a spyglass from his pocket and extended it to full length before turning towards the north. Following the waterfront, passing over the docks, he paused momentarily on the *Gypsy*.

Davine was there, standing beneath a lantern posted upon the centre mast. He could see her lips moving as she barked orders at her crew, pointing this way and that as men carried equipment and supplies about the vessel.

Her hair was back in a braid and her rapier strapped to her side, hidden slightly by her long coat. She was, however, missing her cavalier hat.

It is dark. He smiled slightly. *Hats are usually attire for the day-light hours.*

From what he could see, she was in her element. She belonged on the ship. Her place was at the helm, not in a house, cooped up inside like some caged bird, waiting for him to come home.

He wanted so much to go with her. Dendadia appealed to him more and more each time he gave it thought. The idea of going there became even more tempting when he pictured himself there with her.

But he couldn't go.

He was now the Sub-Commander of Newholt.

He was the Overseer of Arms.

He now had new and greater responsibilities to see to.

How could he just leave?

He lingered on her a little while longer, pointing the spyglass at her to watch her play commander.

With a deep sigh, he moved the scope along the shore. He stopped on a beacon tower posted atop of a high cliff to the city's northern edge.

The flames were high and the polished iron behind the blaze produced an intense light to beam over the water.

"Perhaps we should make a few extra beacon towers," Wake muttered.

"Sir?"

The soldier's question surprised the Sub-Commander. He didn't realise he'd spoken so loudly.

"Beacon towers," he repeated. "I was just thinking that we should construct some more."

"Begging pardon, sir, but two are enough. Both signal the rocks to the south and north. There really is no need of anymore."

"We could have some directed along the road to the north and south and to the woods to our west," Wake told him. The Sub-Commander peered around to the southern beacon as he lowered the spyglass to his side.

The tower was a little farther away from the palace than its counter-part. Still, the beam of light emitting from it was clearly visible to the naked eye.

The soldier standing beside him turned to look at the woodlands. They were dark and indiscernible in the night's blackness.

"Those bastards could be out there right now," the younger man said. "Couldn't they? And we would be none the wiser."

Wake's mind raced back to the battle with the dark creatures that swarmed upon the city. He turned towards the mountains.

"Indeed, they could be," he replied. "With a few beacon towers directing light out there, we'd be able to know for certain."

"It's a good idea, sir."

Sub-Commander Wake stared into the darkness, nodding to himself as the icy wind swept over him again. He folded the spyglass and started for an open door.

"I think I will go back inside, soldier," he said. "I'll need you to fetch a runner for me."

***

"You've had more than enough mead," said a young woman sitting at a small table beside an older man.

"It's wine," he said and smiled sluggishly. "All the way from the vineyards of Crystalbridge. Do you know where that is?"

"Near the Bay of Dreams."

"The Bay of Dreams," he slurred, raising his mug to his lips.

She watched him as he sculled the rest of the liquid with three large gulps.

"Come to bed, Monty," she insisted, taking his arm in her hands.

He shook his head. "Nope." He dropped the empty cup onto the table. "There's more wine to drink. Did you know they have over twenty barrels of this fine, refreshing liquor stored in the cellar here? And there are hundreds more scattered throughout this city at all the other wonderful taverns, pubs, and drinking rooms. Such a nice drop."

"Please, Monty." She frowned and peered sadly at the man.

"You know, Audrey," he said as he waved to one of the waitresses serving another table nearby, "I might see about becoming the official wine tester for Newholt."

"Monty," the young woman pleaded.

"There isn't much else that I'm good at. Is there?"

A single tear slid down her cheek.

"More wine, sir?" the waitress queried.

"You read my mind," Nathaniel Monteacute replied, offering the empty mug to the other.

"Come home," Audrey whispered as the waitress moved away.

"I no longer have purpose," he told her. He wiped his mouth on his sleeve and turned to face her. She looked at him sadly with watery hazel eyes. Her dark hair draped over her right shoulder, just touching her breast. "At least you still have your youth. I don't even have that."

"They'll find you work," she assured him. "They'll find work for all of us."

"They'll find work for you easily enough. Rose and Kateryn, too. There's plenty of work like that around here."

"Ursula doesn't want us to do that anymore," Audrey reminded him.

"You take what you can in the city," he said. "No work for a man of my age on the docks. And there's no need of a sheriff when you have guards posted all over town. Whoring, on the other hand. Well, there are plenty of ships that come in. So, there's your clientele. And it's honest work. Besides, Ursula's not here to watch over you."

"No, but I am," announced a gruff voice from behind him. He recognised it immediately.

"Evening, Maud," Monteacute said.

She moved around the table and sat in a chair across from him.

"We're worried about you," the older woman grumbled. She glanced over to Audrey. "When this one didn't return home with you, Rose sent for me. Now I'm here."

"You see?" He gestured to Maud. "She was given a position as barkeep at the Upright Banker. Or was it the Burping Diplomat?"

"The Upright Banker," the older woman corrected him.

"And a fine establishment, too," he replied with a nod.

"So, why don't you do your drinking there?"

He moved his gaze around the room. The smell of sour ale, vomit and sweat stung his nostrils. There were several men engaged in a civilised conversation at one number while a heated argument ensued between two men playing a card game at another. One individual slumped over the bar, asleep in his drool. Two or three dozed in chairs against the walls, nursing their mugs as others fondled women in the darker recesses of the inn.

"Why? What's wrong with this place? The Petty Beggar is as fine as any other place in Newholt."

At that moment, the waitress brought a fresh mug of wine and placed it before Monteacute. He reached into his pocket and fished out three copper coins and handed them to the woman.

"Anything for the ladies?" she asked.

"No thank you," Maud replied.

Audrey shook her head.

The waitress returned to the bar, leaving the three to their private discussion.

"It's time to come home," Maud insisted.

"I just paid for this," he argued, lifting the mug to his lips. "Besides, what are you? My wife?" He looked at the younger woman, who was silently weeping. "My wives?"

"We're family, Monty," Audrey blubbered. "We need to stick together and look out for each other. Ursula said that."

"And where is she?" he grumbled. "Off finding work for me, is she?"

"Come on, Audrey." Maud lifted herself from her seat and reached a hand out to the young woman. "We should get back to the others."

"We love you, Monty," Audrey said as she stood to her feet. "I love you."

He felt a lump grow in his throat and his chest tighten.

"You shouldn't waste your time on an old useless man like me," he whispered. "I'm not worth the trouble."

"Then we'll leave you to your thoughts." Maud put her arms around Audrey's shoulders and steered her to the door.

Monteacute took a swig from the mug and stared at the table in silence. His mind raced with thoughts and suppositions as to what paths may lie before him. He saw numerous forks in the road. Each led to a dark place. Each; a short journey. Each; a dead end.

Audrey claimed to love him. And while that may flatter many an old man, especially coming from such a beautiful and young woman, he had heard it many times before. Every time he had shared her bed, or the cots of Rose and Kateryn, they had proclaimed their love to him.

He had always assumed their words were simply part of the exchange. Surely, other customers of the Whitekeep whores had heard the same decree.

I love you.

He snorted a laugh.

It means nothing.

He drained the wine and held the mug up for the waitress to see, shaking it slightly to get her attention.

"Another," he called.

***

Captain Davine Staiger stood atop of the quarterdeck, watching her crew take supplies from the dock and down into the hold of her ship. A tall, well dressed, muscular man of dark complexion stood by her side, flipping through pages in a leather-bound ledger.

"How are we faring, First Officer?" she asked, keeping her eyes on three young men who were struggling with a large chest. The companionway leading down into the belly of the vessel was barely wide enough for the container, and their chosen positions to carry it was more of an obstacle than the item itself. Two of the men were each carrying a corner as the third man backed down the steep stairs, holding one end of the trunk on his own.

He was fine; she noticed. It was the two on one end of the box that were proving to be the problem. The stairwell was clearly not wide enough for both of them to descend together. So, they argued over who it would be to carry the cargo down through the ship.

"You take it," one shouted.

"You have the better hold," the other replied. "It would be easier for you to—"

"One of you take the fuckin' load," the third cried as his feet moved down a step or two, placing the container at an awkward angle.

"Go on," the first man urged the second.

"We seem to be on time, Captain," the First Officer said, replying to her query. "We still have several food stores to move from the dock. The last items to bring aboard will be the barrels of wate—"

"You," Staiger shouted, pointing her finger to the two men arguing over the trunk. "Swabbie."

The first man pointed to himself, taking a hand away from the crate and forcing the second to shift position to cater for the weight.

"Me, Captain?"

"You'll do," she barked. "Leave them and go through the galley to the aft. I want you to clean the privy."

"Captain?"

"You two continue to the hold with that chest," she commanded.

The First Officer lifted his gaze from the ledger and placed it squarely on the men.

"Aye, Captain," the other two replied. The second man shot a cheeky grin at the first as he slowly descended the stairs.

"Captain, I was instructed to load the ship," the man said, taking a few steps towards the quarterdeck.

"Are you the owner of this vessel, Swab?" the First Officer asked. His stare was cold and unforgiving.

"No, sir," the young man replied. His voice trembled slightly as he realised his mistake.

"Do you know who the owner of this vessel is, boy?"

"Yes, sir," he answered, and swallowed hard. "Captain Davine Staiger, sir."

"Do you see her standing beside me?"

"Yes, sir." The young man nodded nervously.

"Is she paying you to work on this vessel?" The First Officer's eyes were devoid of emotion. Blank.

"Yes, sir."

"And has she just given you a direct order?"

"Aye," he replied. His hands shook.

"But, you feel it is all right to question such authority?"

"I – I – I—" stammered the man.

"Clean the privy," the First Officer commanded, "or get off this ship."

The man's chin quivered as he looked at the captain. She glared back at him.

"I – I apologise, Captain."

"Another bout of insubordination," she warned, "and I'll throw you overboard myself. Now get yer arse to work."

"Aye, Captain," he replied before vanishing into the recesses of the vessel.

The First Officer turned to his captain. A wide grin spread across his face.

"That was fun," he acknowledged. "I always enjoy it when we have fresh meat to play with."

Staiger was stifling a laugh as she continued to watch other crewmen carting items onto the *Gypsy*.

"The poor sod is probably crying right now, Stalekk Rank'sku," Staiger said. "You are a very intimidating man."

"You wouldn't have made me your First Officer if I wasn't," he chuckled.

"Probably not." She smirked. "Now, you were saying?"

He turned back to the ledger.

"Barrels of water and food stores," he reminded her.

"Take them directly to the galley," she instructed. "Inform Cook that his supplies are on the way and that he will need to store them."

"He won't like that," Rank'sku returned. "We seem to be taking quite a lot of supplies for a journey to Dendadia."

"The food stores are for the return trip also," Captain Staiger informed him. "I don't intend to be away too long. Back within the week, I hope."

"This is unlike you, Captain. Why are you in such haste? Usually, you like to dilly dally and stay awhile when we go east."

"Let's just say that I have interests here, now," she replied. Her face was like flint.

"What's his name?" Rank'sku grinned.

"Mind yer business," she ordered.

He leant in closer, his white smile broadening.

"Captain?" he asked playfully.

She shook her head as her cheeks turned pink and a smile formed.

"Oh!" Rank'sku backed up, pretending to be surprised. "She blushes?"

"All right." She lowered her voice to a whisper. "He's an officer of the guard. Landon Wake."

"Landon Wake?" the First Officer turned to face the main deck. "Not the man with the eye patch?"

"Yes," she answered with a grin.

Rank'sku furrowed his brow.

"Forgive me, Captain, but doesn't he seem a little old for you?"

Staiger changed his demeanour. She scowled at her first officer.

"Mind yer own business," she said again.

He held his hands up in mock surrender, holding a cheeky grin on his face.

"My sincerest apologies, Captain," he chuckled. "Please don't send me aft to clean the piss pots and shit streaks."

She laughed.

After a moment, they both fell silent and returned to watching the crew work.

"When do we depart?" Rank'sku asked.

"Tomorrow evening. As soon as the sun dips below the mountains."

"Just enough time to say our farewells to our loved ones."

"And I suppose you have a few to say farewell to?"

"You have no idea."

***

"Oh my," Alice breathed, rolling onto her back. "I believe you are getting better at this."

"I believe I need more practice," Arthur replied. "Besides, you did most of the work."

She laid her arm over his torso and rested her head against his chest. He wrapped an arm around her shoulders and kissed her brow.

"I'd like to do this forever," she told him, looking at his body in the lantern's light on the table by the bed.

"Wouldn't that be grand?" he responded. "If only I had your strength."

She ran her fingers softly over his skin.

"I should teach you," she whispered.

"Teach me?" He turned his face to hers. "Have you been practising without me?"

She giggled. "No. Not that. I mean, I should teach you to fight."

"Fight?" He sighed and lowered his head back to the pillow. "I don't enjoy fighting. You know that."

"I know," Alice replied. "But that won't stop someone from taking their chances with you. I should at least teach you to defend yourself."

"My father taught me some things," Arthur informed her.

"I can beat your father," she reminded him.

He ran his fingers along her spine. She felt a satisfying tingling spread over her body, causing her to move slightly.

"I have you at the mercy of my fingers," he said as he extended his reach between her legs. "You may be able to defeat all matter of men. But I can control you with the simplest gesture."

"Oh," she whispered. A slight hint of playfulness in her voice. "And what kind of gesture would that..."

She emitted a soft moan.

His lips met hers as he slid his other hand over her waist.

She moved her legs over him, but stopped suddenly.

"Arthur," she hissed, hinting for him to be still.

"Alice," he replied in the most sensual way that he could, continuing to kiss her neck.

"Arthur, stop," she ordered, pushing against his shoulders and sitting upright.

"What?" He looked at her, surprised, confused.

"Shhh," she held a finger to her lips. "Did you hear that?"

He cocked his head towards the door, trying to listen. Shaking his head, he turned his attention back to her.

"Your ears are better than mine," he said. "What is it?"

"Groaning," she answered, lifting herself from him and placing her feet softly on the floor.

She crept to the door and opened it, carefully. It gave a soft squeak as she stepped into the small passage.

Arthur got up and followed her.

The cold of the night air touched his bare skin, sending chills over his entire body. He wrapped his arms around himself and rubbed his flesh, attempting to keep warm.

Alice, however, moved as if she didn't feel the temperature; bare-skinned and unflinching.

He could hear the sound now that the door was open.

"What is that?" he whispered, barely audible.

"Shhh," she hissed as she pointed to the closed door across the passage from theirs. Emily's room.

The groaning grew louder and more frequent.

Alice placed a hand over her mouth and locked eyes with her husband.

"No," Arthur breathed. He could see Alice smiling as the mystery behind the groans became apparent.

"By the gods," grunted an all familiar voice from inside the room.

Both Alice and Arthur stared at each other with disbelief.

Another chorus of grunts and groans emitted through the door from both occupants.

"Go," Alice whispered, gesturing for Arthur to retreat into their own room.

Arthur was quick to respond and was already sitting on the side of the bed as Alice closed the door behind her.

"Unbelievable," he said. "My father and your mother?"

"Keep your voice down," Alice ordered him as she lowered herself onto the bed beside him. "They'll hear you."

"They can't do this," Arthur whispered, pointing to the door. "This is our home. Right under our roof."

"They've been alone for so long, Arthur." She placed her hands on his shoulders and kissed his neck. "They deserve to find each other. In fact, it's about damn time."

"That's *your* mother and *my* father." He pointed to the door again.

"Yes," she said. "I know them well."

"This isn't funny, Alice," Arthur told her. "Essentially, they are making us brother and sister right now. I don't want us to be brother and sister. I like things the way they are."

"We were husband and wife first," she pointed out, rubbing his shoulders. "I don't believe that this was a ploy to disrupt or dispute our marriage in any way. They found each other. They deserve some happiness. Let them have this."

Arthur sighed.

"I don't agree with it." He shook his head. "But I won't get in their way."

"Spoken just like your father," she said before kissing his neck.

Seven

Carefully, quietly, David crept to the door. He carried his boots in one hand as he reached for the handle with the other.

With a slow twist of the knob, the door opened.

A long squeak filled his ears. The sound seemed immeasurably louder in the dark than it did during daylight hours.

"Shhh," Emily hissed from the bed. She was sitting on the edge of the mattress, draping her nightgown over her shoulders.

"Sorry," he breathed, barely audible.

"Close the door behind you," she whispered to him as he stepped into the tiny passageway.

He complied, turning back to smile at her.

Only then did he realise that there was a faint, orange glow seeping in through the door. Emily was staring back at him with wide eyes.

David turned to see a flickering lantern sitting on the kitchen table. Its light streamed through the passage and into the bedroom to where Emily sat.

"Good morning," said a cheery voice from behind the light.

Emily froze, recognising the voice from the kitchen. David squinted, an attempt to block out the bright light. His eyes needed more time to adjust.

"Morning, Alice," he replied, releasing the doorknob and turning to face the girl.

"Is my mother awake?"

"Uh…" David moved into the living area, striding past the cushioned seats and making his way to the table.

"I'm awake," Emily's voice called from the room.

"Tea?" Arthur asked. He was standing by the stove, preparing a pot for breakfast. "The water has just boiled."

"Uh," David said again, moving his attention to his son.

"Of course, he would like a cup." Alice beamed at him. "Wouldn't you, David? My mother would like one, as well."

Emily appeared in the passage. She tightened the straps of her gown around her waist and stepped into the living room.

"Why are you two up so early?"

"There's a full day of work ahead," Alice replied. "Can't waste a day in bed. Can we?"

David sat down across from Alice. She had her blades stretched over the table. A whetstone was in her hand.

"I could," Arthur said as he carried a tray with the pot of tea and four cups to the table. "I hardly got any sleep with all that noise going on."

David turned to Emily. A guilty look came over his face. The auburn woman, however, kept her eyes on her daughter as she sat down next to the bald man.

"Yes." Alice furrowed her brow. "What was going on in your room, Mama?"

David's eyes flashed from Emily to Alice, to Arthur, back to Emily.

Arthur calmly poured the tea and set a cup before each of them.

"Mama?" Alice repeated.

"Come now, girl," Emily smirked. "You know full well what was going on in there."

Alice allowed a smile to spread over her face.

"It's about time you two got together," the white-haired girl said, reaching for a dagger.

David stared to at her, puzzled.

"Wha...?"

"I think this is a good thing," she elaborated.

"You do?" Emily queried.

"Of course I do," she replied. "Arthur, on the other hand, thought you two might try to annul our marriage by becoming husband and wife yourselves. But I told him you wouldn't dare do such a thing."

She glanced at David momentarily. The big man was trying to understand what was happening. He was still half asleep and all the words were dancing in his mind like leaves falling chaotically to the ground.

Nothing made sense.

Arthur sat next to his wife as she started working the blade of the dagger over the stone.

"She told me that," Arthur added, bringing his cup to his lips.

"Of course, we have no intention of breaking you two apart," Emily answered. "As if we could. You two are far more stubborn than either of us."

"Papa?" Arthur turned his attention to David.

"I love you both," he told them. "You're my son. And you are like a daughter to me, Alice. You both seem happy together. I would say that I wish you waited until you were older. I still think that you're too young for marriage. But Emily is right. You're both stubborn, and there was no way that I, or either of us, could have stopped you.

"I think you belong together," he continued. "I see that more since leaving Woodmyst and coming here. You complete one another."

"Then it is agreed." Alice put her dagger down and reached for the cup of tea. "You will respect our marriage and we'll respect yours."

"Marriage?" David questioned.

"Don't think for one moment, David Gyfford, that you get to spend one night under my roof with my mother and not take responsibility for your actions," Alice said sternly. "I expect more from someone like you. She's your wife now. Treat her as such."

David held a blank stare as he allowed the words to soak in.

"Papa?" Arthur cocked his head.

"All right," the big man eventually said as he turned to face Emily. "All right. You're my wife now. And I'm your husband."

"Husband?" Emily raised her brow as she contemplated what had happened.

"Mama?" Alice peered at the other, cautiously watching her mother's reaction.

Emily nodded reluctantly.

"All right," she said. "We should take responsibility for our actions. I'll be your wife, and you my husband."

"Good." Alice sipped her tea and placed the cup on the table. "Now, David. Move your gear into my mother's room. I don't know how many times you and she have done this previously, but I won't have you sleeping in the storeroom any longer."

***

Golden sunlight sparkled through the grass, touched by morning dew. Several cattle and sheep had moved closer to the stream, cautiously eyeing the dragon and the rukyul as they dared to drink from the water.

The two larger beasts were observing the performance of the snowy-haired girl and her husband. Shadow twisted his head one way, then the other as he watched the boy swing one of Alice's blades around his body in a chopping motion.

Arthur pointed the sword directly in front of him, towards the south. The weight was too much, and his arms allowed the blade to dip slightly.

"Keep it up," Alice ordered, tapping beneath his elbow with a rod.

"But it's too heavy," he complained. "I can't hold it."

"We need to build your arms," she told him. "You should start carrying things more often."

"I could carry you," he jested.

"I'm as light as a feather," she replied. "Gharnef's infant son, Kh'shekh, can carry me. You need to cart water to and from the hut every day."

"I do that already," he informed her, lowering the sword a little.

She struck him with the rod again, forcing him to lift the blade.

"Firewood, rocks, sacks of oats," Alice said as she walked around him to check his stance. "Anything with weight. Every day. Then, you may be able to hold a blade."

"All right."

"This sword is one of two," she started.

"I know," Arthur interjected. "You took your father's sword and melted it down, forging it into two swords of your own and a dagger."

"Because it was too big for me to wield," she reminded him.

He looked at her, puzzled. The blade dipped again.

She was quick with the rod. This time, he felt a slight sting.

"What's your point, Alice?"

"If I was to melt this one down again and reforge it into a weapon that you could handle, it would be so thin that it would snap like a twig. You need to learn how to do this. I won't be there to protect you all the time."

He lowered his head and arm, allowing the sword to fall to his side. She was about to strike him again, but saw the pain on his face.

"I know," he said. "What good am I? I can't fight and I can't defend you. Isn't that what a husband does?"

She frowned and moved closer to him. Her hand touched his arm as she reached up to his cheek with her lips to kiss him gently.

"By all comparisons to those who carry weapons," she told him, "you are still a child. Not one of them, the men in our glade or the soldiers in all the cities, learnt how to swing a blade until they were older than you are now."

"But you could do all of this since you were nine."

"Arthur." She rolled her eyes.

"I know," he said. "I felt silly saying it. I know that you're different from the others. And I know I shouldn't compare myself to you. I just feel useless."

"You're not." She stepped away from him. "And you will be able to hold a man's weapon, eventually. Not this thing of mine. You'll have a sword of your own, and you'll be the smartest and bravest warrior that ever lived. Now get that blade away from the ground."

She tapped his elbow with her rod again.

***

"They were too young to marry," David said to Emily.

Both sat on the deck that stretched along the porch to Alice's hut. They fixed their eyes upon the young couple near the stream.

"You think that they should have lived as children a little longer?"

"I do."

"Weren't you as eager as they were to grow up when you were their age?"

"Aye." He inclined his head. "But only to hunt and do things that Richard did for us. I never thought about sleeping with girls until I was older than they."

"We brought that upon them," Emily said. She watched as Alice tapped Arthur's elbow and knee.

"What do you mean?"

"The two of them were so different to everyone else in Woodmyst, and we allowed them to venture off and become the way they are. We probably should have held them closer when they were infants, but we didn't.

"Alice was a wild one. She would explore the woods for hours when she was still learning to walk. And we let her."

"And your Arthur would sneak away to read the books in Henry Cunningham's library, even though you gathered a fine collection for him to call his own."

"I went all the way to Oldcastle and dug through the ruins of the citadel with my own hands to get those," David explained. "After that, I went to Dweagan and asked the merchants to bring me back what they could from Newholt and Dendadia. It was never enough. He'd finish a book within a day. Less sometimes."

"But you never took him hunting or fishing?"

"He wasn't interested in any of it," the other replied. "He'd rather observe a plant growing, or a bird moving about than to kill something worth eating."

"All the while, Catherine would darn clothing and be seemingly content in the kitchen with me, my sister, and Lucy. While Alice was out making swords, and hunting deer."

"And making friends with wild animals," David added.

"That too."

"I was so wrong about her." He wept. "How could I have ever thought that she was responsible for what happened to my family?"

"We were beguiled, David," Emily said, placing a hand on his knee. "The one who was responsible had fooled us all. The bastard was in my house the whole time."

"Perhaps we can put our hopes in her, then." David wiped his eyes and smiled.

Emily glanced over to the hearth amid the encampment. Both Amicia Elynbrigge and Ursula Wadham sat by the fire with a small gathering of others enjoying breakfast.

"I think we have to," the auburn-haired woman replied. "Something has begun here. Something big."

At that moment, Alice whipped Arthur on the buttocks with her rod.

He dropped the sword to the ground and howled, clenching his backside with both hands.

Alice started laughing and ran away from him, towards the centre of the glade where most of the livestock had gathered to feed.

The boy gave chase and closed the gap easily. She let him catch her and tackle her to the ground.

David shrugged as he watched the two play on the grass.

"Children," he muttered.

Eight

"Eighteen of the lambs are dead, my lord," Lewis Drayton huffed. He was trying to keep up with the younger man walking by his side. Both were approaching a small house a short distance from the eastern wall of the city.

The quaint house, fitted with a thatched roof and surrounded by a neat picket fence, stood welcoming by the side of the road. A tiny vegetable garden sat to its side within the yard, as did a tall thin man with a woman and a toddler, a boy, beside him.

"And this?" Takmel gestured to the people as they drew nearer.

"This is the owner of the sheep in question," Drayton replied. "Forgive me, my lord, but his name escapes me."

"Doesn't matter," the other said as he reached the tiny wooden gate. He turned his attention to the man and his family. "I would bid you good morning, but it sounds like you had some trouble during the night."

"We did, my lord." The thin man bowed. His wife curtsied as best she could. The Maji looked them over. Their tattered clothes had seen better days. Hems were fraying, and holes were forming on the seams.

"Take me to where you found the lambs," Takmel instructed.

"Yes, my lord." The thin man passed through the gate and led the other two around the yard to the open field between the house and the river.

A large flock of sheep fed on the grass. A few had separated and stood in a group nearer to the house, bleating loudly.

"That's the mothers," the thin man told the Maji. "They haven't left the lambs all night. It was their crying that woke me."

"Mourning their loss," Takmel acknowledged as they continued towards the animals.

The ewes moved away slightly, eyeing the three men as they reached the dead lambs.

Takmel furrowed his brow as he took in the scene.

"Do you think it was wolves, my lord?" the master bookkeeper asked.

The Maji shook his head.

A small pile of bodies rested on the grass.

"Wolves wouldn't do this," Takmel replied. "They would cart the carcases away or tear them to shreds. Look, there's no blood."

"Then what?"

With a deep sigh, Takmel turned and moved back towards the road.

"Give this man and his family a fresh supply of clothing and linen," he ordered. "Stock them with enough supplies to last the winter and a little beyond."

"Yes, my lord," Drayton answered.

***

Catherine occupied one seat by the fireplace. She threaded a needle carefully, trying to avoid sticking her finger as she had done many times before. A small callous had formed on the side of her index finger after pricking herself too often.

"Use a thimble," Lucy told her from the kitchen table where she was eating breakfast.

"I don't enjoy using them," Catherine replied. "They don't let me feel the material."

"You'll hurt yourself again," Joanne put in as she sat down to a plate of toast and eggs. "And you'll get blood all over that dress of yours that you're trying to mend."

Catherine cocked her head slightly and frowned.

"It's an old one anyway," she replied. "I only wear it when I'm picking in the field."

Joanne gave a grunt, dismissing her niece's apathy.

Lucy kept her eyes on the girl by the fire, staring at her for a seemingly long time.

"What's that in your hair?"

"What?" Catherine reached her hand up to her neck and tucked her auburn hair into her shawl. "Nothing."

"Are you turning grey?" Lucy asked playfully.

Joanne moved her eyes suspiciously to the younger woman.

"I'm younger than you," Catherine answered. "If anyone is turning grey, either of you will be first to do so."

"Let me see," Joanne instructed.

"No." Catherine pointed to the plate of food set before her aunt. "Eat your breakfast before it turns cold."

"Catherine..." Joanne got up and crossed the room.

"I said no." The younger woman stood to face the other. "I won't have you touch me or come anywhere near me. Either of you. Not after what you did to the children."

"Children?" Lucy creased her brow and turned to Joanne. "What is she talking about?"

The woman in black shook her head.

"I do not know," she replied. She took a step towards Catherine.

"Stay back," the girl warned, dropping the needle, thread, and dress to the floor.

Joanne froze in place.

"Something is wrong with you," the woman in black said. "You're different. All I want to do is make sure that you are all right. I'm your aunt. What is it you think I'm going to do to you?"

Images of little Antony and Holly flashed through Catherine's head. She saw them playing on the field together with other infants, laughing and running around.

A memory of a stew that they had all partaken in made her stomach churn. She had smiled when the deed was being done. She had wanted it.

They don't remember.

Now she fought to hold back the tears as her eyes welled with water.

"You stay away from me," she warned again. "Perhaps you should be more concerned with what I will do to you."

The sudden sound of the door closing caused them to turn their heads. Takmel stood to the side of the room, where he removed his cloak before placing it on a peg by the entrance to the house. His eyes were stern as he peered at each of their faces.

"What's going on here?"

"Nothing," Catherine replied, bending down to retrieve the items she had dropped. She plonked herself back into the chair and resumed threading the needle.

"Nothing?" He moved closer to the fireplace, where it was warm. He kept his gaze trained on Catherine, who started working on a frayed hem at the base of her dress. "Joanne?"

"A family squabble," she replied, turning away and retreating to the table. "Nothing more."

"Nothing?" he repeated. "Lucy, will you please tell me what is happening here?"

"It was a discussion between aunt and niece," she answered. "It's not my place to get involved."

"Not your place?" Takmel looked at Joanne. "So, more nothing then?"

He turned and placed his back to the heat of the fire and looked around the room. Joanne ate her breakfast in silence as Catherine continued to stitch her dress.

"Such tension," he said eventually. "I believe that's my fault. I haven't been here as often as I should. A minor problem with having nine wives. Spreading myself rather thinly."

Catherine looked up from the thread work.

Takmel looked down at her with loving eyes. "Did you miss me, my love?"

"Of course," she answered. It was a lie. She had started to loathe her husband. But she couldn't gauge why there had been such a change in her attitude.

"Did you sleep well without me sharing your bed?"

"As well as one can," she replied. "Would you like for me to fix you some breakfast?"

"No." He waved a hand politely. "No, thank you. I had something already. What about you, Joanne? Did you sleep well?"

"What's with the questions regarding our sleep?" the woman in black enquired. "Are you afraid that we are seeing other men? We're loyal to you and you only, Maji."

He pursed his lips and nodded.

"Of course you are," he acknowledged. "It's just that something quite peculiar occurred last night and I'm trying to find out what exactly happened."

"Peculiar?" Lucy asked.

"Some lambs were killed," he informed them. His eyes moved to each of them to see if there was any reaction. All three looked to him with surprised expressions.

"Killed?" Lucy murmured. "Was it wolves? Something else?"

"Something else," Takmel answered as he moved towards the table. "The strange thing is that there was no blood. Not a drop."

"Someone strangled them?" Joanne asked.

"No," he said, shaking his head as he sat down beside her. "I don't believe so. Whoever or whatever did this used sorcery."

"That's why you asked about how we slept last night?" Catherine questioned as she continued stitching.

"Yes," he admitted.

"We were all here," Lucy told him. "One of us would have heard the door open and close if another had left during the night. Surely."

He looked over at Catherine and frowned.

"You're right," he said to Lucy. "Someone would have noticed. Which only leads me to keep investigating. I have another five wives to question regarding this."

"You mean six," Lucy corrected him.

"I was with Tricia last night," he informed her. "I know she didn't leave the bed until the master bookkeeper summoned me."

"Have you considered that my sister or my other niece could be responsible for this?"

Takmel turned his attention to Joanne.

"They're not," he told her.

"How do you know?" she pressed.

"I have eyes on them."

She seemed satisfied with his answer.

"Well then," he said as he got up. "I guess I'll continue on."

He moved about the room and kissed each of the women on the forehead, saving Catherine for last.

She smiled as he caressed her, but inside she felt his lips were like the touch of worms and rot against her skin.

Something was wrong with her, as her aunt had stated. She had loved Takmel with all of her heart and would have done anything for him.

Now, she simply wanted him gone.

A knot formed in her stomach, and a lump gathered in her throat. The sensation that she was about to eject the contents of her guts was overwhelming.

He moved to the door and draped his cloak about himself.

"I'll see you tonight," he said to them cheerfully as he opened the door.

With that, he left.

A quick exchange of looks between aunt and niece ensued.

Lucy remained silent and shifted in her seat uncomfortably.

"I think I'll clean the sheets," she announced, quickly rising from the table and moving to her bedroom. Catherine lowered her gaze and returned to fixing the hem of her dress as Joanne shovelled a portion of eggs into her mouth.

Nine

Alice and Arthur emerged from the forest hand in hand. They each carried a bow with a quiver of arrows slung over their backs. Draped over their shoulders, attached to thin strips of yarn, were their prizes from their hunt. Four rabbits swung from the white-haired girl, two from the boy.

"We'll try again tomorrow," she said as they started across the glade towards the camp.

"What should we do now?" her husband enquired. "More sword practice?"

"No," she answered, lifting her eyes to the sun. It had passed the highest point in the sky and was beginning its slow descent. "We should make a stew."

A loud chirp from the direction of the larger cavern caused them to turn their heads. Liana crawled from the cave, bobbing her head excitedly as they drew nearer.

"Poor thing." Alice sighed. "I should take her up so she can stretch her wings."

"Take her..." Arthur cocked his head. "Surely, she can do that on her own."

"Yes," the other replied. "But I don't want her to get used to not having me on her back while she's up there. I think it would be like a horse. If you don't ride your horse often enough, they get used to it. Then you need to go through a time of training all over again."

"But they let you ride them after a while," he said.

"They do," she admitted. "Most horses take to it almost straight away. But I've seen many a rider with sore arses after being thrown, usually because of their own lack of confidence."

"I didn't think there was a rider in all of Woodmyst that wasn't confident on a horse," Arthur said.

"Not all riders in Woodmyst are from Woodmyst," she reminded him as she peered to the livestock on the grassland to their left. There were sheep, goats, cattle and horses grazing in clusters. "Which reminds me..."

She gave a short, sharp whistle.

A familiar form with a chestnut coat broke from the herd and galloped towards them. The stallion's nostrils flared, and it raced in haste.

Arthur thought the beast was about to run them down when it pulled up suddenly and nuzzled Alice's neck, causing the iron claws she wore to jingle slightly.

"Hello horse," she said, letting Arthur's hand go to rub the steed on the nose.

"Are you going to ride him instead?"

"No," she replied. "I'm taking Liana up as soon as we clean these rabbits. You're taking him."

"Me?" Arthur peered questionably at his wife. "You must be mad. He only responds to you."

"That's what they said about Shadow," she told him. "But he lets you scratch his ears now."

Arthur looked to the cabin's porch where the rukyul was sleeping.

"That's until he decides to eat me," he responded.

"He likes you." Alice smiled. "He trusts you. And, so does this one."

As if agreeing, the stallion nickered.

"I'm not too sure," Arthur said, shaking his head slightly.

"Confidence," she remarked. "You must have confidence."

"Confidence," he echoed. He reached his hand over and rubbed the stallion's shoulder. "And a saddle."

***

Takmel stood upon the parapet walk above the southern gate. He peered through the crenels, observing the train of wagons, beasts and men moving away from the city towards the mountains in the distance.

"The first supply run is underway, my lord," Andris Hill announced as he approached the Maji.

"I can see that, Commander," Takmel replied.

"Of course." Andris lowered his head apologetically.

"You will go with the next shipment," the younger man instructed. "I need you in Dweagan to oversee the operation at the docks. When the ships have departed, you will take the ground forces by way of Belburn and head north to Newholt. If all goes to plan, you and the fleet should arrive at the same time and..." He turned to see the commander gawking at him. "What is it, Commander?"

"You promised me I would stay here," he replied. "You said that I could remain in Woodmyst with my wife and command the city guards."

"I changed my mind," Takmel said blandly. "You will accompany one of my wives to Newholt instead. You will protect her with every ounce of your being. Or there will be consequences, Andris."

"Consequences, my lord?"

"Perhaps your wife would enjoy being my wife," the younger man taunted. "Perhaps you won't have a wife to return to."

"Forgive me, my lord." Andris bowed slightly. "I would never disobey an order. But there is no need to threaten me or Sevrina."

Takmel sighed as he turned to face the officer.

"We've known each other for a long time, have we not?"

"Yes."

"Since I was ten." Takmel pulled his cloak around himself tightly and leant against the battlement. "So, what's that? Six years?"

"Yes, my lord."

"We've come to be well acquainted, wouldn't you say?"

"Our families are related through marriage," Andris replied. "We have spent a great amount of time together."

"You see," Takmel retorted. He squinted and pointed a finger at the commander. "That's the thing. Your families are related while I feel I am not."

"But you and Catherine?"

"Yes, I know. But it's not quite the same. That was more of a burning in the loins. A fire that I needed to quench, if you get my meaning," he explained. "But you married Sevrina Verney, sister of Lor Verney. And he married Linet Warde, sister of Tomas Warde. And, well, we all know about Tomas Warde. Saviour of Blackrock Haven. Hero of Woodmyst. Vanquisher of the White Witch. My mother."

Andris felt an immense fear overwhelm him as Takmel stepped closer to him.

"Don't misunderstand me, Commander," Takmel continued. "I love Catherine more than any of my other wives. She was there with me when this all began. She saw what I was and helped me to become what I am. I didn't need to manipulate or twist her mind for her to succumb to my will. She wanted it as much as I.

"Others in this city needed a little push in the right direction. Some sweet words to soften the blow. A few promises here and there. A few lies.

"Then there are those like you." He placed his hand on Andris' shoulder. "Not so easy to control with magic. I think your time in the presence of Yasmeen Svoboda may have taught you how to see through certain tricks. But fear, however, is something that is deeply embedded in you."

The Maji slowly walked past the soldier.

Andris felt his body shake slightly. His jaw quivered and his heart raced.

"You saw the things the Sovereign could do," Takmel said. "Crushing men into balls of meat with a simple movement of the hand. Horrible. Ghastly. But know this, Andris. I am far more powerful than she. More powerful than all the witches of the Mirikin combined. If I wanted, I could turn your beloved Linet, and the life inside of her, into vapour with a click of my fingers."

Takmel did just that. The sound caused Andris to spin and drop to his knees.

"Please, no," he begged.

The Maji turned to face the commander. A smug grin stretched over his face.

"I won't do that, Andris," the younger man replied. "Of course, I won't. Not if you do as I say."

"Anything," the commander offered.

"It's simple, really," Takmel explained. "Oversee the loading of the fleet. Take my army north. Escort and protect my wife. You proved your ability to do so in the past. In fact, it was the Sovereign who gave you this task in the first place."

"Joanne?" Andris furrowed his brow.

"That's right," the Maji said. "Protect her. See to her needs and your wife and unborn child will remain safe from harm. I promise."

I promise.

Andris had heard those words spoken by manipulators of sorcery before. He didn't believe them then. He didn't believe them now.

But what was he to do?

His wife's life was in the hands of a boy.

A boy who could influence and bend everything to his will, gaining control within a very short time.

"What do you say?" Takmel asked, peering down at the man on his knees.

"Yes," Andris breathed, feeling a great weight upon his shoulders. "My lord."

***

Liana banked slightly to the right, dipping her wing towards the glade. She gave a great cry that echoed through the air as Alice lifted her hands into the sky.

The wind built as the dragon climbed higher and higher. She beat her powerful wings, pushing herself towards the clouds as the snowy-haired girl laughed uncontrollably.

"Higher," Alice called to the beast.

Liana chirped as she sped into the air.

Alice could feel the angle getting steeper and steeper as the dragon pointed her nose directly up. The girl's heart skipped a beat when she realised Liana was continuing on her arc, turning upside-down.

A shrill scream filled the air.

"What's she doing?" David queried, peering into the sky. "Is she mad?"

Yuri pointed and laughed a guttural chortle.

"I can't watch," Emily said, looking away.

The dragon completed the turn and dived towards the ground.

Screaming all the way, Alice kept her hands high and a wide grin on her face.

Liana tucked her wings to her sides, allowing her to fall faster and faster.

The ground rose towards them with intensity, rapidly.

Alice's eyes grew wider and wider.

Her screaming turned to uncontrollable laughter.

Cattle, sheep, goats and horses ran to the far side of the grassland. Amongst them was Arthur, on the chestnut stallion.

She could see him yelling something to her, but the wind in her ears was too loud. Like a roaring waterfall that surrounded her head.

The blending colours of lush greens and earthy browns that covered the ground separated. She could see the bundles and patches of grass, weeds and wildflowers.

They were getting very close to crashing.

Liana flung her wings out to her sides and swooped along the surface, aiming her flight towards the boy on the horse.

"No," he called. "Alice. Don't you dare."

He desperately tried to turn the stallion out of the path of the on-coming monster. The horse, however, had other ideas.

It fled.

Arthur wasn't used to riding at such speeds. He pressed his knees against the steed as hard as he could and gripped the reins so tightly that his knuckles turned white.

His ears picked up the sound of the stallion's hooves thudding against the turf, the rapid breathing of the beast escaping its nostrils, and the wild laughter of his wife approaching from behind.

Suddenly, a great shadow cast over him, and his charger as Liana passed directly above him.

The force of air that followed the beast almost lifted him from the stallion.

"Alice," he called angrily.

Her laughter drifted away as she and the dragon climbed into the air again.

***

"You and that dragon almost knocked me off the horse," Arthur told her as they sat together by the campfire. The sun had just moved below the mountain tops to the west and a large pot of rabbit stew was bubbling away on top of the hearth. Several others had gathered for the nightly assembly after putting in a day's hard labour of constructing huts and gathering supplies for the camp.

"Liana knows what she is doing," Alice replied, resting her head against his shoulder. "She would never hurt you."

"Still," he put in, "I would ask that you never do that again. It spooked the horse and made him run. I couldn't control him."

"And you shit your pants," Oliver jested.

"I did no such thing," Arthur retorted, not seeing the humour.

Others chuckled quietly as they watched the flames tickle the base of the pot.

"I almost died watching you," Emily admitted. "What if you fell?"

"I was strapped into the saddle, Mama. I wouldn't be able to fall unless I unbuckled myself."

"And it looked as if you had no control over that beast," her mother continued.

"You're right," Alice agreed. "I didn't have control. I let her do whatever she wanted to. I was simply along for the ride. But when I want control. I have control. I lean to the left; Liana turns to the left. I lean to the right; she turns to the right. I call a command and she heeds to it. Today was fun for her. But any other day might not be so."

"You think you will need to use her for battle?" David said.

"I do," she acknowledged. "It's only a matter of time."

"The three of you haven't been able to determine when Takmel or his witches will strike?" Baldwyn Palmer asked, peering around to Amicia and Ursula, who were both seated beside their men on opposite sides of the hearth.

"Our abilities don't work that way," the queen answered with an understanding smile. "We're not prophets or soothsayers."

"But there are some that are?" Palmer pressed. "There was the prophecy about the Maji, and it came true. Perhaps one of you other ladies..."

With frustration, he looked at Emily, Karlena, and Akasati.

"Baldwyn," Elka said soothingly, gently placing her hand on his in an attempt to calm his nerves.

He turned to his wife. "I'm sorry," he said sheepishly. "I guess I'm getting a little worked up. Perhaps it's my age setting in."

"It's all right," Karlena told him. "I too am worried about what is to come. But, sadly, none of us can foresee the future."

"He will attack us first," Akasati stated. All eyes turned to her as she stared blankly at the flames. The sky had grown darker and a chill, but a gentle breeze started down from the northern peaks, running through the camp and over the glade.

"How do you know?" Schoenbach asked, leaning forward in his chair.

"It's his strategy," she replied. "It's one that he adopted from those who came before him."

David furrowed his brow and looked at Richard, who was leaning back in his seat and musing over what was being spoken.

Oliver shook his head and turned to the Erilian warrior.

"What do you mean, those who came before him?"

"The Sovereign," she replied. "The Mirikin. The White Witch. Years and years of hiding and plotting passed before we saw anything of them openly. Yet, they were always at work.

"The black ships attacked my home," Akasati continued. "Ships that belonged to the Sovereign. The same ships that took Sumaiyya away from Dakmel. The same ships that took your Meaghan away from you, Captain."

"Aye," Jeremy said. "They took many things from many people. But, I don't think I understand your point."

"My point is the Sovereign used them to instil fear into everyone she could reach. She eventually planted her witches into strategic places on the coast to prepare for an all-out assault. Blackshore, Meadowmoor, Ostford."

"Newholt," Amicia interjected.

"Yes," said the Erilian woman. "She then started reaching her claws inland to take more *potentials* for her cause. Your sister, Emily, and the others of the Seven amongst them. And even though she was defeated, betrayed by the Seven, the damage had been done.

"The assault of the Mirikin happened. The Maji was brought into the world and he, along with the Seven, betrayed us all."

"So," David mused. "Let me see if I understand this. You're saying that, like the Sovereign, Takmel has planted seeds that are only starting to bear fruit now."

"Yes," Akasati agreed. "I'm sure there was a time when he was just a boy and nothing more. But something changed in him. Or perhaps he was always who he was, and he knew exactly what he was doing since the day he was born. I don't know.

"What I do know is that he started sowing his seeds when he was first brought into our lives. We trusted him and invested a great deal in him to make him a part of us. Then he called his pets."

"Those black devils?" Glaun asked.

"The same," she replied. "They have the task of wiping out the isolated villages before moving into the more densely populated areas. All the while, Takmel picked corn and ate at our tables and laughed at our jokes as if he was one of us."

"Hidden in plain sight," Oliver muttered.

"He didn't adopt the strategy," Ursula put in. "It was the strategy from the beginning. Since before he was even born."

The gathering looked to the woman from Whitekeep; all except Alice and Amicia, who kept their eyes on the flames dancing in the hearth.

"The tactics of the Sovereign and the Mirikin were all part of one plan," she explained. "The ascension of the Maji. Everything that was done has been done for his passage. Every victory and loss they had benefited him. It was meant to happen, because it was meant to happen."

"So, he will win?" Lor asked. "No matter what we do, he will be victorious."

"None of us are soothsayers, remember?" Ursula reminded. "There truly is no way of knowing what will happen. But we can't give up.

"Good men and women, and their children, have all been slain because it is his will to dominate through fear," she added. "We can't simply allow fear to have control. And something tells me it is not just the realms of men and other free-folk who don't wish to live under the shadow of fear."

She reached her fingers to the sky.

"Four have been chosen," Ursula said as sparks of electricity danced in the air above them. Several children gasped as the adults watched in awe. "This has never been done before. And three of the four are here with you. That leads me to believe that you were chosen, as well."

"But he has Death on his side," David grumbled.

She lowered her hand and pursed her lips.

"Death doesn't take sides, David," Alice interjected. "It just takes. It has no allies. It has no favourites. If Death is in Woodmyst, then it may not be to the Maji's advantage."

Ten

Posted lanterns were lit along the path that encompassed the Great Oak, illuminating the giant tree and the surrounding lawn in a flickering orange glow. The Seven had gathered beneath the outstretched, twisted limbs. Cloaked in their colours, they softly murmured words together as they knelt in a circle, holding hands and swaying gently.

Takmel watched from the gate. His eyes fixed upon Joanne as she kept her chin to the sky. Her eyes were closed and a wide smile had formed on her face.

This was a moment of strengthening the coven before they departed.

He knew they needed this before their separate journeys began.

Their voices grew louder, turning from groans to loud calls, as if they were being pleasured by someone, something.

Two or three of the women giggled as others appeared to reach a point of climactic ecstasy.

He creased his brow and turned towards the guards standing sentry just outside the fence. They were both trying to sneak a peek, but straightened themselves when they saw the Maji glaring at them.

Returning his eyes to the Seven, he saw they had dropped their hands and had relaxed their posture. Joanne opened her eyes and peered around to the others.

"I will miss you all, sisters," she told them. "We will be apart, but we can still be together. We must be together." Joanne reached beneath her cloak and produced a sharp dagger. She lifted the hem of her garment and cut a thin strip away, about the length of her arm, from along the seam.

Carefully, she folded it once, twice, then a third time. With the blade, she split the thin strip of material into six pieces and placed them on the ground before her before passing the knife to her left.

Tricia took the blade and repeated the process, removing a piece of her scarlet robe. When six pieces lay in front of her, she passed the blade on to the next of the Seven.

And so it went until all of them had completed the task.

Six pieces of material sat before each of the Seven.

The woman in black got up and moved into the circle. She took the blade again and slid it over her palm. Stretching her fingers apart, she held her hand over the piles of different coloured fabric, ensuring that at least one drop of blood landed on each piece of material.

"Unify," she said in a low voice.

After passing the blade to the scarlet woman, she watched as each of the women slit the skin of their own palms. Instead of sprinkling their blood over the fabric, however, they offered their wounds directly to Joanne.

"Unify," Tricia breathed as the woman in black scraped her tongue over her blood-stained skin.

"Unify," Isabel, the white witch said, offering her wound for Joanne to taste.

"Unify." Christina, in gold, held her palm out at the ready.

Takmel watched quietly, excitedly, becoming slightly aroused as Joanne moved around to each of the Seven. She completed the circuit with Gilda, the jade witch, before resuming her position in the circle. She lifted the six strips of black material into her hand.

The others copied her action, taking the piles that sat before each of them.

Together, almost as one, they passed the bundles to their left. Each woman took one strip of fabric as they handed the piles over. Eventually, each of them had six different coloured strips that represented the other women of the coven resting upon their laps.

"Now we are united," Joanne told them. "You are all a part of me."

They rose to their feet, tucked the fabric away inside their cloaks.

One by one, each of the Seven departed after embracing Joanne, their prime.

The ritual was complete.

In single file, they moved silently to the gate where Takmel waited, offering his open arms. The women looked at him adoringly as they wrapped their arms around him before moving away into the night.

Joanne was the last to approach, walking slowly along the path to give him time to farewell each of the others.

"So, it is done," he said when she drew nearer.

"It is," she replied sadly.

"You're upset." He frowned. "I am sorry about that. But there really is no other way."

"I understand. You need us as your representatives. You need us to maintain your authority."

"Exactly." Takmel inclined his head. "You're to be my ambassadors."

"Overlords," she corrected.

He looked surprised.

"You may have me, Maji," she told him, grimacing slightly as they stepped out of the fenced grounds of the ruins and into the street. "And you may have my coven. But don't think me to be dim-witted. We are going to instil fear. Just as the Mirikin did for Svoboda. We are to be *your* Mirikin."

They started walking side by side. The two guards maintained a distance far enough behind the Maji to allow him and Joanne to talk privately.

"And you disagree with this tactic?" he asked, testing her submissiveness. A deep concern flashed through Takmel's mind. If she could overcome his ability to control her, to manipulate her, could she be able to release the others of the Seven from his will?

"I didn't say that," she answered. A look of confusion swept over her face. She stopped walking and faced him. "Why would I oppose you? You're my husband. My lord. I will forever be yours, my love."

Takmel allowed a wide grin to stretch from ear to ear. It wasn't that long ago when she opposed him, when she fought his attempts to control her.

But she was still his.

Joanne wrapped her arms around his neck and planted her lips on his.

"Come home," she said. "And I'll prove my devotion."

He slid his arm around her waist and started towards home with her by his side.

"As you wish."

***

Alice stirred and peered at the other two women with piercing blue eyes. They were both staring at her with alarmed looks.

They had sensed it, too.

"What is it?" Emily asked, sitting upright. She had been leaning against David and was almost asleep until she saw her daughter's countenance change.

The snowy-haired girl moved her eyes around the group.

Several had retired for the night, including the children, leaving only a handful of people behind.

"Blood magic has been performed," Alice replied.

"A bonding," Amicia added.

"Unify," said Ursula, repeating the words that were spoken during the ritual.

***

"Unify," Catherine hissed.

Her eyes glazed over as she stared blankly at the kitchen wall. A pot was in her hands, partially submerged in a tub of warm water. Her hair tucked neatly into her blouse.

Lucy was a short distance away, using a towel to dry cutlery and plates before placing them into a cupboard. "What's that?"

"Nothing," the auburn girl replied as she snapped out of her trance.

Lucy squinted in the lantern light, peering directly at Catherine.

"What's the matter with your eyes?" she asked the young woman.

"What do you mean?" Catherine let the pot go and took a towel from the back of a chair to dry her hands.

"Come," Lucy instructed. "Let me see."

Catherine complied as the other put her towel on the table. She stared into the young woman's eyes and saw pink and red tendrils spreading across the whites like spider webs.

"Did you get dust or something in there?"

"No," Catherine answered.

"Are they itching?"

"No."

"They're so red," Lucy told her. "And it looks as if the colour is changing. They don't appear to be hazel. They almost appear to be blue-ish."

"What?"

"It could be just the redness and this light." Lucy squinted. "I think you should go to bed and rest."

"But Takmel is coming," she argued. Secretly, she didn't care if she saw him or not, but she felt she had a part to play, and that included acting interested whenever Takmel was involved.

"I fear you may be infected," Lucy told her as she stepped back from the young woman. "I think Takmel can wait until you're feeling better. I can finish here. Go to bed. I'll bring you some tea with honey when I'm done."

Catherine agreed reluctantly and moved away.

She closed her bedroom door behind her and sat on the chair positioned before her looking glass. Carefully, she moved the lantern that rested on the dresser so that she could look into her own eyes.

She first noticed the twisted veins and redness. But in the centre, she saw what Lucy referred to. The colour was changing.

Her hazel eyes were turning blue.

She leant back into the seat and lifted her hair from her blouse and ran the length through her fingers until she reached its end. There, she held it tightly in her grasp.

A white band had formed at the base, as if she had dipped the strands into dye.

"What's happening to me?" she asked the girl in the looking glass.

Tears welled in her eyes as she quietly sobbed.

***

"Blood magic?" Emily queried.

"That doesn't sound too good," Oliver opined.

"Indeed, it doesn't," Jeremy agreed. "Have any of you known of blood magic being performed before?"

"Not since the days of the Mirikin," Amicia replied. "We used blood magic to unite the coven before separating across the land. It kept us bound to the Sovereign. We could sense her and each other."

"And you think that's what has happened just now?" Linet enquired.

"It is," Ursula answered. With her eyes closed, she pointed her face to the sky. "The Seven are one."

"For what reason?" David looked at each of them, understanding the conversation but becoming more and more befuddled.

Ruttger leant forward and reached for the pot of water steaming at the edge of the fire.

"They are about to separate physically," he said matter-of-factly. "I'm making tea. Does anyone else want some?"

"Separate?" Courtney asked from his side. "And, yes. I'll have some."

"They are about to move to other locations," he explained as he poured. "They are about to establish strongholds for their master. Just as you did when Svoboda sent you all across the land."

He looked directly at Amicia.

"I was a younger man," he continued to explain. "Perhaps thirty-something. Heading to forty. Still a colonel in the Ostford guard when the Lilac Mistress gained supporters. I must admit, her beauty drew in me at first. Then her words gripped my heart. She talked about the corruption of the magistrate and how the people could rise above it all.

"Once she had enough of us on side, and when we had overthrown the powers that be, she revealed her true self. She used fear, persuading others to her side. She used death or imprisonment resulting in death for those who would not submit."

"We all used such tactics," Amicia informed him. "It was the Sovereign's way."

"So, it was." Ruttger turned to Jeremy Schoenbach. "Did you know the black ships attacked a great number of the smaller coastal villages between Ostford and Oldcastle? Raping and killing. Taking young women and girls. Never once hitting any of the ports where the Mistresses lived. And we, the soldiers, the protectors of the people, knew about it. And we did nothing."

Jeremy felt a sharp lump form in his throat. He swallowed hard.

"How could you?" he replied. "You were under the control of a Mistress."

"Yes," he agreed. "She had control. But, at the time, I wanted to serve her. She was the most beautiful creature I had ever seen. And, as I grew older, my hair turned grey and lines filled my face. She didn't age. Not a day. How is that possible?"

He turned to face Amicia. Her features were also those of a young, attractive woman.

"I don't know," she replied. "There are powers I cannot explain."

"When did you begin to see past her beauty?" Arthur asked. "The Lilac Mistress, I mean."

"Oh..." Ruttger handed a steaming cup of tea to his wife and leant back in his chair before taking a long slurp from his own. "I guess just after she appointed me as her personal guard and commander of her forces. I was still taken by her beauty for some time, but then I saw the way she treated a young girl that she appointed as her cupbearer. As the cupbearer grew into a young woman, she too grew more and more beautiful, and my heart became entranced by her and less so for the Mistress. Eventually, I saw that bitch for what she really was, and I looked for an opportunity to steal the cupbearer away so I could free her from that kind of life."

"And so it came to be," Arthur said. "Here you are."

"Here we are." The old soldier confirmed. "But I think I was too late. It wasn't until the Mirikin were on the move before I seized my opportunity. And it wasn't until after my men and I sacked all the villages along the coast to the south of Dellmoor that the opportunity presented itself.

"So many were killed senselessly," he continued. "We cut open mothers and children. Placed the heads of infants beneath the heels of our boots. Burnt down houses with families inside. I still wake at night, hearing their screams."

He stopped speaking and wiped his eyes.

Courtney put her mug on the ground and wrapped her arms around her husband.

"You're here now," Arthur told him. "You're one of us and will forever be. You vanquished the Lilac Mistress, and the Mirikin is no more."

"But they are," Ruttger interjected. "The Mirikin returns. The Seven are the Maji's Mirikin."

"Perhaps," David put in. "But the Mirikin were nine. Ten if you count Svoboda. The Seven are only seven."

"Power, in this case, is not determined by numbers," Amicia stated. "It's not the same as having an army where the more soldiers in your ranks, the higher chance you have at victory. Magic doesn't operate in the same way as man does. It's not physical, but it is. It's not spiritual, but it is. It's beyond our way of thinking and does not behave in the same manner as the things that surround us.

"The Seven are far more powerful than the Mirikin. The Seven defeated Svoboda when they were only little girls. Around the same age as you." She looked at Alice. "And look at us. Three of the four, where a thirteen-year-old girl holds the position of prime. The most powerful of all of us.

"It has been quite some time since the Seven defeated Svoboda. Their power has only grown and their abilities have become more focused. We should not underestimate them."

"You're also forgetting about Catherine," Oliver offered. "She has some abilities herself. And if what you three have told us is true, then she is one of the four, which means she has some other tricks up her sleeves that we don't know about.

"And then there is the Maji, himself," he continued. "Who knows what that boy is capable of. Just how powerful is he?"

They sat in silence for a while.

The fire crackled, and the air hissed softly through the trees.

"So, what do we do?" Jeremy asked. "Do we go into Woodmyst and murder them in their sleep to prevent them from departing? Do we wait until they have gone and hunt them down one by one?"

"And allow them to build armies just as the Mirikin did?" Ruttger asked.

"There's not much of a population out there now," Captain Thornton informed them. "Most of the larger cities that have people are north of the Griralith Pass. Ostford and Dellmoor have been emptied. Only nomads walk the lands between the Lunkhul Forest and the Western Sea."

"And you know this how, Captain?" Karlena asked.

"We sent scouts from Newholt after the battle of Woodmyst to try and contact anyone still alive out there," he explained. He jerked his head towards Brondt. "The commander could tell you more about that than I."

"It is true," Brondt replied. "We sent riders and ships to all the major ports and townships. We reached as far north on the western coast as Blackshore and found the people were still loyal to Sumaiyya Tarkin."

"Even though she is dead?" Jeremy queried.

"Even though she is dead," the commander answered.

"They must breed them strange over there in the west," David remarked.

"I'm from the west," Jeremy told him.

"Case and point, then," David quipped.

Soft laughter spread around the fire, bringing some light to a dark conversation.

"We can't attack them," Alice said, resting her head against Arthur's chest. The rukyul slunk around them and lowered himself to the ground beside the boy's chair as she spoke. "The Maji has eyes on us, even though Shadow here has been doing his best to thin their numbers."

"The dark creatures are out there?" Lor turned around in his seat and looked towards the tree line near the camp.

"I'm sure they are," she replied, peering at the black beast on the ground. "But they are also a delicious treat. Aren't they?"

Shadow lifted his head and looked over to the girl. He moaned softly and licked his lips before plonking his head onto Arthur's lap.

"Awph!" the boy let out. "You're so heavy."

Arthur started stroking the rukyul's ear.

"We need to wait," Alice continued. "We need to see what Takmel's next move will be."

"We need eyes of our own upon Woodmyst," Thornton added.

Alice peered across the flames to Yuri, who was listening quietly to the conversation. He locked eyes with her and gave a small nod.

"Indeed, we do," she replied.

Eleven

With his eye attached to the spyglass, pointing to the ocean, he watched one small light upon the horizon from the rooftop of the palace. It blinked periodically, dipping in and out of view with the tide.

Every time the light vanished; his heart sank a little more. He had known her for such a short time. A month at best. But she had become everything to him.

The small, yellow dot floating on the sea of black disappeared again.

Flickered.

Gone.

She was gone.

He lowered the spyglass, folded it, and placed it into a pocket inside his coat.

"Sir?" a soldier said from his side.

Wake turned to face the other, a look of sadness on his face.

"I apologise for interrupting." The soldier moved his gaze to his feet.

"No need for that, son," the sub-commander replied, moving by the young man to make his way to a door leading back inside.

"I just thought you may want to inspect the beacons."

Wake stopped in his tracks and turned to face the soldier.

"They're done already?"

The young man shifted his stance. "Not yet, sir. But the frames have been constructed and the mirrors are in the process of being moulded."

"Mirrors?"

"That's what the blacksmiths are calling the polished panels that reflect the light," the soldier answered. "I know, it's not an appropriate name. But who am I to argue with blacksmiths."

"They can call them whatever they like," the sub-commander agreed. He turned for the door again. "I think I will pay them a visit. Are they working at this late into the night?"

"They're working shifts, sir," the soldier replied, following his superior into the palace. "The work has been ongoing, not ceasing, since you gave the order. We have given priority to the beacons over everything else."

They were moving through a long passage with many doors on either side. Wake stopped again and faced the soldier.

"I don't want everything else to stop," he directed. "Tell the Vice-Admiral Morris to prepare arms for the fleet. Tell the senior officers and field marshals to run drills and keep our men on their toes. We don't know if, or when, those things will return. We need to be ready. We can't wait for the beacons to be built. Fetch runners and get the message out."

"Yes, sir." The young soldier saluted before racing along the corridor.

***

Arthur stood nearby as Alice and Yuri spoke together near the tree line, close to the Agrodien shelters. He felt a little out of place as the two spoke in the reptilian language. Now and then, his ears picked up a phrase or two. Obviously, every time Yuri mentioned the word Kayl'sro, he was referring to Alice in a manner of respect. But Arthur surmised the two were debating something they did not completely agree upon.

"I know it's dangerous," Alice said to the reptilian in his tongue. "And that's why I'm having a problem with seeing this through. There are eyes and ears everywhere, watching us."

"They are Agrodien warriors, Kayl'sro," Yuri replied, gesturing towards the shelters. "They know that danger awaits them. They offered themselves."

"After you approached them," she interjected. "I didn't ask you to do this for me, Yuri."

"I apologise." He bowed his head slightly. "But even you can see that we need to know what is taking place. These warriors are proficient at hiding. They will not be seen. Let me send ten."

"No." She shook her head. "Not ten. That's too many."

"Five," he bartered. "At least five."

"Three and I'll choose them. That way, only I can be blamed if something goes wrong."

He nodded reluctantly.

"Yes, Kayl'sro."

"Call them out," she instructed.

As Yuri turned to summon the warriors, Arthur tapped his wife on the shoulder. "What's happening?"

"It seems that Yuri has organised a party of scouts on my behalf."

"You're sending spies to Woodmyst?"

"I didn't want to," she replied defensively. "But he's right. We should know what Takmel is up to."

"Alice," he hissed. A concerned expression swept over his face.

The corners of her mouth turned down deeper as guilt gripped her heart.

"They volunteered," she told him, knowing his resentment regarding her decision. His disappointment couldn't measure up to the amount that she felt for herself.

Ten Agrodien warriors arrived, weapons in hand, packed satchels strapped to their sides, ready to go. Amongst them were Nakrah, Bein and Nola'ee.

"No," Alice said in the Agrodien tongue, pointing to the three warriors. "You will remain here."

They peered at her, confused.

"Kayl'sro," Yuri objected. "These three are your best warriors. They will not let you down."

"I don't doubt their abilities," she told him. "But I won't risk them. I need them here. And besides, Nola'ee is my personal guard. She does not have the privilege of volunteering without my explicit permission."

The female reptilian lowered her eyes in shame.

Yuri grunted and snorted a deep, frustrated breath. He pointed to the three warriors.

"Go back to your dwelling places," he ordered.

They bowed and moved away into the night, returning to the shelters.

Alice moved her gaze over the remaining seven warriors. They stood proudly, tall and robust.

The girl pursed her lips and shook her head slowly. Yuri noticed her apprehension.

"Kayl'sro," he said in a low voice. "They are all well-trained. They are all strong. They will all do their duty."

She pointed to the three standing closest to the older reptilian.

"Those three," she told him.

"Good choice," Yuri approved. "Vaktor, Y'sku and Plo'shyk. Step forward. The rest of you return to your dwellings."

The three warriors took a step towards the snowy-haired girl as the other four moved away.

"Do you know what is expected of you?" Alice asked them.

"We do," one of them replied. "We are to watch the city and report on what we see."

"There is to be no contact," she commanded. "Stay hidden and keep your weapons sheathed unless you have no other option. Do you understand?"

"Yes, Kayl'sro," they replied.

"Keep to the western forests and watch from the trees," Yuri instructed. "Try your best to not venture onto any roads, paths or tracks. Do not pass through the quarry and avoid all things of man along the way."

"Yessir," the three acknowledged.

"Cross the river downstream where the watchers on the wall can't see and position yourselves so that you can observe the western and southern gates," Alice ordered.

"What of the northern and eastern gates?" one warrior asked.

"Your name?" the girl demanded with a stern look.

The warrior swallowed hard.

"Y'sku," he answered.

"Y'sku," she repeated. "That is a good question. One of you will remain on the northern bank of the river to watch both the western and northern gates. There is no safe place to watch the eastern gate. But those on the southern bank should be able to see if there is any movement on the ground to the east if you position yourselves correctly."

"If they see you," Yuri added, "run as fast as you can to the west. Run all the way through the forest until you hit the plains. Follow the mountains north and cross back to us when you get the chance. Avoid capture at all costs."

The three warriors nodded as they shifted their gaze to one another nervously.

Arthur moved into the clearing slowly, making his way towards the camp. He tried not to show his discontent about his wife's decision, but found the entire episode of sending others on a mission that could cause peril a bit too much to handle.

Alice moved along the line and embraced each of the warriors, wishing them luck. They were hesitant to return the gesture, as their traditions didn't include physical interactions with their leader.

Yuri grinned slightly as he read the uncomfortable looks on the three young reptilian faces.

"Keep safe," Alice instructed.

"And keep to the shadows," said Yuri. "Go."

With that, the three Agrodien warriors dashed away, disappearing into the dark woods.

"They'll be all right, Kayl'sro," Yuri assured the girl.

"Let me know the moment you hear anything," she said as she turned to follow her husband.

"Yes, Kayl'sro," he replied, bowing slightly as she walked away.

***

The incessant sound of movement and pleasure coming through the wall from the room next to hers filled Catherine's ears and kept her on edge. She believed that both Takmel and her aunt were attempting to outdo each other during their embrace, getting louder and louder.

It was unnecessary.

It was late.

She was tired, and there was no chance of sleep ever occurring tonight.

She rose, dressed and laced her boots. She then draped herself in her shawl and quietly left the room.

The noise was louder in the corridor. She winced as she passed by the closed door to her aunt's room, trying not to imagine what was occurring inside.

There was once a time when she wouldn't have cared. Perhaps she might have even wanted to observe or partake.

But now, something inside her felt repelled by the thought.

She didn't understand why.

She simply knew that she no longer desired such tastes.

A light flickered from the living room. She could hear soft sobbing underneath the sounds of loud moans and groans. She moved to the doorway and peered around the corner, keeping herself hidden.

Lucy sat facing the fireplace. Her back was towards Catherine, but the girl could see clearly that the woman was crying.

"What's the matter?" Catherine asked, pulling her shawl over her head like a hood.

The sound of the girl's voice startled Lucy. She jumped slightly and turned in her seat.

"Nothing," she replied, wiping her eyes on her sleeves.

"Don't lie to me," Catherine whispered, moving into the room. "Tell me why you're upset."

Lucy frowned as the girl lowered herself into a seat across the room.

"He didn't choose me," she replied. "He refused me."

Lucy wept again.

"Is that all?" Catherine shook her head slightly.

"Is that all?" Lucy looked at the other, surprised. "He's the Maji. He's my husband. I ache for him."

"He's my husband, too." The girl looked into the small flames dancing in the fireplace. "I don't ache for him."

"You were his first." Lucy wore a confused look. "You should hurt even more than I. Can't you hear him in there?"

"I'm trying not to."

"So, you are hurting?"

"I'm repulsed," Catherine hissed. She fixed her piercing blue eyes upon the other woman.

Lucy winced, feeling the stare penetrate her heart. "I don't understand."

"Neither do I," Catherine replied, turning back to the flames.

"His touch means everything." Lucy relaxed and also peered into the fire. Her eyes were still wet with tears.

"If you say so," the girl said as she got up.

"Where are you going?"

Catherine quietly crossed the room and stood behind Lucy. She gently placed her palm on the woman's head.

"Slumber," she whispered.

Lucy closed her eyes and sank into the chair.

Catherine turned and made her way to the front door. The sound emitting from her aunt's room didn't appear to be coming to any conclusion. So, instead of returning to her room to get some sleep, she slipped out through the door and into the night.

Twelve

They ran swiftly, silently, through the darkness. The deep shadows beneath the trees, as well as the hollows and ground coverings, kept them from being seen.

Every once in a while, Vaktor signalled for them to stop.

The three reptilians listened intently for sounds of any pursuers. They sniffed the air for the scent of others who might be watching.

Only the familiar aroma of the forest surrounded them.

Continuing on, they hustled over ridges and clung to the darkness.

It was a long trek, and the morning was approaching. They would need to find places to hide, places to spy upon the land before the sun crept over the mountains.

Pausing by the side of the Western Road that stretched from Woodmyst to Oldcastle, they listened again. Vaktor peered to his left, towards their intended destination.

The walled city was too far for him to see, but with the wind blowing from the east, the smell of fire, baking bread and defecation was unmistakable.

There was no sign of anyone nearby, so the Agrodien warriors crossed the path and moved towards the river.

The sound of flowing water grew louder as they ventured closer and closer to the wide stream. Carefully, they pushed through the undergrowth and squatted on the bank.

"I'll cross and move the farthest so that I can watch both the southern wall and the ground to the east," Vaktor whispered. "One of you will need to cross with me to keep watch of both the southern and western gates."

"I'll go," Y'sku volunteered. "But I think we should stick together, you and I."

"No," Vaktor replied. "I aim to watch the east. It's a long way to the other side of the city and I will concentrate most of my attention there. You will need to watch the two walls, in case I miss something. And you, Plo'shyk, will need to watch both the north and west."

"I know," the third reptilian answered. "I hope you two think of me while you're out there."

"What do you mean?" Y'sku asked.

"All the gates into the city are on this side of the river," he told them. "All except for one."

"Perhaps we should keep two on the northern bank," suggested Y'sku.

"Kayl'sro Alice was specific," Vaktor reminded him. "Two on the south. It makes sense. If this Maji is going to try anything, he will send forces through either the southern gate to Dweagan or the eastern gate to the caverns."

The other two dipped their heads.

"We do our duty," Vaktor added as he started towards the water.

"May Q'sharh watch over you both," Plo'shyk whispered.

"And you also," Y'sku replied.

Plo'shyk moved stealthily back towards the road as the other two warriors slid beneath the surface of the water. With a thrust of their tails, they swam across the river at great speed, passing through the strongest part of the current, over the deepest section of the channel with the greatest of ease. Before long, they were on the southern bank and moving into the woods.

Once back across the Western Road, Plo'shyk moved into the shelter of the forest and started towards the city.

The scent of man became stronger with each step that he took.

Eggs, bacon, sausage, toast and tea.

The bouquet of aroma was filling his senses.

Beneath it, he could grasp the distinct odour of horse and dog.

Even with the breeze working in his favour, he knew he needed to be cautious. The hounds could be trouble for him.

Another fragrance struck his nostrils. It was weak, but close. There was a sweetness to it, but it reeked of foulness.

He turned his head towards it. Just slightly out of his way, a little towards the road.

Hesitating, Plo'shyk considered whether to investigate the unfamiliar scent.

It could be dangerous, he thought. *It could be a trap.*

He peered towards the city. Through the trees, he could see small orange sparks dancing high above the ground.

Torchlight.

There were guards on patrol, walking along the wall.

Venturing closer to the road could place him in their view.

It's on the way. Sort of. And there is still a lot of forest between you and the wall, he tried to convince himself.

He grunted softly, giving in to his curiosity, and moved carefully towards the source of the fresh smell.

His eyes kept returning to the flickering lights through the trees.

Keeping his breathing slow, he tried to steady his heart as a small amount of fear crept in.

He came upon the edge of a small clearing, still a short distance from the roadside and well hidden from the guards on the wall by tall trees and thick shrubbery.

The scent was coming from here.

Slowly, he stepped into the clearing, peering towards the city now and then as he moved onto the open ground.

The smell was strong.

He moved his eyes to the ground before him.

His heart seemed to stop.

His mind became perplexed.

Birds.
Many, many birds.
Sparrows, robins, starlings, ravens.
Lifeless.
Still.

***

Vaktor and Y'sku paused by the edge of the tree line, keeping to the shadows as they peered towards the great stone wall of Woodmyst. Torchlight danced at intervals along the parapet. They could see a few dark forms of men standing on the towers by the gate and along the length of the western wall.

"Do you think I should remain here?" Y'sku muttered.

"No," Vaktor was quick to reply. "We should move to the south. You need to see both the southern gate and the western gate at the same..."

He squinted, staring towards the western gate, just on the other side of the river.

Y'sku followed the other's eyes and saw men atop of the wall, some conversing and some calmly gazing towards the woods.

"What is it?"

"There." Vaktor pointed with his chin.

Scanning the wall and only seeing the guards, Y'sku noticed nothing that couldn't be regarded as ordinary behaviour. He shook his head.

"Just where the western gate tower protrudes from the wall," the other explained. "Something clings to the stones just below the parapet."

Focusing his vision, Y'sku trained his eyes on the location that Vaktor was describing.

Sure enough, there was something on the wall.

It looked like laundry that had blown onto the stonework and had become attached.

"It's nothing," Y'sku told him.

Then it moved, creeping slowly to the top of the wall.

"By Q'sharh," Vaktor whispered. "Did you see that?"

"Yes," the other answered. "What is it?"

The guards above turned their attention towards the reptilians. The two Agrodien warriors lowered themselves to the ground and remained as still as they could.

"Do they see us?" Vaktor whispered.

"I hope not," Y'sku responded as he watched the men on the gate tower.

The men moved their faces along to the south before turning their attention back towards the Western Road.

Both reptilians relaxed. Their eyes moved back to the spot where the thing on the wall had been.

It was gone.

"Do you think it went into the city?" Y'sku asked.

"I think so, yes," Vaktor said. "I wonder what it was."

"I think we should get moving," offered Y'sku as he turned his face to the sky. "It's getting lighter."

The two moved away silently through the undergrowth, away from the river and the guards above the western gate.

**

Catherine stood in the kitchen, staring at her hands. Filth covered them.

She dipped them into the tub of water, used for cleaning the previous night's dishes. It suddenly annoyed part of her that no one had bothered to empty the tub from the night before. All of them were too preoccupied with the visit from Takmel.

Lucy had been the most excited to see him, acting like a pup who hadn't seen her master in a while. That was until Takmel made his ambitions clear and took Joanne, and only Joanne, into her bedroom.

Catherine, at the time, could not care in the slightest who he chose. She simply didn't want to be in his presence.

But she didn't understand why.

If he had chosen her, she would've acted appropriately, feigning excitement and making the same sounds that her aunt had been making behind the closed door.

She scrubbed her hands together frivolously, splashing a little water onto the table. Eventually, her hands were spotless.

She crossed the room and unbolted the back door, which opened onto a tiny courtyard. There, she emptied the tub onto a small vegetable patch before returning inside.

She wiped the table down with a towel and set it for breakfast. She returned to the courtyard and fetched some wood for the stove and fireplace.

Using two wooden pails, she fetched water from a barrel just outside the kitchen door and filled two large soup pots sitting on the stove. With a towel wrapped around her hand, she opened the firebox of the stove and placed a chock of timber inside.

Satisfied, she tiptoed through the living room, where Lucy still slept in the chair by the fireplace, and into her room to change out of her dirty clothes.

The sound of soft breathing reached her ears as she passed by her aunt's bedroom door. She could tell that the occupants were fast asleep.

After laying a fresh dress out on her bed, she stood back and stared at the garment for what seemed an eternity. The colour reminded her of the deep blue in the sky on a clear day.

She remembered her mother helping her to sew the material together. It was fabric bought from Dweagan a little more than a year ago.

The corners of her mouth drooped as she remembered sitting by the fireplace, her mother seated on one side guiding her, and Alice on the other giving advice periodically, clearly not understanding how to make a dress.

"Just loop it over and over and pull it tight," her younger sister had instructed. *"You're taking too long with those tiny stitches."*

"It's a dress, Alice," Emily told her. "Not a piece of leather."

"I know." The girl scowled. "She's just taking too long."

"What's the hurry?" Catherine asked. "I've nothing more to do today."

"But it's so dull," Alice whined.

"Not everything needs to be horses and hunting."

"Well, it should be," the girl replied. "Shouldn't it?"

She looked at the two younger children playing on the floor by Lucy's feet. One nursed a rag-doll while the other raced a small horse, carved from wood, around his body.

"Horses," the boy cheered, holding up his toy.

"See?" Alice gestured to the lad. "Antony agrees with me."

"Don't bring him into it," Joanne called from the kitchen.

"It looks nice," Takmel said, leaning over the back of Catherine's chair to see over her shoulder. "I can't wait to see you wearing it."

She smiled. Her cheeks turned rosy red as she continued moving needle and thread through the material.

"She can't wait for you to tear it off her," the younger girl jested.

"Alice," her mother chided.

Catherine felt a small smile grow on her face, but a deep sadness filled her heart as she remembered a fonder time. It seemed an eternity since she and her family were together. Such a long time had passed.

Tears streamed over her cheeks as she remembered the faces of her half brother and sister. She missed them.

She wished she could hold them again.

Apart from Takmel, no one remembered them any longer.

Her thoughts turned to her mother and sister.

She wondered if they still harboured memories of Antony and Holly. Or were they too affected by Takmel's spell?

Not Alice.

She pictured her younger sister with long white hair tied back in a braid. She saw the girl wearing her leather chest plate with swords in each hand. She recalled the rukyul and the dragon by the young warrior's side and the Agrodien nation standing behind her.

Alice can never be subjugated to the power of the Maji. That's why he doesn't have her. That's why he can never have her.

She is too strong for him.

Catherine flung the dress to the floor.

No matter how much she wished she could turn back time and have her whole family together again, she knew it was impossible. It was she who was responsible for Takmel's rise to power.

His ascension started long ago with the two of them scheming, plotting the course that needed to be taken. Subtle incantations, whisperings in certain ears and manipulations birthed attitudes within the influential people in Woodmyst.

Small actions had taken place to help the progress towards gaining control.

A small push here.

A little tug there.

A tiny accident involving horses on a bridge.

She was responsible, and she did it of her own free will.

Catherine sat on the edge of her bed and wept.

Whoever she was, she was not that person anymore.

She hated that girl.

But she wasn't sure if she liked the person she was becoming either.

"Mama," she whispered. "I wish you were here to help me."

It was a call in vain.

She no longer believed that her mother would help her any more than any of those living in the caverns. In her mind, they all, including her mother and sister, possibly hated her as much as she did.

She was alone.

So alone.

Thirteen

Using a knife and fork, Takmel sliced a portion of sausage and shovelled it into his mouth. His glance moved around to both Lucy and Joanne seated across the table from him, also enjoying a hearty breakfast of sausage, eggs and toast.

"This is good," he said with a mouthful of food. He swallowed and cleared his throat loudly. "Who do I thank for such a lovely meal?"

"Catherine cooked this for us." Lucy pointed to the young woman with her knife. "She was up very early."

"Well," he said, turning to look at Catherine. "Thank you, my love. It truly is a wonderful meal."

She faced the fireplace, away from him. Her shawl was over her head again, and her hands were working with needle and thread.

To Takmel, it appeared as if she was mending an old, grey blanket that she had draped over her lap. It looked to have stains in places and more than its fair share of tattered edges.

"Are you enjoying this wonderful meal that your niece prepared for us, Joanne?"

"I am," the auburn woman answered cheerily. She looked at her husband, but his attention fixed on the woman by the fire.

"Why don't you come and sit with us, my love?" he asked.

"I'm fine here," Catherine answered.

"You really should come over here," he said. "Your aunt is leaving today, and this may be the last chance you get to spend time with her for a while."

"I'm fine here," she answered.

The fire crackled as a deep silence fell over the room. A heavy tenseness filled the air, causing both Joanne and Lucy to sit still and watch on nervously.

Takmel pursed his lips and stared at the back of the chair in which Catherine sat.

"It is a good meal," Joanne finally said, trying to lighten the atmosphere. "I really appreciate it, Catherine. I've got a long way to go."

"Where are you going?" Lucy asked. "And why didn't you tell us about this sudden arrangement to travel?"

"Takmel wishes for me to be his ambassador in Newholt," she replied.

"Should we come along?" Lucy asked. "Should I come?"

"No." Takmel turned to face her. He forced a smile onto his face. "I need you here. At least one of my wives who is on good speaking terms with me should stay. Unless you would like to discuss whatever the problem is, my love?"

Catherine ignored the prompt and continued to move the needle through the thick material.

"The Seven are leaving?" Lucy furrowed her brow. "All of them?"

"I'm afraid so," Takmel replied. "It's necessary. Things are moving a little quickly. I understand your confusion. I really do, but there have been some developments of late that have forced me to speed up our plans. I need the eyes and ears of people I can trust in places far and wide. And who else better to trust is there than my own wives?"

Lucy tilted her head, seeming to understand. Catherine, however, shook her head slightly, as she knew his answer told her nothing. Lucy was lapping up what he offered like a dumb animal under its master's control.

"I really wish you would turn around and at least look at me," he said. His voice sounded hard and irritated.

"I'm fine here," she said, repeating her words again.

She sensed his rage, like hairs sticking up on the back of her neck. A tiny, wry smile turned the corner of her mouth.

"I haven't seen you in days," he said, pushing his chair back to rise to his feet.

"You can see me just fine from where you are," she replied.

The atmosphere tensed. Both women seated at the table went rigid as Takmel took a slow step towards the sitting room.

"I mean, your face. Your eyes. At least, let me see your eyes."

"You don't want to see my eyes," she answered. "I've changed. I'm hideous."

"Hideous?" He stopped in his tracks. "What do you mean? Let me see."

"No." She shook her head.

"I'm your husband." He took another step towards her. "I've known you since we were children. Let me see."

"No."

Joanne peered at the table before her as plates and cutlery trembled and shook.

"Catherine," Takmel said as he moved towards her.

Suddenly, the table slid across the floor violently, knocking both Joanne and Lucy off their chairs. Plates and cutlery crashed to the floor, spilling sausage and egg in all directions. A great roaring sound filled the room as the wooden legs of the table slid across the timber boards, right out of the kitchen. It sped past Takmel, turned, and blocked his advance towards the young woman in the seat by the fire.

There it stopped.

He stared at the piece of furniture, perplexed, dumbfounded. He turned to see both Joanne and Lucy lifting themselves from the floor. Their eyes turned to him as they tried to understand what had occurred. His expression told them he was as puzzled as they. Takmel's eyes flickered between the table and the back of the chair where Catherine sat.

"I said no," she told him calmly as she continued to face the fire, working with needle and thread.

***

"We have fifteen-hundred men taken from our ranks," Lewis Drayton said, standing atop of the parapet that stretched over the southern gate. His face appeared perplexed as he read through the numbers and notes on the parchment in his old hands. "Is this correct? That's quite a large portion of our soldiers."

"It is," Takmel replied. His eyes were upon the large parade of troops and supplies moving through the market square between the Assembly Hall, the northern bank of the river. Amongst them, near the middle, seven women robed in seven colours rode amongst the men.

He felt nervous and sad as he watched his wives start across the centre bridge, heading towards his position. The corners of his mouth drooped as he looked at each of their faces. They talked amongst themselves cheerily. Clearly, they were excited about the prospect of being his *ambassadors*. Only Joanne held a sombre expression as her eyes kept their gaze upon her husband. Takmel sighed as he heard the ruffling of paper by his side.

"Is that wise, my lord?" the old bookkeeper asked. "We'll be practically defenceless. I mean, we already have nearly ten thousand troops in Dweagan. Surely that would be enough to take Newholt."

"Twelve hundred remain here with us, Lewis," Takmel answered, watching Joanne as the procession started along the wide street towards the gate. "That's more than enough to defend the walls."

"But we've practically no horses left."

"We have enough to pull wagons," the younger man told him. "There are still those that belong to the farmers that we can sequester if need be."

"But what if we're attacked?"

"By whom?"

"My lord?"

"Only Alice and her vagabond band of castaways pose any threat," Takmel informed the other. "And what are they? Around two hundred in total. Most of which are women and children. I'm sure our twelve-hundred will hold their own against them."

"She has a dragon," the old man said fearfully. "Have you heard what dragons did to this place?"

"That was long ago." Takmel smiled to Joanne as the parade drew nearer to his position. He turned to a guard standing by the tower. "Open the gate."

"Open the gate!" the guard shouted.

The sound of loud clunks and jingles resounded as levers were pulled and bars were removed from the large timber panels that faced towards the southern plain. With a loud creak, the gate opened wide, thudding noisily as the heavy wooden hatches slammed against the stone walls of the gatehouse.

"Our walls are larger, wider and better constructed than the stone fences of old," Takmel told the bookkeeper as he watched Joanne start for the passage beneath him. He gave her a nod and blew her a kiss. She smiled sadly and blew him one back. The other six women riding behind her looked up to him and waved as they disappeared from view.

He crossed the parapet to the southern edge of the wall. There, he leant against the battlement and peered through an embrasure. The procession moved into the open, following the southern road that moved between the recently emptied cornfields on either side. Several farmers and their families leant against the rickety fences that surrounded the meadows, waving and calling to the Seven as they rode by them.

"No dragon could crush the stone," Takmel said. "Not even two dragons could break this wall."

"But they breathe fire and fly over walls," Drayton reminded him.

The young man's eyes flickered to the woods just past the fields.

"Alice won't attack with her dragon, Master Bookkeeper," he said confidently. "I believe she won't attack at all. She has family here. Her friends have family here. I assure you, we are perfectly safe from Alice and her people."

"Of course, my lord." Drayton bowed slightly, not sounding entirely convinced.

"Now..." Takmel turned and started along the wall towards the west. "If you'll excuse me. I have a little errand to run."

"You're not staying to see your wives away?"

"I've seen them," he returned, moving off as he wrapped his robe tightly about himself.

"Oh," the old man said with a quick nod. "I'll leave you be then."

He turned to move towards a door set in the tower, only to be startled by the sight of another standing on the wall a few yards from him.

A figure, draped and hooded in a grey tattered cloak, stood near the edge of the wall, facing south.

"Ah..." Drayton's voice quivered. He felt an intense fear as he looked upon this new vision. "Hello. Can I be of assistance?"

"You have much to do, Master Bookkeeper," the other replied. The voice was familiar, but filled him with dread. It sounded like a whisper that surrounded him, having no point of origin. Yet, he knew that the voice belonged to this shrouded woman.

"Lady Catherine?"

"Don't let me keep you," she told him.

He tilted his head to see her face, but she was well concealed.

"Perhaps you would like to accompany me for some tea?"

"I'd like to stay here and see my aunt away, if you don't mind," she said.

He peered at her for what seemed a long time. "Of course, my lady."

The old man moved into the tower, vanishing down a winding stairwell that returned him to the ground below.

Catherine looked over the procession, watching her aunt in black and the six other women in coloured garments moving away. Her gaze moved to her right. She looked to where her husband had been heading.

He hadn't noticed her approach.

He hadn't seen her move upon the wall to watch the Seven depart.

She wondered if he had noticed her now.

But he was gone.

It didn't matter. She knew where he was going.

Her attention moved to the forest, just beyond the empty cornfields.

There, momentarily, she saw a whiff of black vapour moving along the tree line before disappearing from view.

She lowered her head and let out a soft sigh.

***

Vaktor, crouching low in the brush, observed the long procession, counting horses, wagons and riders. He hoped Y'sku was doing the same.

His gaze moved to the seven colourfully clad women.

He recalled seeing them once before, in the glade by the caverns. Yuri had later informed him of what they were.

"Witches," he hissed.

He spat in the grass as he continued to observe them.

A chill ran down his spine to the tip of his tail. A gentle breeze swept over his back as if something had passed by swiftly.

Turning, he peered into the forest and saw nothing.

Just the wind.

Only there was no wind.

The trees didn't move.

The grass didn't rustle.

His heart beat faster as he noticed a shadow forming around him.

Dark.

Dense.

He turned back to face the walled city. Instead, his view was obstructed by a thick pillar of black vapour.

Vaktor started to his feet, reaching for his sword.

A thick, membranous arm formed at the side of the misty object. It shot out towards the reptilian with long, claw-like fingers, gripping him tightly by the neck.

Tighter and tighter the fingers squeezed.

Unable to breathe, Vaktor tried to kick at his attacker with his legs.

The vapour lifted him off the ground so that the tip of the Agrodien's tail just touched the surface.

Vaktor gripped the arm with his own claws, trying desperately to pull the aggressor away; trying desperately to breathe.

His legs and tail swung wildly in order to connect with the lower regions of the dark cloud. But it was in vain. The only solid portion Vaktor could find of this creature was the limb that grasped him by the neck.

Tighter and tighter, the claws gripped.

The reptilian felt several places pop inside.

The pain was immeasurable, but he could not scream or call out.

A thick splatter of blood ejected from his nose.

The world around him grew darker and darker.

Tighter and tighter.

A loud crunching sound filled his ears.

His arms fell to his sides, and his legs stopped kicking.

The dark vapour continued to squeeze tighter and tighter.

Suddenly, the creature shook Vaktor violently, tearing his head away from his body.

The headless corpse thudded to the ground in a heap.

Slowly, the membranous arm transformed back into vapour, drawing the reptilian's dismembered head into its bulk.

For a moment, it hovered over the body, observing as the Agrodien's tail continued to twitch before silently wisping through the trees towards its next victim.

***

"You need to flee," a voice said from behind him.

Plo'shyk turned quickly away from the city, causing the undergrowth where he hid to rustle loudly.

A woman in a tattered grey hood stood before him.

He stared at her, confused.

"Do you understand?" she asked. She pointed to him, and then, using the same hand, pointed to the west. "Flee."

He cocked his head.

He didn't understand.

The woman turned her head to the south.

"He is coming," she hissed. "I cannot stay."

She pointed to him.

"You," she said, before pointing to the west again. "Go."

He stood slowly, warily.

"Go to Alice," she instructed.

Alice.

"Kayl'sro," he grunted.

"Kayl'sro?" she queried. "Alice."

"Kayl'sro Alice," he growled, staring wildly at the woman. He bared his teeth and gripped the hilt of his blade.

She moved her eyes to the south again.

"Go to Alice," she said once more.

Plo'shyk turned his head to the south to see what had her interest.

He saw trees, shrubs and more of the same beyond.

Annoyed with the silly game, he tightened his grip on his sword and prepared to cut the woman down.

Turning back, he saw nothing.

He turned in a complete circle to find her.

The woman was nowhere to be seen.

But to the south, he could see a shadow approaching through the trees.

It moved like a snake, writing and twisting through the air, like a dark cloud with a mind of its own.

A deep sense of fear overcame him.

He no longer felt the need to stay and watch Woodmyst.

The sudden urge to run away became far more powerful.

So, that was what he did.

His legs pumped as fast as they could as he sprinted through the woods.

With a quick glance over his shoulder, he saw the smoke creature pursuing.

It was faster than he.

It was gaining.

He knew blades and claws would be no match against such a creature.

The only hope he had was to make it back to the glade where Alice or one of the other sorceresses might be able to save him.

"Q'sharh," he spat as he turned slightly to the north, directing his route towards home.

Fourteen

Oliver Weston strolled across the open grassland, balancing his wood axe on his shoulder. Several children galloped happily through the tall grass not too far from him, causing the sheep to scurry away. A few of the hounds gave the children chase, catching them only to smother their faces with licks and slobber.

It was then the younglings' turn to give pursuit. Two dogs ran just slowly enough for the children to gain upon them, allowing their little hands to pull them to the ground. Oliver laughed as the dogs relented, rolling onto their backs so they could have their stomachs rubbed.

It was a win-win situation for the hounds. They got to lick people and get their tummies scratched in return.

"Papa," he heard a small child call from the grass. The youngling was barely visible as he moved through the tall growth.

"Who is that?" the man called, lowering his axe to the ground. "Are you friend or foe?"

"Papa," the child called again. The grass rustled and parted as the child ran towards his father.

"I hope you're not a bear," Oliver teased. "I may need to run away if you are."

"I'm not a bear," the other replied. "I'm Ivo."

"Ivo the bear?"

"No!" The boy giggled. The other children stopped to watch the exchange, enormous smiles on their faces. Some hounds took advantage of this tranquil moment and tackled them to the ground to lick their faces.

As laughter erupted from the tall grass, Oliver hoisted his youngest boy high into the air.

"Ivo the bear," he roared. "I caught you at last."

"I'm not a bear," the lad protested.

"No?" the man asked in jest.

"No."

"Then, what are you?"

"I'm your son."

Oliver held the boy in front of him with outstretched arms, inspecting him by tilting his head this way and that.

"Hmmm," he agreed. "It appears to be so. You look like my Ivo."

"I am."

"There's only one way to be sure," Oliver said wryly. "I'll need to give you the test."

"Test?" Ivo looked concerned.

"I need to give you," he paused for effect, "the claw!"

With that, he fell to the ground with his boy in his arms and tickled the lad's ribs with his fingers. Ivo instantly fell into a laughing fit as Oliver raised his hand to the sky triumphantly.

"The claw," he growled before attacking his son with another barrage of tickles.

The game continued for some time before the boy pleaded for his father to stop.

"I'm going to piss myself!"

"Not near me," Oliver objected, rolling away from the boy. He retrieved his axe and returned to his feet.

"Where are you going?" Ivo asked.

"Back to the fire," he replied.

"Why?"

"For something to eat," the man said. "You want to come?"

The boy turned to see the children still playing with the hounds.

"No," he decided. "I want to play more."

"All right," Oliver said. "Don't go too close to the forest. Stay in the open where I can see you."

"Yes, Papa," Ivo called as he ran off to join the others.

Oliver continued across the pastureland, taking a route that led him over a newly constructed small timber bridge spanning the stream. It creaked slightly under his weight. He could have walked through the water, as it wasn't much deeper than ankle-high.

He started up the embankment that passed the large cavern and continued on towards Alice's cabin. There, he found several members of the small community seated around the fire drinking tea and eating bread.

"So," he said, leaning the axe against one cart that doubled as a dwelling, "what's the topic of the day?"

"Where's all the wood you've been cutting?" David asked from his seat by the fire.

"I'm not bringing it back by hand," the other told him as he sat in his seat. "I'll take a horse and one of the canvas sheets to collect it all after I eat and have had time to recuperate, thank you. And what have you been doing all morning, David?"

"You think I've been sitting here drinking tea since dawn?"

"Yes," Oliver quipped.

Soft laughter made its way around the hearth. David enjoyed the banter that he and Oliver often engaged in. It reminded him of his younger days.

"To be truthful, I've been working on some final touches in the Agrodien dwellings."

"Well," Oliver replied as Agnes, his wife, approached from the cabin with a mug, "that's just wonderful."

"Here," Agnes said, handing her husband the vessel. "Careful. It's hot."

"Thank you," he said before taking a sip.

She started away, back towards the cabin. "I'll fetch you some food," she said over her shoulder.

"Wait," he called after her. "Have you seen Tomas? He wasn't on the field with his brother."

"I told him to keep an eye on Ivo," she replied, and a deep look of concern fell upon her face.

"Great." Oliver rose from his seat.

"Don't fret," Lor interjected. "He and Alan were walking along the bank downstream when I last saw them. They'll be fine. What harm could they get up to?"

"He's right," David told them, directing his speech to Agnes. "The hounds are with the children. They'll keep them safe. And there is always this sentry watching over the glade."

David gestured to the large black form of Shadow, lying on the veranda of the cabin.

Oliver relaxed, returning to his seat.

Agnes allowed a deep sigh of relief.

"I'll fetch you something to eat," she said again before turning back to the cabin.

It wasn't long before others returned from their chores. The gathering by the fire grew larger and larger until almost all the inhabitants of the glade crowded about in the encampment. Only the children kept away, playing in the pasture where they chased the hounds and each other.

Alice appeared at the edge of the wood to the north of the clearing, with Queen Amicia and Ursula by her sides. Commander Brondt and Captain Thornton followed closely behind. The latter led his horse by the reins. The fresh carcass of a doe was slung over the beast's back.

"Well..." said David with a grin.

"Wait," Oliver said as he looked to the young, white-haired girl, then to the veranda of the cabin where the rukyul rested. "Shouldn't that thing be with her?"

"What thing?" David asked, turning to face his friend.

"That big, ugly thing," the other pointed to Shadow.

"He's more or less Arthur's pet, now," Lor put in, standing up to face his niece.

"Or Arthur is the rukyul's pet," Linet joked.

"A fine kill," Lor said to Alice, clasping a hand on her shoulder.

"Not mine, Uncle," she replied.

"No?" he replied, scrutinising the slain animal. It had a wound just above its eye from a bolt. "I don't know many who can shoot aim a bow this well. Except for you and perhaps Akasati."

"Ursula made the shot," the white-haired girl told him. "She says it was her first time shooting a bow. I have my doubts."

"It was," the other young lady assured her with a look of satisfaction on her face.

"The best shot I have ever seen," Thornton rumbled.

"She must have cheated," Amicia said in jest. "You used magic, didn't you? I tried shooting that wretched thing and couldn't even get the arrow to stay on the string."

"I didn't cheat," Ursula huffed playfully.

"Then it was a fluke," Alice stated. "Probably will never happen ever again."

The woman from Whitekeep placed her hands on her hips and gave the other two a stern look. They were both grinning cheekily.

"Don't listen to them, my love." Thornton took her gently by the arm and started away with his horse and the doe. "It was the best shot ever. You made it all by yourself and you should be proud. In fact, I believe you could make that same shot any time you want to. Now, let me show you how to skin and clean one of these."

Ursula leant against her man as they walked towards the cabin. She glanced over her shoulder at the other two women and poked her tongue out.

Alice chuckled as she peered around the fire at the many faces seated nearby.

"Where's Arthur?"

"He's inside helping your mother in the kitchen," David replied. "Pull up a seat and have some tea."

Brondt's and Thornton's men rose to their feet to offer their queen and commander a seat. Alice took her place in a chair that she had moved from the cabin just for herself.

"Busy morning," she said as David poured her a mug of tea.

"Life in the wild," Richard said, peering off towards the large cavern a short distance from his seat. "Always hunting and gathering. It was like this just after the Night Demons destroyed Woodmyst."

"I hate to admit this," Oliver said, grimacing, "but they were good days. Fun. We learnt so much back then."

"Great days," David agreed.

"Not for me." Richard looked at them both sternly. He reached over and took his wife's hand. "Not for the older children, like Becka here."

David and Oliver both lowered their heads apologetically.

"We did all the hunting," the old man continued. "We patched your clothes. Made new ones with what material we had. We thatched roofs and built shelters because all of you were too young or too small. Or you were too busy playing games like those younglings on the pasture over there. All except Tomas, who understood the importance of survival."

"We were children," Oliver argued. "We were too young to understand. But we heeded to your word and obeyed you like our own father."

"Yes," Richard agreed. "That is true. You were all good little girls and boys."

"And we learned to survive," David added. "We learned how to construct homes and how to hunt."

"Tomas taught you how to do that," said the elder. "Not me. I taught you how to farm and raise crops. By the time you were old enough to hunt large game, I was feeling old in my legs."

Richard took a deep breath. He looked to the blue sky and watched thin white clouds stream across the expanse.

"I think it's time that some younglings learnt how to fish and hunt small game," Richard told them. "I think they need to know how to raise crops and livestock. We had it too good in Woodmyst. Others did all of this for us. We had farmers and butchers and a market to buy our needs. Most of you have skills to survive out here," he continued. "But your children do not. Alice here is the only exception."

The girl sipped her tea and listened to the old man's words.

"That young lady could bring down a doe on her first try." Richard gestured to Ursula, who was working the blade through the carcass under Thornton's careful watch. "I feel glad for her. But we have children nearly the same age as Alice who have not yet caught a fish, let alone milked a cow. It's time they learnt."

"I can teach them," Alice offered.

"No offence, my dear," Ewan Cunningham spoke up. "But most of the younglings are afraid of you. Don't misunderstand me. They love you and respect you. But you differ from most children. They see you more like one of us. An adult. And even then, they see you as something more, because *we*, the other adults, listen to you and treat you as our leader."

"I'm thirteen," Alice argued. "And Richard just said that it was my father who taught the others how to hunt and build. And he was my age when he did all of that."

"That's true," Linet acknowledged. "Your father, my brother, wasn't given much of a choice. Richard was the only adult we had. It was only natural that someone like Tomas would rise and lead the rest of us.

"But things have changed. We are adults now and we have our own children. We should teach them these things. We shouldn't leave it to you when you have so much more to contend with."

"But, I can—" the girl started.

Suddenly, a terrible shrill scream echoed across the glade.

Shadow lifted his head and glared towards the pastureland.

Thornton turned from the carcass to see the mixed herds fleeing away from the eastern tree line and further into the opening.

At first, he thought the children were giving chase, until he saw they were all standing rigid, facing the trees.

"Fuck me," he said.

"Shouldn't swear," Glaun told him as he passed by, heading towards the pasture to get a better look. He called over his shoulder. "There's something down there. Near the trees."

Alice was already on her feet, running towards the open land.

Down the embankment, leaping over the stream effortlessly and speeding through the tall grass, Alice sprinted as fast as she could.

The sound of her heart thumping filled her ears. Her breathing became more and more hurried. The smell of fresh blood filled her senses.

She slowed when she reached the first of the younglings. A small Agrodien child pointed towards the trees.

Alice moved on, sidestepping a hound who was standing by another child. The beast's hackles were on edge and it bared its teeth as it glared towards the woods.

She passed another child and another until she came face-to-face with three reptilian warriors. The white-haired girl recognised them immediately.

They were the three volunteers that she had chosen to spy upon Woodmyst.

Their eyes had been plucked from their sockets, leaving gaping black holes. Their mouths were pried open, and their long tongues hung listlessly from the side.

Each head rested upon a pike and left in place, as if to watch the glade from the edge of the trees.

Standing at the base of the pikes was one child.

He peered at her blankly, shivering as she stepped nearer to him.

"Ivo?" She reached her hand out, hoping to take him away from the ghastly scene.

Instead, he shook more violently.

The sound of approaching feet caused her to look over her shoulder.

Yuri came to a sudden stop when he saw the mutilated heads of his warriors.

"By Q'sharh," he hissed before dropping to his knees.

Nola'ee was hot on his heels. Her mouth dropped open in shock as she looked at each of the Agrodien faces. Her eyes paused and lingered on one before filling with tears.

"Plo'shyk," she blubbered. "My Plo'shyk. Where is his body, Kayl'sro?"

Alice felt her stomach tighten into a ball. She did not know that her personal guard was in a relationship with one of these warriors. Perhaps she would have chosen differently if she had.

"I don't know," she answered.

Nola'ee lost breath as she fell to the ground, weeping. Alice fell to her side and wrapped her arms around the other, wishing she could turn back time and choose a different stratagem. Wishing she hadn't sent watchers to Woodmyst.

Others appeared on the scene.

"Ivo," Oliver called to his son. "What's the matter?"

The boy's shoulders moved as if someone held him and shook him aggressively. His head rolled around wildly, while his arms and legs remained rigid.

Slowly, slowly, he lifted from the ground.

Rising.

Rising.

"Ivo?" Agnes screamed as she ran through the grass.

"Alice, help," Oliver cried. His eyes filled with water.

The white-haired girl watched on. She did not know of how to deal with such a thing.

Higher and higher, the little boy lifted in the air. His feet dangled above the heads of the Agrodien warriors. His head lolled to the left side as his body stopped convulsing.

His eyes rolled back in his head, exposing the whites, and his mouth opened wide.

"Alice," a voice boomed from the child.

Ivo's lips didn't move. But the voice continued to resound from the child's mouth.

"Alice," the voice said again. "I'm very disappointed, Alice."

"Takmel," the girl said.

"I thought we had an agreement," he continued. "You were to remain here in the glade and I would allow you to live. You have broken this agreement. You can't be trusted."

"Let the boy go," she hollered.

Ivo's head lolled to the right side.

"I found your spies," the voice told her. "I ate their eyes."

Yuri got up, balling his hands into fists.

"I have plans for their other parts," said Takmel.

"I'll kill you," Alice growled, reaching her hands up to grab the boy. "Let him go."

"You can't stop this," Amicia whispered in Alice's ear. "There's nothing we can do for now."

"I need to remind you of who I am," Takmel's voice thundered. "I intend to hunt down any outsiders who you might consider worthy allies. Whether they be human or otherwise, I will find them, and I will destroy them. One by one, I will rid the land of all who may oppose me. I will start with your friends, the dragon keepers in the Core Lands. Eventually, you will have no one left in this world. And to show you I mean what I say, watch carefully."

The boy's arms flung outwards, as if something was pulling him from either direction. His mouth opened wider and wider.

A loud, wet crunch burst from deep inside of the lad. Dark blood spurted from his mouth and spilled over his chin.

Agnes screamed hysterically.

Oliver could do nothing but hold his wife and watch on in horror.

A stain appeared on the chest area of the boy's tunic and expanded down his body.

His jaws pried open wider and wider.

His cheeks tore apart, exposing raw flesh and white bone.

Sinew and tendons snapped as the little one's crown came to rest against the back of his neck.

A thick puddle of fluid and blood collected beneath the child.

Alice fell to her knees in a sobbing mess as the boy came crashing back to the ground.

Fifteen

They had set the pyre using the wood that Oliver had cut during the morning. The flames rose high, lapping the deepening evening sky. Glowing embers lifted and circled before being caught by a cross wind zipping down from the mountains, that sent them shooting towards the south.

Alice turned her head slowly, absorbing the faces of all who had gathered. They wore expressions that ranged from grief, sombreness, confusion, guilt and anger.

The Agrodien stared into the flames quietly. They concealed their emotions mostly. All except Nola'ee and two other young females who stood beside Alice, weeping profusely.

Out of respect to them, she wore the black bearskin and brandished the iron claws of the Kayl'sro. In truth, she blamed herself for the deaths of the three warriors. Alice wished she had words for them. She wished she could produce the slain bodies of the Agrodien, instead of placing only their heads upon the timber.

She looked over at Oliver and Agnes. He had his arm wrapped over her shoulders as they both clung to Tomas, their elder son. The cheeks of all three glistened in the firelight from the tears that they shed.

Alice felt Arthur's fingers interlace with her own. She peered to him and saw that he was crying.

She leant into him, resting her head on his shoulder. Uncertain whether it was the right thing for a leader to do, showing emotion in public, she didn't care. Her husband was upset, and she didn't like that.

He made the typical manly response by wrapping his arms around her, probably believing that he was comforting her.

But she didn't feel sad or despondent. She didn't feel confused or angry. And even though she blamed herself for the fatality of the three Agrodien spies, she didn't feel guilty.

She felt empty, as if a dark void had opened in her heart.

***

Liana seemed to sense Alice's determination as the girl strapped the saddle and bridle to the dragon's back. The dragon had noticed the leather armour and two swords sheathed upon her rider's hips and knew that they were not about to take a pleasure ride over the small village. She stayed rigid, allowing the girl to pass under her neck and chest as she moved the leather bonds into place.

"What do you think you are doing?" Arthur called. His footfalls were heavy, and his paces were quick. His voice emitted a hint of anger amongst confusion. "A boy has been murdered and you want to take a ride on your dragon?"

"I have to warn Gruloch," the snowy-haired girl replied as she tightened a buckle just beneath the magnificent beast's wing. "I may be too late already."

"I forbid you to leave," Emily called as she approached. Amicia and Ursula followed closely behind.

"I am leader here, Mama," Alice replied, standing to face the small gathering. "I will not take orders from you or anyone for that matter."

"Will you take advice?" the queen asked calmly.

The girl took a deep breath and locked eyes with the other. She nodded.

"Be careful out there," said Amicia. "He will have eyes on you."

"I know." She strode a few paces to her husband and wrapped her arms around his neck before planting a long kiss on his cheek.

"You're a bloody fool, Alice," he said, taking her into his arms and holding her tightly.

"Tell Yuri to keep the warriors alert," she instructed him. "Takmel may try something in my absence. Keep watch over Oliver and Agnes for me."

Arthur nodded, he would do so. "Don't be gone long," he told her.

She stopped by the side of the dragon, pressing her hand against the rough skin of Liana's neck. Her head dropped as she slowly turned to face the gathering.

Without warning, Alice raced to the auburn woman and fell into her arms.

"I'm sorry, Mama," she whimpered.

"Me too," Emily replied. "You are right. It's not my place to instruct you. Not anymore. You're too much like your father, and no one could tell him what to do."

"I'll be back as soon as I can," the girl said, pulling away from her mother.

With one leap, Alice was upon Liana's back.

The dragon spread her wings wide as she turned to face the open ground of the glade. She thrust her wings and bounded upon her back legs, and both dragon and girl left the ground and lifted into the sky.

"Be careful out there?" Emily directed to the queen as she watched her daughter and the beast bank to the north. "That's your advice?"

"It was the first thing I could think of," answered Amicia.

Emily pursed her lips and continued to silently watch the dragon fly away with her daughter.

***

Liana climbed into the air, far above the rugged mountain range. The western plains stretched on and on before them, blurring where the sky met the ground on the horizon.

Alice pulled her cloak about her tightly and positioned her scarf over her mouth and nose as the chill of the air swept over her face. She turned her head to the east and saw nothing but countless jagged mountain peaks. The taller ones had snow gathering on top. Others were a little too low to receive such a dusting.

Returning her face to the west, she noticed Liana had adjusted her bearing a little to the north. She knew where they were heading.

Alice allowed the reins to slacken and relaxed her posture.

The gentle thrumming of the dragon's wings filled her ears with each long thrust.

Before long, the edge of the range passed beneath them and they were flying over the great sea of grass that hemmed the western slopes.

White specks fluttered from the trees far below. Birds spooked by the sight of a giant beast in the sky above them.

Eventually, the grass changed from a lush green to a dirty brown and the trees thinned out, so it became a rarity to see one.

She could see here small patches of vegetation and there, but their colouring reminded Alice of the charred timber left in the fire after the flames had died.

They were now over the Core Lands.

As Liana continued to press on, Alice took time to peer about her. She noticed the mountains in the distance behind her and to her right. The entire range seemed to go on forever into the north. Its immensity was something she could never comprehend from the ground.

From so far above, where everything looked so small down below, she appreciated the tremendousness of the world around her.

She felt a smile form as she soaked in the view.

Liana let out a guttural call.

Alice looked to the ground ahead of them.

The obscure form of large, towering rock formations appeared.

The Pillars of Mohaa.

They were still some distance away, but they would be there sooner than Alice had originally believed.

"My, you're fast," she told the beast.

The dragon started gently towards the ground.

"Not yet," the girl said as she took the reins again.

The beast continued on her descending path.

"Up, Liana," Alice ordered. "Up."

The dragon ignored the calls and continued towards the ground.

Alice peered ahead, towards the Earth below, and saw what had drawn the beast's attention.

A swarm of black figures were scurrying over the ground towards the distant towers. Hundreds and hundreds of creatures.

"All right," Alice said to Liana. "You know what to do."

The dragon dived for the swarm, rushing towards the ground at great velocity.

She opened her nostrils and mouth and let a long jet of flame sweep over the tail end of the horde as she swooped back into the sky.

At least thirty of the black creatures fell to the dirt, writhing and screeching in agony as they burned alive.

The rest of the swarm ignored their fallen comrades and continued racing towards the towers of rock.

Liana sped into the air, tucked her wings against her body and turned back towards the ground.

Alice lowered herself to place her frame against the dragon, gripping tightly to the horn of her saddle.

The terrible sound of roaring wind filled the girl's ears as they plummeted towards the earth.

With a flash, bright flames spewed from the dragon's mouth, filling Alice's vision.

Suddenly, she saw the bright blue of the sky again as Liana took to the air, preparing for another attack run.

Alice glanced over her shoulder.

Dark smoke trailed away from the back of the swarm towards the west.

She couldn't count how many she hit in the barrage, but she could see that hundreds were still making their way towards the Pillars of Mohaa.

This could take all day and night, Alice thought.

Liana rolled over and dived again.

Again, she ignited the ground where the creatures ran.

Again, she set many of them aflame.

But her efforts had a limited effect on their numbers.

Onward they scurried.

With each sweeping pass, more creatures fell.

With each sweeping pass, they grew closer and closer to the towers of rock.

There were still too many.

A great trumpet blast resounded.

Alice moved her attention to the north and saw seven winged beasts approaching.

The Haigok were coming.

The horn blew a long, deep note.

Six of the dragons responded by diving towards the swarm. They formed into a line and attacked head-on.

A colossal wall of flame swept over the horde like a rolling wave of light and smoke.

Screams and roars erupted from the ground as the fire bit into the flesh of the black creatures.

Alice turned Liana towards the rider holding the trumpet. She hoped it was Gruloch, the leader of the Haigok, but as she passed by, the rider gave her a friendly wave. It was one she did not recognise.

He gave two sharp blows on the horn, recalling the other dragons.

Her eyes could scarcely believe it when they circled around her. Not one of them had a rider.

They simply responded to the calls of the trumpet.

The Haigok let out another long note, instructing the dragons to strike again.

Alice turned Liana in a wide circle as she observed the attack run.

Another wall of flame swept over the ground, engulfing the creatures and scorching everything on the surface below them.

This time, the screaming ceased.

With two sharp calls from the trumpet, the dragons regrouped in the air and the rider led them back towards their home. He waved his arm, beckoning Alice to follow.

He needn't have done so as Liana was already turning towards the stone towers.

Sixteen

"Alice?" a familiar voice called as she dismounted from her saddle.

Liana craned her neck towards the figure approaching from along the path and let out a soft, pleasant chirp.

"Lord Gruloch," the girl replied, bowing slightly.

"You look different," he said as he drew nearer, reaching up to pet the dragon on the snout. "Your hair. I almost didn't recognise you."

Alice touched the white braid that had fallen over her shoulder.

"Some things have changed," she told him.

"I know," he replied. His voice went low with a tone of solemnity. "We have much to discuss."

A tall Haigok male stepped from a nearby cavern and approached Liana. The dragon turned to inspect the newcomer, sniffing his head as he started unbuckling the straps of the saddle.

"I should see to Liana first," the girl said.

"We will look after her," the Lord of the Haigok informed her. "This is Hogul, one of the dragon keepers. She is in expert hands with him."

Hogul sang softly to Liana in a tongue that Alice didn't understand. Liana chirped quietly and purred.

"Hogul cares for the infant dragons," Gruloch explained. "Liana knows him well. You have nothing to be concerned with. Come. There is food and a hut has been prepared for you."

"Hut?"

Gruloch took the girl by the arm tenderly and led her back along the path, away from the dragon caves and towards the village in the valley

125

below. Torches had been lit along the edge of the trail, and throughout the community in preparation for the night.

"We saw you approaching," he said, pointing to the south with his free hand as two guards fell into step behind him. "Just before your dragon attacked those creatures. We dispatched our own dragons and readied a place for you. I hope I wasn't being too presumptuous."

"No." Alice smiled politely. "Of course not. I appreciate the gesture. But I must be truthful with you. I didn't come to destroy those creatures. I came to ask for your help."

Gruloch could hear the upset pitch in her voice.

"Something horrible has happened," he presumed.

"Most horrible," she admitted as they continued along the path.

***

"So, this Maji intends to wipe my people and me out," Gruloch restated. "All because we are friends."

"You are the first that he intended to attack," she said, lifting a portion of lamb from her plate. "I opposed him. I guess I offended him, and he sought retaliation."

"For sending spies?"

"I presume so." She slipped the meat into her mouth.

Gruloch pointed his blade at her. It still had a small piece of charcoaled flesh clinging to its edge.

"That would be a false presumption," he told her before pointing the knife towards the other villagers sitting about them, sharing the meal. "We have been watching for some time, Alice. This Maji of yours has been plotting something for a very long time."

The Lord of the Haigok sliced another piece of mutton from the roasted lamb resting on the table before them.

"We have seen these dark creatures that you attacked before today," he said through a mouthful. "They come from the north. From the Frozen Waste. They lurk deep in ice caves and feast upon wolves and bears.

"They sleep in the warmer seasons, only coming out during the coldest times of the year. The fact that they are roaming these lands before winter has come only causes me to suspect that something sinister is occurring."

"They answer to him," Alice informed the Haigok.

"The Maji?"

"Yes," she confirmed. "And his mother before him."

"His mother?"

"The White Witch of the Mirikin."

"From Wintermarsh," Gruloch said.

"She was in the White Keep by the Eastern Sea before that," explained Alice.

"We know of her," Gruloch told her. "We know your father killed her. We also know that she left a sizable army behind in Wintermarsh and the Ironfields before the attack of the Mirikin began. We know those armies have been recruiting and training new warriors and that they have more than doubled their sizes since the White Witch was destroyed.

"The ports of Blackshore and Meadowmoor have been reinforced and Ostford and Pryholt have been rebuilt. It would appear that your Maji has grand plans.

"The latest report we have is that there is a large encampment in the mountains to the south of Woodmyst. They are heading south. Our guess is that they are making their way for Dweagan, where there are many ships and a large force of men waiting."

"How do you know this?" Alice asked.

"We have spies too." Gruloch smiled, his bulbous eyes squinting menacingly. "Ours, unlike yours, take to the skies and watch from high above. It's a rare thing for a man to look up when he's a sentry. Instead, he will look to the ground and watch for movement between trees. We use the clouds and the glare of the sun to hide. No one has not seen yet."

Alice looked to the ground blankly as several images churned in her head.

"He's establishing outposts," she said finally. "He's replacing the old Mirikin strongholds with his own wives."

"Wives?" Gruloch looked at her curiously.

"He has a hold over them," she said, moving her eyes to the Lord of the Haigok. Tears welled in her eyes. "He's using sorcery to control their will. They have all done terrible things in his name. So terrible that I don't think there will be room for forgiveness."

"Explain, *terrible*," he requested.

"They fed upon their children," she muttered.

A sudden silence fell over the gathering.

A flooding memory of stories, a history involving his people and hers, filled his mind. He peered at the stars and swallowed the lump that had formed in his throat.

"He must be destroyed," Gruloch whispered. "Perhaps his demise will break the spell."

"I agree," said Alice. "He must be destroyed. But as far as his spell breaking afterwards, that is yet to be seen. I wonder how many of them are acting upon their own will now. Perhaps they have turned so far that there is no way back. Perhaps some were twisted badly after their encounter with the Sovereign in Blackrock Haven. Perhaps some of them have always been this way and were waiting for an opportunity like this to present itself.

"One thing is for certain," she continued. "He won't venture far from Woodmyst. It offers natural fortifications and is positioned far from the coast. Ships can't attack it with cannons and armies need to cross mountains or move through forests to reach it.

"Its walls are high and thick, fortified and reinforced with iron and stone. A dragon's weight would not even be enough to tumble it."

"But an attack from the air might succeed," Gruloch interjected. "Which is why he tried to reach us with his creatures first. He has considered the threat we pose."

Alice furrowed her brow as she considered the growing forces in the west.

"How do you think he could get messages to Wintermarsh without leaving Woodmyst?"

"He uses the shadows," Gruloch informed her. "We've watched them come and go over the years, darting this way and that. We don't think they've seen us watching them. They appear like puffs of black cloud and usually keep hidden well. But we have seen them."

"Shadow Demons," Alice said. She had heard of them in tales. David and Richard had recounted a time when her own father had encountered one. Even Takmel had told her of Vonavo, the shadowy form imprisoned in a cage of armour and set to watch over him as a boy.

"They call themselves Gomatha," Gruloch said, slicing another portion from the lamb. "We have not seen them in some time. One of our scouts saw them converging on Woodmyst a while ago. That was the last we noticed them."

"Perhaps they're still there," one of the Haigok males seated nearby suggested.

"This is Malukh." Gruloch gestured to the figure across the table from Alice. "He was the scout who last saw the shadows."

"Or perhaps this Maji ate them," Malukh added with satisfaction as he reached for a portion of lamb.

Alice felt a chill slice through her heart. The Haigok's words weren't far from the truth. A flashing vision filled her thoughts of twisting tendrils of vapour being drawn into Takmel.

"He absorbed them," Alice said, putting a hand to her chest.

"Alice?" Gruloch leant towards the girl. "Are you all right?"

"The Maji absorbed them," she reiterated. "That's why you haven't seen them."

"They're dead?" Gruloch questioned.

She nodded, lowering her hand and repositioning herself more comfortably on her seat.

"So," Malukh remarked, "he *did* eat them?"

***

Takmel Hamond slouched in a high-backed chair atop of the assembly hall's platform. A deep scowl had formed on his face as he stared angrily at the large doors of the building.

Several lanterns had been lit along each of the side walls, casting deep crisscrossing shadows throughout the interior, formed by the thick pillars that supported the roof. The flicker of distant flame created a sharp glint in his eye, which made the guards by the base of the platform slightly uncomfortable. Frightened.

The darkness of the enormous, nearly empty auditorium filled him with energy and gave him focus.

His hatred and fury fuelled his being as he channelled his thoughts to elsewhere.

His mind had moved from the disaster that had unfolded near the Pillars of Mohaa, where a legion of his dark creatures had turned to ash, to the people living on the glade by the caverns.

He sensed the power of two.

But the third, the one he concerned himself with the most, was elsewhere.

Their protector is away.

Takmel felt the dismay of the small community living by the mountains. He recognised their sadness and fear.

They were troubled.

They were disheartened.

They were lost.

This made him glad.

A tiny smirk crept upon his face.

The glade dwellers' weakness was his gain.

While they mourned the loss of the boy, and while their leader was absent, they would be distracted.

"Summon the captain of the guard," he commanded as he lifted himself from the chair.

"My lord?" a guard said, bringing himself to attention.

"I want a garrison ready to ride immediately," Takmel replied. "As many men as we can spare. Leave only what we require upon the wall. The time to strike is now."

Seventeen

Silently, the bowmen stepped over fallen branches, carefully placing their feet on the ground to not cause a stone to roll or a twig to snap. They held onto their weapons tightly, nocks already pressed against the string.

Behind them, waiting in the dark shadows of the woods, a mass of riders anxiously tried to keep their chargers quiet. But the horses were restless, thumping their hooves against the leaf-littered floor of the forest.

"Shush," the captain hissed angrily to the men sitting on their beasts nearby.

His men responded with apologetic glances.

The archers crouched by the edge of the tree line, peering across the glade from the east towards the camp.

Growls from amongst the livestock drew the men's attention. They loosed several arrows, silencing the hounds before they could alarm any of the folk dwelling near and in the caverns.

Forward they moved, crouching in the long grass, keeping their gaze upon the flickering orange glow of the low fire in the midst of the encampment. They retrieved their shafts from the bodies of the dogs and moved across the pastureland, trying their best to not spook the sheep and cattle.

Kneeling by the edge of the stream, the archers aimed their weapons high and pulled back hard on the bowstrings.

A soft creaking sound emitted, barely audible over the bubbling water passing by.

But it was enough.

Shadow heard the strange noise and bolted upright from the cabin's porch, scratching his claws loudly over the timber flooring.

"What was that?" David huffed, rolling onto his side before lifting himself out of bed.

Shadow sped through the camp and down the hillside as fast as he could.

His breath emitted clouds of white vapour from his open mouth. Gradually, each huff grew louder and louder until a deep guttural sound escaped with each rapid stride.

David barely made it to the porch, still fumbling with his boots, as the rukyul leapt over the stream to taste the blood of his first victim.

It was too dark to see what the beast was so excited about.

But the screams of men from the glade were enough.

"Wake up," he hollered. "Wake up. We're under attack."

Grumbles and curses from neighbouring tents filled the night air.

The noise of bumping and stumbling followed as the men pulled their trousers and boots on before grabbing what weapons they could lay their hands upon.

David turned to see his son running through the cabin towards the door.

"Is it Alice?" he called. "Is she back?"

"No." His father shook his head. "There's someone out there."

The sound of more men screaming resounded across the grassland.

Arthur stepped onto the porch, reaching for a wood axe resting by the door.

"Where are you going?" David asked. "We don't even know how many are out there!"

"Does it matter?" the boy replied impatiently. "Shadow fights for us. We should be down there with him."

Arthur started across the ground, running behind the tents as people appeared from their dwellings.

"They could be after the queen," Emily suggested, appearing beside David. She had wrapped a blanket around herself before stepping into the cold air.

"Are you dressed?" he asked.

"Yes," she replied.

"Good. Grab your sword. Your skills may be required."

"I'll get Akasati and Karlena," she said, stepping back inside. "We'll find the queen and Ursula. You go after your son. My daughter won't be too happy if we lose him."

"Aye," David agreed, starting after the boy. "You be careful."

***

A roar bellowed from across the stream.

Arthur glared into the darkness as he ran, trying to see what was happening.

A giant dark form was turning and twisting its head this way and that, flinging men into the air. Several attackers had surrounded the beast and were slinging arrows wildly into the dark form.

It bellowed again and again as each shaft sank deep into its black flesh.

As he drew nearer, the sound of deep whimpering reached his ears as the enormous beast fell to the ground.

They flung more arrows into its back and chest.

Still, it clambered back to its feet and continued tearing apart another three bowmen before collapsing again.

"Shadow," Arthur cried as he reached the river bank.

The creature lay still.

A deep snorting breath fell from its nostrils as one last grunt escaped its throat.

Shadow was gone.

"You bastards," Arthur shouted.

Thirty men armed with bows turned their attention upon him, pointing their arrows directly at his torso.

"Not him," called a man on horseback. "The Maji wishes this one to be kept alive. Loose your arrows upon the camp."

Without hesitation, the archers aimed their weapons up the embankment towards the encampment.

The sound of tight strings being let free filled Arthur's ears.

Thirty arrows flew through the air, unseen against the pitch-black night sky.

"Nock," the rider called. The archers loaded their bows with more arrows. "Draw. Loose."

Another thirty arrows arced towards their targets.

"Nock," the rider commanded again. "Draw. Loose."

Tears filled Arthur's eyes.

The first arrows hadn't even reached their target, before sixty more were already in the air.

He gripped his axe tightly and waded into the stream.

"There are children up there," he yelled. "Little children."

"Nock," the rider hollered, ignoring the boy's plea. "Draw. Loose."

The sound of creaking bows and twanging strings became deafening.

Arthur raised his axe and ran at the rider as hard and fast as he could.

Before he could reach the man on the charger, one bowman swung his weapon around like a sword and cracked the boy on the back of the head with the upper limb of the bow.

Arthur saw stars as he lost control of his limbs. His world turned upside-down before he felt the firm kiss of grass and dirt against his face.

"Nock," the rider called. His voice was distant and far away, as if in a deep cavern. "Draw. Loose."

The world gradually grew darker and darker before Arthur's eyes fell shut.

**

"Bastards!" David yelled from across the stream as he watched two bowmen lift Arthur onto the rider's horse. His son lay slumped over the lap of the horseman. Arthur's arms over the left side of the charger's shoulders, legs dangling over the right. "Let him go."

David felt something bite him in the thigh, forcing him to his knees. His eyes quickly fell to an arrow's shaft protruding from his leg.

"David," a shrill scream called from far behind him. It was Emily, running at full pace across the open ground between the camp and the stream.

"Kill her," the rider commanded the archers before pointing to the big bald man. "Kill him too."

The archers aimed their weapons and started pulling back upon the strings. David heard the creak as tension upon the bows increased. He pursed his lips and prepared for death.

Suddenly, the earth around him shook, knocking the archers off their feet and causing the horse to stumble.

Arrows were flung wildly in all directions as the bowmen crashed to the ground.

The rider steered his beast expertly, keeping himself and Arthur from falling.

David watched wide-eyed as puffs of dirt and grit exploded from the ground along the far side of the stream's edge.

The rider moved his steed back into the pasture land, away from the water as wide cracks formed.

Wider and wider they grew as the earth started spewing grass and soil into the sky.

Emily collapsed by David's side, dropping her sword to wrap her arms around his shoulders.

He wanted to look at her, but his attention was transfixed.

The ground on the other side of the stream continued to open and fall away, swallowing several archers.

"Retreat, you fools," the rider bellowed.

But it was too late.

As the bowmen attempted to flee, the ground quickly collapsed beneath them.

All archers disappeared into the earth, calling and screaming as they fell.

Without warning, the ground closed in behind them with a terrible thud that echoed across the glade.

David turned his face towards the camp where he saw Queen Amicia crouching low, her hand touching the ground.

She had saved his life and Emily's.

His eyes then fell upon the rider who now stood alone in the pastureland.

His archers were gone.

He was alone.

But he still had Arthur.

The rider met David's glare and raised his sword above his head.

A signal.

"Get ready," David told Emily.

The tree line at the eastern edge of the glade erupted with charging horsemen dressed for battle and armed with long swords.

As they raced across the field, David peered back at Amicia.

She was being helped back to her feet by Brondt, who was never far from her side. Her movement was slow. She appeared weary.

Standing about her were several other armed men. They weren't guarding her. They were just watching. Waiting.

What are you waiting for? David furrowed his brow. He turned to see the rider with his son riding back towards the forest. Arthur's legs and arms were flopping and flapping this way and that as the steed galloped away.

"He's taking my boy," David cried, trying to get back to his feet. The pain in his thigh was too much, and he fell back onto the grass again.

"Don't move," Emily told him.

David looked back at the men near the camp. The Agrodien warriors were there now, standing by Akasati and Karlena. As he watched, more men arrived with weapons in hand.

But still, they didn't race down to the stream.

They just stood there.

Waiting.

Watching.

"Why don't they come to help?" he asked, looking at Emily for an answer. His eyes flashed back to the approaching riders racing across the pastureland.

"Help is here," she assured him, nodding towards the northern edge of the camp.

He turned his face and saw Captain George Thornton and his men moving slowly down the long embankment.

Behind them stood a lone figure; a woman.

Ursula.

Her arms stretched towards the sky.

A chill wind instantly swept down from the mountains all around them, swiftly moving towards her. She redirected her hands towards the riders, channelling the breeze, funnelling it across the glade.

A flash of light, from deep inside the clouds above, erupted.

A deep rumble of thunder followed.

Thornton threw up a hand, gesturing to his men to halt and crouch low.

Another flash.

Another rumble.

The riders raced towards the stream, closing the ground quickly.

The sound of their steeds' hooves thundering across the ground grew louder and louder.

The wind fanned across the grassland, lifting dust, grit and discarded arrows, flinging anything that lay loosely upon the earth towards the riders.

Several were smacked in the heads with broken bows, knocking them from their chargers.

But it wasn't enough to slow the attack.

A bright explosion directly above Ursula drew David's attention back to the woman on the hill.

A great and deafening clap caused a ringing in his ears.

"By the gods," he cried as a blinding stem of light streamed from the clouds, engulfing Ursula.

Crooked beams shot from her fingers, passing closely over Thornton and his men's heads before streaking across the field towards the horsemen.

Sparks erupted from armour, buckles, and swords as lightning struck deep into man and beast.

David could hear the cries of pain as men fell from their steeds.

The piercing screams of horses filled the night air.

Within moments, the entire attacking force was lying on the ground.

Ursula lowered her arms, releasing the sky from her control.

"Finish them," Thornton roared, returning to his feet and racing forwards.

David heard a great cry as all those waiting with weapons in hand raced down the embankment towards the stream.

They rushed past David and Emily and through the shallow water.

As he rested in the auburn-haired woman's arms, staring up at her sadly, he could hear blades hacking and slashing from the pastureland.

"We've lost so many tonight," Emily said, frowning as she looked back towards the camp.

David shook slightly as a mixture of anger and gloom filled his spirit.

They had his son.

And even as the last of these riders of Woodmyst were slaughtered, he knew they had been defeated.

They had suffered substantial loss at the hands of the bowmen.

Eighteen

"Alice," hissed a voice from the entrance of the cavern.

She stopped dragging the saddle across the gravelly cave floor and turned to see Gruloch approaching slowly. His eyes moved from the girl to the very sluggish dragon, watching both of them curiously.

"What are you doing?" he asked, keeping his voice low. "Where are you going?"

Her eyes were red and wet. She was both tired and upset.

"Something has happened," Alice replied. "I need to go home."

"What could be so terrible that you would risk taking to the air before your dragon has had enough rest?"

Gruloch placed his hand gingerly upon hers.

"My husband," she said and cried. "I saw him in a dream. Darkness and pain surrounded him."

"It could be nothing more than a dream," the Haigok said, trying to calm her.

"I sensed the others like me," she replied. "They were in battle."

Gruloch looked at her hair. Thin, tiny strips of black ran through her mane of white, barely visible in the torchlight.

He remembered her dark braid that snaked over her shoulder.

Reaching up with both hands, he wiped her tears with his thumbs and ran his fingers through her snowy strands.

"I believe you," he whispered, dropping his arms by his sides. "But you cannot leave."

Alice glared at him angrily.

"Why not?"

"Liana won't make it more than five leagues before she will need to rest again," Gruloch gestured to the dragon. The noble beast had lowered its head back to the dirt and had fallen asleep. "She needs to rest after such a long flight."

"Arthur," she cried, tears streaming down her face.

Gruloch looked to the ground, trying to find words of comfort.

"I know not what to say," he grumbled. "There is nothing I can do to help you for the time being. All I can say is that you and your dragon need to rest. But I know you won't. I can see that this burden weighs heavy upon you."

He took Alice's hand and pulled her lightly, coaxing her towards the mouth of the cavern. She dropped the straps of the saddle and followed him, leaving Liana to sleep.

"When the dragons have fed," he said, "I will prepare a detachment of riders to accompany both you and me back to your home."

Alice stopped and stared at the Haigok with wide eyes.

"We will assess the situation and stay with you until this problem with the Maji has been sorted out. Would that be sufficient?"

Without warning, she wrapped her arms around Gruloch's shoulders. He wasn't prepared for such an emotional outburst and was nearly knocked off his feet.

"Thank you," she whispered into his ear.

"You are more than welcome, Alice."

***

The rider threw Arthur against the trunk of a large tree. His back felt alive with immense pain as he fell onto his side. He made loud wheezing gasps as he desperately tried to fill his lungs with air.

"Shut it," growled an angry voice from the darkness. A horse snorted loudly and stomped its hooves eagerly as Arthur felt himself being pulled upright.

His hands were forced behind his back as the other bound his wrists with thin cords. As his eyes focused, a figure moved into his view.

It was a man outfitted in battle attire. His armour appeared dark and well-seasoned.

Arthur studied the soldier's features as his legs and ankles were bound in rope. He didn't recognise the face. Not that it mattered. He couldn't claim to know every man in Woodmyst.

"Do I know you?" the boy asked.

"I'm captain of the guard," the other answered with a hint of pride in his voice.

"No, you're not," Arthur snorted. "That title belongs to Andris Hill."

"I do not know of this Andris Hill," the soldier said as he tightened the cords around Arthur's legs. "My name is Dakoth Risha. And *I am* the captain of the guard."

"Where are you from?" the boy questioned. "You're not from Woodmyst. I can hear it in your voice."

"You're an inquisitive fellow, aren't you?"

"I would recognise most of the armed men of the city," Arthur told him. "My father was chief."

"But he isn't now, is he?"

Arthur pursed his lips.

"I bet you're a bright lad, too." Risha leant in close and smiled. Arthur could smell the overwhelming stench of the man's sour breath. "The Maji summoned me. I and a number of others. We travelled from Ironfields to Blackshore. There, we came by ship to Dweagan. From Dweagan to Woodmyst. From Woodmyst to you. And now, you go to Woodmyst to see the Maji."

"Why?"

"How should I know?" Risha replied, twisting a long piece of cloth in his hands. "The Maji instructed me to find the girl witch's husband. Said he was a boy who would most likely be accompanied by a large, black beast."

Risha shoved a dry rag into Arthur's mouth. He felt pressure around his head as the soldier tied the gag in a knot at the back of the boy's head.

"That was you," the man said. "Except the beast got to the battle before you did. But you weren't far behind. So, I took a gamble and assumed that you were the one that I came for."

Risha got up and moved to his steed. "I suppose that was your father who arrived shortly after you. Big man with no hair?"

Arthur glared silently at the soldier.

Crunching sounds of leaf litter being crushed underfoot grew louder and louder.

"Doesn't matter," growled the other he checked the harness on his horse. "He won't be going far with an arrow in his leg."

"Did you see it?" a new voice called from the darkness of the woods. "The bloody ground opened up and bolts of lightning struck down the horses."

Arthur watched silently as four men on horses appeared from the shadows.

"Perhaps the Maji has his work cut out for him?" another suggested.

"Don't you let him hear that," Risha warned.

"You sound frightened of him," the third chortled. "He's just a fucking boy."

"Yeah," said another. "He's no White Mistress."

"No, he's not." Risha turned to face them. "He's much more powerful. She knew it. The others knew it. And he's only just beginning to figure it out. You watch your tongues. You never know who or what might be listening."

One man locked eyes with Arthur.

"So," the man said, crouching beside the lad. "This is the one?"

"He doesn't look like much," said another. "What does the Maji want with him?"

"It's not our place to ask," Risha said. "Help me get him on my horse."

Within moments, they were moving through the woods at a slow pace. They draped Arthur over the shoulders of Risha's steed.

Every step felt like a solid punch in the gut as they pressed on through what was left of the night.

Every step brought a tightening knot to his stomach as they drew closer and closer to Woodmyst.

***

Her eyes filled with tears and her mouth open wide in a mournful cry. Her arms wrapped around the frame of her husband, who lay lifeless, riddled with arrows. She knelt by the fire, rocking him back and forth. His arms splayed awkwardly to his sides as she pulled him to her breast.

"Becka," Emily whispered, crouching behind her and placing her hands upon her shoulders. "I'm so sorry."

"My husband is dead," the other howled.

"I'm so sorry," Emily heard herself repeat. It seemed such a silly thing to say. But there were no other words that came to her.

"My husband is dead," Becka cried out loud. "My husband is dead."

Mournful tears were shed throughout the camp as mothers held their silent children and husbands cradled their still wives. Roars filled the glade as the Agrodien lamented in their own way, carrying their fallen onto the open ground to the west of the camp. Some warriors had already carried the timber, preparing to build the pyre for the departed.

"My husband is dead," Becka called again, tears streaming down her cheeks.

David stood by the campfire, leaning his weight onto a wood axe as he peered across the tents and ground in front of the cabin. Countless shafts protruded from the ground, stuck from the make-shift shelters, and poked from bodies strewn around the encampment.

He saw it on the faces of those gathered by the fire, tending to their own wounds or those of others. Their hopes had been shattered.

His eyes fell upon the forms of Baldwyn and Elka, lying in each other's arms near their tent. Ewan Cunningham, who was caught off guard while he slept in his cot, was now carried from his bed by two Agrodien males.

He looked across the camp to see Yuri on his knees, roaring into the dark sky with his wife and children by his side. Lying before him were the bodies of Gharnef and his entire family.

Galonia, Yuri's wife, fussed about the bodies of her fallen friends. She pulled Evalad's cloak tightly around the fallen female's body, covering both mother and infant son.

David then moved his eyes to Oliver, who sat by the fire, staring blankly into the flames. The big man limped over to his friend, glancing this way and that as he approached.

"Oliver," he called. The other seemed not to hear. David called again.

"Yeah," the other answered, snapping out of a trance.

"Where are Agnes and Tomas?" the big man asked, suddenly wishing he hadn't.

The tear-filled stare from his friend was enough for an answer.

"They're sleeping." Oliver frowned. "They're all sleeping now."

***

Takmel stirred awake and rolled onto his side.

He felt a warm hand slide over his chest and creep across his belly.

"You're not leaving?" Lucy whispered. Her breath felt hot against his neck. "I want you to stay."

"I'll stay a little longer," he told her, placing his hand over hers.

"Good," she breathed, snuggling against his back.

He closed his eyes and drifted away.

The sound of birds chirping from the dark outside, summoning the morning, caused his eyes to open again. The honking calls of water fowl and distant bleating of sheep drew him back to reality.

He needed to get out of bed.

He needed to be ready to receive news from the captain of the guard.

He hoped to receive his gift before the light of dawn struck the city.

In one swift motion, he flung the covers away and sat upon the edge of the bed.

"Takmel?" Lucy complained.

"I need to go," he said, reaching behind him to touch her bare skin. She shivered.

"It's cold," she replied, reaching for the covers.

He got up and placed the blankets back upon her before dressing himself.

Before leaving the bed-chamber, he kissed her forehead.

Passing through the sitting room, he saw Catherine seated by the fireplace. Her grey hood covered her, obscuring her features from his view.

"Hello, wife," he said coldly, moving into the kitchen.

"Husband," she slurred, keeping her face away from him.

"Tea?" he asked.

"I have some," she replied. "I've made a fresh pot not more than a few minutes ago."

He found it sitting on top of the stove.

After pouring himself a cup, he turned his attention to her.

"Why do you avoid me lately?" he asked.

"Do I avoid you?" She cocked her head slightly.

"Don't mock me," he warned, moving closer. "You no longer look at me. Do I disgust you that much?"

"Perhaps," she answered, lifting her cup to her lips.

"Why?" he pressed. "It wasn't that long ago when you would stand by my side and work with me. Both of us had a vision. We started this together. What changed? Why don't you stand by my side any longer?"

He waited for an answer.

Instead, she lifted her cup to her lips again and sipped loudly.

"Is it the others?" he asked. "The other wives? Are you jealous of them? You knew they needed to play a part in this. It was required. We talked about it. You said that you understood."

She sipped her tea.

"I'll get rid of them. I'll end it. It will be just you and me again."

"Liar," she said.

"What?"

"You need them," she said. "You need nine. It's the only way for the prophecy to be fulfilled."

"I'll give it up. I will." He tried to sound convincing. "I will give it all up just to have you look at me again."

"Liar," she repeated.

"You were the only one." He stepped closer. "The others, I had to manipulate and turn. But you, I didn't need to. We were both the same. You did it all wilfully. You did it without any influence on my part."

"I did it because I loved you," she replied.

He stopped in his tracks and stared at her.

"Loved?" He furrowed his brow. "You don't love me?"

"I did once," she answered honestly. "But something has changed."

"Not I," he assured her. "I'm still the same Takmel I've always been."

"But I'm not the same Catherine." She stood and faced him, pulling her hood away from her face.

Her piercing blue eyes bored into his.

He felt his heart stop momentarily as he took in the vision before him.

Streaks of snow-white hair extended from her temples and fringe.

"You're one of them," he spat.

She shook her head slowly.

"I don't know what I am," she replied. "All I know is that I don't love you. I know you have no hold on me. I know you never will."

"So?" He raised his brows. "You plan to kill me, then?"

"No," she answered. "I plan to leave you."

"And join your sister?" he chided. "I can't allow you to do that."

"I don't plan to join anyone," she told him. "But I also won't be held prisoner."

"You're my prisoner?"

"We all are," Catherine answered.

"You can go anywhere in this city," he said and gestured to the world outside. "I can prepare a coach for you and take you to Dweagan.

There, you can board a vessel for any port within sailing distance. If you wish it to be, we can go today."

"I don't wish to sail away," she said. "I wish to be left alone."

A sudden knock at the door brought the discussion to a halt.

"We'll continue this later," Takmel stated as he moved to the door.

Catherine resumed her seat.

"Forgive me, Maji," said a familiar voice.

"Master Bookkeeper," Takmel replied. "Isn't it a little early, even for you?"

"Ah," the other faltered.

"What news, Master Drayton?"

"The captain of the guard has returned, my lord," the old man announced. "He has captured Arthur Gyfford, as you commanded."

"What?" Catherine was back on her feet. "Why do you hold Arthur captive?"

"It's complicated." Takmel turned to her, holding his hands up in defence.

"He's family," she argued. "He's like a brother to you."

"I thought you just got through telling me you didn't really care about any of them," he said, giving her a curious glance.

"I never said I didn't care," she corrected him. "I just said that I wanted to be left alone."

"Isn't that the same thing?"

"If you hurt Arthur…"

"It's not Arthur I'm interested in," he assured her. "He's a means to an end."

"So that's it." She frowned. "That's been your plan all along. It's my sister you want. You think that by holding her husband hostage, she'll climb into bed with you."

"There was a time that I would have liked to have her on my side," he conceded. "But I think we both know that possibility has long passed us by. No. I plan to make her lay her weapons down and allow me to fulfil my destiny. She, and the others like her, are the only threat to my success. I can't manipulate her, seduce her or influence her as I have with this city. As I have with Lucy and the Seven. So, I'm left to play tactician. I will sway her by dangling the lives of those she loves before her. I will threaten Arthur's life to force her hand."

"If you hurt him…"

"No harm will come to him." He held his hands up in surrender. "I promise."

Nineteen

Again and again, he was struck on the side of the face. Cast iron knuckles continued their barrage, connecting with his cheek and jaw, over and over.

He wanted to die.

With his hands bound to a wide beam, and his frame pressing upon his aching knees, there was nothing he could do but take the punishment.

His ears rang, and his left eye had closed over. The taste of blood and bile filled his mouth, and his tongue had swollen where his teeth had bitten into it.

Another blow.

The back of his skull smacked against the beam, shaking embers from the flickering torch posted high above his head. He couldn't feel the pain there any longer. He couldn't sense the difference between the sweat or the blood that spilt down his back.

"Enough," Takmel commanded, waving his hand.

Arthur took a deep, wheezing breath and glared up at the cloaked figure standing before him.

"Tell me," the other began, crouching in front of the boy, "do you think she will save you from this?"

Arthur's head drooped, spilling long strands of saliva and blood over his chin and onto the straw-covered floor.

He could no longer smell the sweet scent of horse and straw. They had broken the bridge of his nose before Takmel arrived.

"Wha...?" Arthur groaned, hearing only loud ringing in his ears. Takmel's lips started moving again. A small smile crept upon Arthur's face. "Carn ear yooh."

The boy chuckled, oozing pink liquid from between his broken teeth.

"Maji." Risha bowed slightly, the blood-stained gauntlet dripping small pieces of Arthur onto the floor by his side. "Let me finish him off. There isn't much more he can take of this. He is only a boy, after all."

Takmel lifted himself to his full height and turned to face the captain of the guard. He saw the looks of concern on each of the men's faces, including Master Drayton, who stayed by the doors of the stable.

He looked down at Arthur, covered in his own glistening filth. Each breath that the boy took was an effort.

"You feel pity for him?" Takmel asked. "He is our enemy."

"He's just a boy." Risha frowned, regretting his words the moment he spoke them.

Takmel instantly turned and glared at the man.

The captain of the guard lowered his head apologetically.

"Forgive me, Maji," he whispered. "I spoke out of turn."

"Untie him," Takmel ordered the men standing nearby before turning his attention to the old man by the door. "Master Drayton."

"Yes, my lord."

"Fetch the apothecary. Tell him to come to the cells in the guardhouse."

"Yes, my lord." Drayton bowed and quickly disappeared into the darkness.

Takmel turned to face Arthur, who was being hoisted to his feet by two brawny men.

"I hope you heal quick," he snarled, gripping the boy's jaw tightly in his hand. Arthur winced and moaned in pain as Takmel tightened his grip. "I have much more in store for you."

Releasing his grasp, he signalled the men to take the prisoner away with a nod of his head. Arthur's feet dragged across the dirt, leaving two long shallow trenches behind in his wake.

"The horses?" Takmel asked, watching the men carting the boy away. Risha removed the gauntlet and peered curiously at his master. "The livestock? Where are they?"

"My lord?" The captain of the guard glanced quickly around him at the horses in the stalls.

"I commanded you and your men to retrieve the horses from the glade," Takmel reiterated. "Where are they?"

"My lord," Risha bowed slightly. "The witches overpowered us."

"They numbered two." He held up two fingers as he stepped slowly towards the captain of the guard. "You had over fifty men at your disposal. You couldn't outflank them?"

A lump formed in Risha's throat. His hands trembled.

"It was fast," he tried to explain. "The beast came from nowhere and attacked the bowmen. I ordered a barrage and grabbed the boy before the ground opened up. Then the bolts of light. I barely got out of there."

"Without a scratch." Takmel patted the captain's cheek gently with his hand. The man peered at him, confused. "And they still have my cattle, sheep and horses."

Risha felt himself being flung through the air.

The world passed by him in a rushing blur as he fell through the open door of the stable house and onto the paved road outside. His face scraped against the stonework, scratching his face with countless tiny marks.

Slowly, Risha rolled onto his side, feeling aches in his arms and legs. He had hit the ground hard, but could still move.

He placed his hand on the ground and started to his feet.

Suddenly, he lifted into the air again. Straight up and back down.

CLUNK!

He cried in pain as he landed heavily on his knees. The poleyns covering his knees dented, pressing against his joints.

"Please don't misunderstand me, Captain," Takmel said in a soft, kind voice. He folded his arms beneath his cloak and circled around

Risha slowly. "I appreciate what you have done. Capturing Arthur was your prerogative. But I wanted their livestock."

Risha felt his body being held rigid and upright as his knees continued to be pressed towards the ground. He could hear the grinding sound of steel kissing stone, and could feel the dents of his armour digging into his skin.

"Capturing their cattle and sheep would have deprived them of food and wool for the winter," the Maji continued. "Bringing me their horses would have prevented them from a quick relocation or escape."

The captain of the guard groaned as a sharp pain shot along his legs and into his groin. Several other guards had gathered and watched in awe as Takmel cruelly berated their commander.

"Nevertheless, what's done is done." Takmel waved his hand. Risha fell to the ground and let out a moan as the ache in his legs subsided slightly. "I think what we need to learn from this is that if I give you an order, Captain, I expect it to be followed. I hope we understand."

"Yes, Maji," Risha grunted. "I won't disappoint you again."

"I know you won't." Takmel placed his hand upon the captain's shoulder and offered a friendly grin. He then turned to the men surrounding them. "Help your captain to his feet and tend to his wounds."

Risha watched the Maji walk away into the darkness as several men came to his aid.

"He's no White Mistress," he heard a familiar voice whisper in his ear.

"No," Risha growled, feeling a sharp pain in his knee as two others helped him to stand. "He's much worse."

***

Sub-Commander Landon Wake stood by one of the newly constructed searchlights. He pressed his spyglass to his eye as he scanned the forest to the west of the city.

Hundreds and hundreds of blinking eyes, like tiny twinkling stars, glared back across the darkness towards Newholt.

Clanging and banging resounded through the air. The din of distant construction echoed through the darkness.

The heat from the torch fire that fuelled the searchlight was unbearable. He quickly folded his spyglass and placed it back into his inner coat pocket before stepping away from the large iron frame of the structure.

"Why don't they attack, sir?" a young soldier asked. "I thought they had retreated."

"Clearly, they have not," Wake replied. "Ready the catapults and prepare the archers."

"Already done, sir," the soldier replied. "They've been ready all night for this lot."

"What news of the other beacons?"

"Four more are being erected along this line," the soldier reported. "Another three to the southern edge of the city and three to the north."

"Are they operational?" Wake queried.

"Not all," the other answered. "One to the south has lit its beacon. But the others are yet to be ignited."

"Tell them I want all beacons alight for the coming night." Wake turned to look at the ocean. A dull, pink glow rested upon the horizon. His eyes lingered there, hoping to see a sail belonging to the *Gypsy*, but there were no ships coming or going. "Dawn approaches. Change the guard. Give these men relief for the day. It's been a long, cold night."

"And what if these devils attack?"

"Then you had best be quick about it," Wake replied, giving the nervous soldier a stern look.

"Aye, sir." The soldier saluted and moved away.

Wake turned his gaze back upon the dark woodland. Countless blinking eyes peered back, stretching as far as he could see to the north and south.

They were vastly outnumbered.

"Why are you waiting?" whispered the sub-commander to himself.

***

Alice had spent most of the night staring up at the ceiling of the hut that Gruloch had assigned to her. She had flung the covers from her body, feeling hot, only to gather them back when she suddenly felt cold. This occurred several times, accompanied by tossing and turning in a futile attempt to get comfortable.

Eventually, she gave in. She realised very early on that it wasn't the bedding or the temperature that was causing her anxiety. It was her train of thinking.

Arthur was at the forefront of her mind. When she closed her eyes, she saw his face. Only, it wasn't the face she had kissed and caressed before her journey to the Haigok village. His face appeared beaten, swollen, and broken.

Something inside her knew that this wasn't a simple concoction of an active imagination. She knew that what she saw was actual, real, that it was Arthur now.

Alice dressed, donning her cloak and swords, preparing to travel. She braided her hair tightly and stepped from the tiny mud hut into the communal area of the village where banquets were held.

The fire was still blazing and a few older Haigok were preparing food. Some were roasting portions of meat on tiny spits over the flames, while others dribbled fluid dough onto large frying pans.

At least, they appeared like frying pans in Alice's eyes.

"You sleeping," an elderly female whispered, pointing at the girl. "Not wake time."

"I can't sleep," Alice answered. "I've too much on my mind."

The Haigok female cocked her head, not understanding Alice's words.

"Too much on my mind," Alice repeated, pointing to her head.

The elderly female nodded, seeming to comprehend.

"Tea," she mumbled, turning back to the fire. "You drink tea. All good."

It wasn't long before Alice sat by the fire on cushions. As one elder served her tea, another draped a blanket over her. Another brought her a plate of fresh, flatbread with some steaming meat on top.

"Eat," grunted a male. "Need strength. Big journey."

Alice suddenly sat upright and looked towards the caves where the dragons were kept. Light flickered through the open mouths of the caves.

"You no worry," the old male smiled, baring his pointed teeth. "Dragons being fed. You being fed. All strong. Big journey."

"They're being fed now?" the girl asked.

"Yes," he replied, patting her on the shoulder with his long fingers. "You eat."

Alice relaxed and crossed her legs. She then placed the plate of food on her lap and the mug of tea on the ground by her side. Carefully, she rolled the bread over the meat, creating a tube.

"Good," said the old male, turning back to the fire.

Alice ate slowly, delicately, trying not to make a mess.

"You're up early," a voice called softly.

She turned her head to see Gruloch emerging from his hut, dressed and ready to travel. He sheathed a curved sword at his side, and he twisted it slightly with his hands in order to sit on the ground. One of the other elders brought him a plate of food.

"I couldn't sleep," she admitted.

"Of course," he said. "You should try to rest during the flight."

"I don't think that is possible," she said, thinking about the joy she experienced every time she and Liana would take to the air.

"Oh," Gruloch said as he stuffed a handful of meat into his mouth. "It is."

Alice watched the other eat with interest. Here she was, trying to maintain a certain level of civility. Trying not to make a mess. Gruloch, on the other hand, was simply shovelling his food in as though it was his last meal. Slivers of meat and bread fell back to his plate with each intake, only to be scooped back up in the next handful.

A tiny smile formed on her face as she lifted her tube of bread and meat to her lips. It didn't last very long.

Her eyes fell upon the flames, and she saw Arthur in her mind again. Beaten and bloody.

The smile vanished as a tear welled in her eye.

Her stomach tightened, and her appetite dissipated.

"You eat," the elder male said, pointing at her. "Need strength. Big journey."

She took a bite, forcing herself to chew the morsel and swallow it down.

A few younger Haigok males appeared by the fire, dressed in battle attire. Alice presumed these were to be a part of her escort back to the glade.

As they all sat to eat, her stomach tightened more. Her thoughts were upon Arthur and what may have become of her home. She thought the worst.

If Arthur has been treated so terribly, what might have happened to the others?

What might have happened to my mother?

She was eager to leave.

I need to get home.

I never should have left them.

She forced another mouthful of meat and bread down her throat as tears crept over her cheeks.

Gruloch observed her carefully, seeing a little girl who desperately wanted to go home.

"We'll leave soon, Alice," he breathed. "You'll be back by nightfall. I promise."

***

Loud thudding footsteps of the multitude following her filled her ears. She had turned her steed to the north, spying a glint of sunlight breaching the horizon.

Turning in her saddle, she saw Andris in his armour. Behind him were five bannermen carrying five black standards. Her standard.

Beyond them, four rows of mounted troops flanked by hundreds of infantrymen. Their armour jostled loudly with each step. They walked in unison, generating a tremendous cadence with each stride.

Further to the south, at the mouth of the Twisted Road, another great mass marched south, towards Dweagan. Six more colours, displayed upon three banners each, were carried before the throng. Ahead of them were six women. Her coven.

She already felt as if she was breaking away from them. As if she was being torn away.

But it was for the better.

At least, that is what her husband had told her.

The husband she shared with all of them.

You will be my ambassadors, he had told them.

His words sounded pure. She had to believe him.

This *was* for the better.

Her face returned to the north.

A stern determination set into her heart.

She wouldn't let him down.

A small smile rested on her face.

This is for the better.

The sun climbed a little higher and sent a warm touch upon her face as a lone tear fell from her eye.

Twenty

Glaun and Kygra spent much of the morning digging a wide hole in the pastureland by the stream. They then sought help from both Porf and Hygo to help with moving Shadow's body to the freshly dug grave.

Most of the inhabitants of the glade were preparing their dead, or gathering wood for the pyre. David, limping awkwardly, opted to help with gathering timber. When the two men of the north came seeking help, he offered his services as well.

"No, you don't," Emily barked suddenly. "You'll stay here and help with this or go back to the camp to rest that leg."

"I can help," he argued stubbornly. "I should help."

"You are helping," she said sternly.

"I should be there to bury him." David's voice trembled. "He should have someone there who knew him."

Emily stared at the large man, touched by the sentiment.

"She's not here for him," he continued, tears welling in his eyes. "But I am. I was horrible to her."

The four northern men lowered their heads.

"We'll go back," Kygra said quietly. "You two should talk alone."

David watched as the men moved away, out of the woods, and back into the glade.

"She loves you, David." Emily put her bundle of kindling onto the ground and put her arms around his shoulders.

"I was so horrible," he sniffled. "I never supported her or showed compassion to her. I treated her like one of the guards. I was only ever interested in how she performed. And that was only because I feared her."

"That was him," she told him. "That was Takmel inside your head."

"I believed it was her that killed my family," he blubbered. "How could I do that? How could I be so cruel?"

"He tricked all of us, David." Emily placed her hands on his cheeks. "He lived under my roof. I treated him like my own son."

"I need to be there," he said. "I need to be there for her. I should be there for her. The bastard took Shadow from her. I can't find the stallion. And I let him take her husband." He fell to his knees, weeping. "I let him take my boy."

"You did no such thing," Emily whispered into his ear as she wrapped her arms around him tightly. "It was all him. You had nothing to do with that."

"If I never was chief, this wouldn't be happening," he sobbed.

"Yes, it would," she assured him. "If you weren't chief, then someone else would have been and they would blame themselves instead of you. Grovelling here is just another way of letting him win."

Emily got up and stared down at the large man. She reached her hand out to him.

"Now," she said with authority, "get up and come with me. We'll both go together. For Alice and Arthur."

He gaped at her for what seemed a long time. She looked strong. Stoic.

Reaching out, he took her hand and lifted himself off the ground.

"For Alice and Arthur," he agreed.

She slid her arm around his waist, and he placed his around her shoulders. Together, they started for the glade, leaving their gathered timber behind.

After the last shovel of earth was placed onto the grave, Glaun peered around to the others gathered nearby. The crowd had grown a little, consisting of the four northern men and their wives, as well as David and Emily.

"Should we say something?" Glaun asked, looking at Emily. "I mean, I will if you wish it. It wouldn't be all that meaningful. The truth is, Shadow frightened me so much that Lilen needed to wash my underclothes frequently."

The gathering chuckled quietly.

"It's true." Lilen's face softened.

"Lady Emily," Terix, Kygra's wife, called quietly. "Shadow was your daughter's pet. Perhaps you should say something."

"Shadow was no one's pet," the auburn woman replied with a grin. "He was a friend to Alice. She could always find the best in even the most despicable beast and draw them to her. They trusted her. But Shadow loved her, I think.

"Even when most other creatures would go about their merry way after she had spent time with them and played with them, Shadow remained. He stayed by her side and became a part of her family."

Emily crouched by the grave and placed a hand on the fresh soil.

"Thank you, Shadow," she sighed. "You came when she needed someone like you most of all. You were taken from all of us far sooner than you should have been."

***

Yuri could barely walk. His knees grew weaker and weaker as he counted the swathed bodies of the dead. He watched sadly as each of them was laid carefully upon the long, neatly stacked woodpile.

"One hundred and seven," he growled in his own tongue. Galonia stroked his arm as he shook his head slowly. "So many younglings amongst them. What kind of creature could do this?"

"He waited until the Kayl'sro was gone," she replied. "He knew she would leave."

"He baited her," Yuri admitted. "He used that little *Ivo* boy to tear at her heart. He knows it is her weakness. Her love for others. That's why he told her of his plans for the Haigok. To lure her away. This would not have happened if she were here."

"You blame her?" Galonia asked, hearing the anger in her husband's voice.

"No," he answered. "I blame this Maji."

She rested her head against his shoulder.

"Do you remember the time when some of our people made a pact with the Mirikin?"

"I was not privy to that," he told her hastily. "I did not support the decision that those quislings made. Look where it got them. Not one of them came back."

"Kayl'sro Marrok was part of that decision," she reminded him. "And you were loyal to him."

"I am loyal to the Kayl'sro," he replied, looking to her from the corner of his eye.

"Without question?"

"What is your point?"

"Did you not question the orders of Kayl'sro Greil when it was his turn to wear the iron claws?" she pressed.

"Of course I did," he turned towards her. "He placed everyone in danger."

"And Alice has not?"

Yuri stared at his wife, perplexed and confused.

"There's no comparison to be made here," he eventually said. "Greil was greedy and cruel. Alice is kind and generous. She gave us shelter. We share her land and we eat meals together. She brought us to a safe place."

"And yet, we were attacked during the night when she is nowhere to be seen," Galonia wept.

"You blame her," Yuri stated. "It is *you* that places blame on Kayl'sro Alice for this. Not me."

"Look at all the dead," she snarled, tears streaming from her eyes. "Look at how many younglings lie upon the woodpile. Look at our friends, Yuri. Evalad and Gharnef. Their beautiful children. Dead. Dead, Yuri. My friends."

He pulled her into his chest. She fought him, trying to pull away, but he held her steadily in his enormous arms. Slowly, she gave in and allowed herself to let go.

Loud cries vibrated through his body as she wept boisterously.

"They were her friends too, Galonia," he whispered. "They were her family. Imagine how she will feel when she hears the news of what happened here. Imagine what she will do when she has had time to grieve. Imagine what terrors she will bestow upon anyone that stands in her way when she seeks vengeance for this.

"Place your blame where it belongs," he continued. "It was this Maji who is responsible for what happened here. Not Kayl'sro Alice. She will be responsible for what is coming next."

**

The surviving twelve Agrodien warriors lit the pyre. Nola'ee was first to touch her torch to the woodpile.

Within moments, the entire length of the pyre was alight. The flames stretched high into the air, almost as tall as the surrounding trees. The heat grew too intense for the onlookers, who stepped back and away accordingly.

They shed tears and lamented loudly along the edge of the flames. Some were so overcome with grief that they fell to their knees. Their fathers or mothers, brothers or sisters, sons or daughters rested before them, slowly being engulfed by the bright flames.

David's gaze kept moving to the smaller forms in the fire. The children. His heart felt as if a thousand blades had run through it as he remembered the young boy who had tried to kill them all.

Takmel, in his mind, had been a good lad. He had shown a deep interest in the people of Woodmyst and had always attempted to offer assistance where he could. David remembered a ten-year-old boy who volunteered to sweep the stables and clean the bedding of soldiers not long after he arrived in the village.

He recalled how, as the boy grew and became a part of Woodmyst, Takmel would pair up with Catherine Warde and vanish into the woods on many occasions. David treated it lightly then, believing it was innocent young love and nothing more.

Now, he and Catherine both resided in Woodmyst, working together as husband and wife.

He wondered just how much of the little, innocent things that Takmel Hamond did were stepping stones towards becoming the Maji.

His eyes landed upon the form of an adult and youngling lying side-by-side. A woman and a child. A mother and her son. Agnes Weston and Tomas.

A deep sorrow swept over David as he considered his friend Oliver. None had been struck so hard as he during all of this.

First, Ivo was taken away. Ripped apart by Takmel's sorcery.

David shook his head, feeling Emily's hand tighten around his, as he thought about the bolt-riddled bodies of Oliver's wife and last remaining son.

It's not fair.

He looked along the line of mourners, expecting to see his friend there. But Oliver was nowhere to be seen.

David wiped his eyes, bending and twisting slightly to see past the others. Turning around hoping to find Oliver sitting back in the camp by the hearth.

Nothing.

"What is it?" Emily queried.

"Oliver," he replied softly. "I can't see him."

She turned her head, trying to find the missing man.

"He can't be far," she said, trying to sound calm. "Perhaps he just needs to be alone."

"No," David told her. "When I lost my family, I most definitely did not need to be alone."

He broke away from the gathering as stealthily as he could, leaving Emily by the pyre after kissing her hand. He started for the encampment first, hoping to find Oliver in his tent.

"Where are you off to, then?" a voice called from behind him.

David turned to see Lor following him.

"Oliver is missing," he answered.

"I'll come along," the other offered, jogging a little to catch up to the big man.

They searched through the camp, checked inside each tent, and even went through Alice's cabin.

Still no sight of Oliver.

"How long since you last saw him?" Lor asked.

"I'm not sure," David replied. "I think maybe when we were gathering wood earlier today. I saw him by the campfire. After that, I don't know."

"He didn't go down to help with the rukyul?"

"No." David started across the camp, wincing with each step towards the woods on the northern edge of the glade. "You didn't see him?"

"Not then," Lor said, walking beside his friend. "I also saw him by the fire when we were stacking timber onto the pyre. You were gathering wood with Emily. I remember that because I wished I was doing the same with Linet. It looked... well... romantic."

"Gathering wood?"

"Yeah."

"You're a strange man." David grinned.

"Just being in the forest with someone you love," Lor tried to explain.

"A very strange man, indeed."

The two moved into the forest. David peered at the sky and noticed the sun making its way to the treetops on the western edge of the glade. Its golden orb barely penetrated through the black smoke of the pyre. His eyes landed upon Emily, who was standing beside Linet near to where the bodies of Agnes and Tomas Weston had been placed.

"Wish we had a hound," Lor muttered. "We might have a chance at finding him quicker."

"I wish we had Shadow," David said. "He had a far better nose than any dog I've hunted with."

The two pushed on through the undergrowth, making their way along the inside edge of the forest, not moving too far into the woods. David tried keeping the glade within sight to his right at all times. Lor moved a little deeper into the woods, but kept David in his view.

"So," Lor said. "You and Emily."

"It appears so," David answered. The tiny hairs on his neck stood on end. He had been waiting for one of the family members to say something. "Why? Do you disapprove? Does Linet?"

"No," the other answered, holding up a hand defensively. "Not at all. We were surprised that it took this long."

"What do you mean?" David furrowed his brow. "We didn't plan this."

"I know," Lor said. "We just thought that you two would find each other sooner. That's all."

"We?"

"Linet and me." Lor crouched low atop of a small rise. He ducked his head as if looking under an obstruction that David couldn't see from his position.

"Who else has been discussing my life?"

"Shhh!" Lor hissed.

The big man tried to crouch, feeling an immense pain shoot through his thigh.

"Bastard," David blurted, pressing his hand upon his leg. He could feel the bandage beneath his trousers. It had slipped up his thigh a little.

"Shhh!" Lor repeated.

"What is it?"

"Some fluttering," the other replied. "I thought it was the stream at first. But it's not consistent. Not like flowing water."

"Are you sure?" David asked. "The stream is just a little way from us."

"I'm certain," Lor said, pointing ahead of him. "It's just over there. Blackbirds are dancing on the ground."

"Dancing?"

"Come see," the other beckoned.

David climbed the embankment slowly, holding his hand against his leg. He felt something wet and sticky in the palm of his hand. When he reached Lor's side, he peeled back his hand to see a small patch of blood soaking through his trousers.

"Bastard," he spat.

"We should fix that," Lor said.

"I'm not pulling my pants down for you," David snapped. "What if someone was to come up here just as I do?"

"Are you worried that new rumours of your love life will begin?"

"You would be a part of such rumours," David said, raising his eyebrows.

"It's your bloody bandage," Lor said. "It needs to be tightened. Other-wise, that wound will rub against your trousers and it will get worse."

David pursed his lips and scowled at the other. He knew Lor was right. But he didn't want to have to partially undress, let alone have a man see to his bandage.

Frustrated, David unbuckled his belt.

"Emily wrapped this," he said as he pulled his pants down to his knees. Lor reached over to fix the bandage, only to have David take a step backwards. "I'll be the one to fix it. Not you."

"Fine."

"You just keep watch on whatever it is down there." David pointed towards the area that Lor had shown interest in.

"Fine," the other repeated with a chuckle.

Before long, David had redressed the wound on his leg and buckled his belt back in place. The two men walked gingerly towards the sound of fluttering birds.

Several ravens were resting on the ground at the base of a large oak tree. The trunk was extremely wide, culminating of strange twisting formations, as if many smaller trees had braided together to form one.

A strange creaking emitted from high above, causing both men to peer upwards. Tree branches mixed with red and yellow leaves obscured the source of the sound.

With each step, the long creaking sound ensued.

CREEEAK!

CREEEAK!

The flutter of wings and grumpy warbles from the ravens on the ground competed with the sound above.

David moved his eyes to a small group of birds standing by the trunk of the tree. Some were roosting upon large roots that had broken through the ground.

All were glaring back with wide, yellow eyes.

CREEEAK!

CREEEAK!

CREEEAK!

The big man stared curiously at the ravens, sighting long strands of something dark and wet dripping from the tips of their beaks.

CREEEAK!

CREEEAK!

CREEEAK!

CREEEAK!

Lor kept his eyes high, squinting and tilting his head to see what it was high above them. Too many branches and leaves were in the way for him to have a clear view. But he could see a form moving back and forth. Back and forth.

CREEEAK!

CREEEAK!

CREEEAK!

David glared at the ravens, focussing his vision upon their beaks and talons. He concentrated his eyes on the glistening, wet stains forming on the ground with each drop.

Blood.

CREEEAK!

CREEEAK!

CREEEAK!

"Bugger me," Lor gasped. His head tilted high. "Oh, bugger me."

David followed the other's gaze to see a mess of ravens clinging to and pecking at a large object swinging from a rope.

"No." David shook his head.

Lor bent and picked up a stick, roughly the length of his arm, and threw it at the object.

A raucous chorus of cries bellowed through the air as the ravens took flight. Several of them flew only a short distance, landing in the branches nearby. Others got such a fright that they disappeared from view altogether.

"No," David said again. His eyes welled with tears.

He recognised the form swinging from the rope high above them. The sandy blond hair was unmistakably that of Oliver Weston. There were no bindings around his legs or hands, just one piece of rope looped around his neck.

CREEEAK!

CREEEAK!

CREEEAK!

CREEEAK!

Twenty-One

"Ride ahead," the scarlet woman barked to a rider. The throng heading south climbed over the crest of a smooth hill. In the distance, beyond the folds of land, they could see where the ocean met the sky. "Tell the captains to ready their ships. We sail tonight."

"Yes, my lady," the rider said, bowing slightly before charging away.

"Begging pardon, my lady," said an older soldier, a commander of the guard. "Shouldn't we wait until dawn and allow the men to rest?"

"We will rest on board the ships," she told him coldly.

"Yes, my lady," he replied, wishing he hadn't spoken at all.

A well-worn road appeared as they progressed towards the coast. Eventually, the horses and men formed up into two long columns.

"Smoke, my lady," the commander said, pointing towards the crest of a hill west of their position.

Tricia squinted, peering through the haze of the sinking sun to see a dark, mist-like patch.

"From the chimneys of Dweagan," Claire, the olive woman, suggested. "We're getting closer."

This news brought pleasure to the other women in the troop.

"I can smell the salt air," giggled the lilac witch.

"Calm yourself, Sarah," Tricia said. "One would think that you've never seen the ocean before."

"I haven't," she replied. "At least, not since the black ship that brought us from Blackrock Haven."

"Takmel doesn't want us talking about that," Isabel snapped, turning her head so quickly to face the other that her white hood fell from her head.

"My apologies," Sarah replied sheepishly.

They rode in silence for a short distance before Christina, the gold woman, couldn't contain herself any longer.

"Why doesn't he want us talking about it?"

"About what?" Tricia asked.

"Blackrock Haven?" she clarified. "It's where we came together. It's how we became what we are."

"Christina," Isabel chided.

"No," Tricia held up her hand. "Let her speak."

"But Takmel…"

"Takmel isn't here," the scarlet witch interjected. "Continue, Christina."

"I simply mean, it was an important part of our lives," she pointed out. "We met one another. We were united under Joanne. We found a new home in Woodmyst. None of us would be here right now if it wasn't for what happened in Blackrock Haven."

"Perhaps," Gilda, the jade woman ventured, "he simply doesn't want us to recall the terrible things that we were subjected to. I've all but forgotten the trip that took us to that palace. That may be the reason for his wish for us to never speak of it. It's not discussions of Blackrock Haven he disproves of. It's the journey that took us there."

Tricia suddenly remembered the constantly uncomfortable rocking back and forth as they traversed over the sea. She recalled the smell of salt, and the croaking and creaking of wet timber as she held onto others locked inside the dank pens deep inside the black ship. She saw the dirty, brawny, grotesque captain of that dreaded vessel in her mind. She could smell the stench of his stale sweat and sour liquor-drenched breath on her bare skin as he forced himself on to her again and again.

"We shouldn't speak of it," she said. "We should try to forget that time. It plays no part in our lives any longer. The will of the Maji is all that matters now."

***

Alice turned Liana sharply to the east, passing just over the treetops of the mountain peaks that overlooked the glade. She turned back to see the other twelve dragons riding in single file behind her.

Gruloch raised his arm, waving to her; a signal that all was fine.

She returned her attention to the sight before her and saw a thin trail of smoke rising from the nearest edge of the clearing. Her heart skipped a beat as she passed the tree line from high above. She saw the long, dark remains of what could only be a pyre.

She quickly took in the view, spying several people on the ground near her cabin and by the campfire. She next noticed the upturned ground along the stream's edge and several slain horses in the meadow.

Circling back, she urged her dragon to make for the ground by the large cavern. Liana knew exactly where to go, straightening her body and stretching her legs forwards before lowering to the ground.

They landed with a soft thud. Liana crept a few paces forward, continuing the momentum for a short distance. With a snort and a shake of her giant head, she stopped and plopped her frame to the ground.

Alice unbuckled the straps that held her onto the saddle and slid from the dragon's back. Gruloch and the other Haigok landed their beasts a short distance away.

"Alice," a familiar voice called. She turned to see Emily sprinting across the grass towards her. Before she had time to call back, she was swept up into her mother's arms and laden with kisses on her cheeks and forehead.

"I'm fine, Mama," she said, grinning from ear to ear. "I'm pleased to see you as well."

Emily pulled away a little, still keeping her arms wrapped tightly around her daughter. Alice then noticed the tears streaming down her mother's face. They were not tears of happiness.

"Something terrible has happened," Emily said.

"I know," Alice replied. "Arthur was taken."

"Yes." Emily peered at her daughter, perplexed. "I won't ask how you know this. But something worse has occurred."

Gruloch and his men moved to Alice's side, preparing to introduce themselves. They paused when they saw the state of the auburn woman.

"Many have been killed," she informed the other.

"Many?" Alice queried. "Who?"

Emily looked to the Haigok standing behind the girl.

"Perhaps we should tend to your friends and their beasts first," the woman suggested. "You must all be weary after your journey."

"Indeed, we are," Gruloch replied.

"Mama..." Alice gestured to the Lord of the Haigok. "This is Gruloch. Leader of the Haigok. He and these other warriors offer their help."

"You are most welcome here," Emily offered.

Alice's eyes darted around from one side of the glade to the other, searching frantically.

"Where's Shadow?" she asked.

***

Night had fallen when she had knelt beside the fresh grave of her friend, weeping silently. Her hand rested upon the soil, petting it as if it were a part of him.

"I'm so sorry," she whimpered. "I'm so, so sorry."

She peered up to the cavern where the Haigok tended to their dragons. Yellow and orange torchlight flickered at the mouth of the cave. She watched through wet eyes as several men led some cattle inside.

Rising to her feet, she brushed dirt from her knees and looked down at the earth again.

"I shouldn't have left you, Shadow," she whispered.

"You did what you had to do," a voice growled from the bank of the stream. She had smelt the other approaching before he spoke.

"I'm not sure that all would agree with you, Captain Thornton," she replied. "This wouldn't have happened if I had remained."

"You don't know that," he told her, moving to her side. "No one knows that for sure."

"I don't think he would have attacked if both I and Liana were here to defend this place." Alice stared at the rukyul's fresh grave.

"Granted," Thornton conceded, "a dragon and the prime sorceress do pose a grand threat. I believe he fears you. But that may just be something that delays an imminent attack.

"In any case," he continued. "This bastard would have attacked the glade, eventually. Or you would have attacked him. Whichever it be, many would have perished. This is what it means to be at war. And you are at war, Alice. Whether you like it or not."

"I know," she replied, meeting his eyes. "But I left to help an ally. I returned with help but I've lost more than I gained."

"True," he said. "You lost friends and family. Some were even good fighters. Not great. But good. You lost men, women, and children who owed their allegiance to you and have all shown it one way or another. We burned people you love in your absence, and you feel guilty about that.

"Perhaps you should," he said, cocking an eyebrow as he stared at her. She felt a cold shiver run down her spine as he glared at her.

"I've never been a leader of a people," Thornton told her as he surveyed the camp. "I've led soldiers, but not a community. I don't think I ever want to, but I know tactics, Alice. I know that most of those that we said goodbye to were nothing more than farmers who tilled soil, or woodcutters, stone men, hunters and fishermen and not much more. They were not soldiers. Not all of them.

"But you have Commander Brondt and his men. You have me and my squad of well-trained bastards. You have twelve of those reptile people, armed and ready to fight. And now, you have thirteen big, fucking dragons."

She gave him a stern look. Alice didn't appreciate the use of vulgar language, and she let him know it with her silent glare.

"Sorry," he said. "I'm just excited. Forgive me."

She gestured with her hand. "Go on."

"I've heard..." he stopped himself. "We've all heard the stories of how two dragons destroyed Woodmyst once before. Two."

He held up two fingers to illustrate the fact.

"You have thirteen." He pointed to the cavern across the clearing. "I don't have enough fingers for that. You could destroy the city on a single night. Swoop in and douse the place in fire."

"There are people there," she countered.

"People who are loyal to the Maji."

"People who are like family to me," she argued. "People who *are* family. My uncle's sister and her husband are still there, for all I know. My husband is most definitely there, being held prisoner."

"We get them out," Thornton told her. "During the attack. We get them out and burn the city down."

"No," she said firmly. "No one needs to die just because they live in that city. It's not their fault that they serve him. He seduced them and manipulated them. He has a hold over all of them."

"So?" He gave her a perplexed look. "You don't intend to use the dragons."

"Of course I do," she said, starting back towards the camp. Thornton fell into step by her side. "Things will be burnt, Captain. Just not the entire city. But I will need your help to come up with a plan of attack."

***

They moved through the streets of Dweagan with their banners held high before them. Horns blew and people lined the sides of the avenues to get a glimpse of six of the nine queens of Woodmyst.

"The fleet has been loaded with supplies," reported the rider who went ahead, now reunited with his unit and reporting to the scarlet witch. "The master of the port has informed me that the warships have already departed three days ago to make their way around the horn and then north."

"What of our escort ships?"

"Still docked and ready for battle if necessary."

"Good." Tricia smiled. "How long before we can be underway?"

"To load the men and horses," he replied, "would take an hour or so if we hurry."

"And hurry, we must," she replied. "Go back to the port and inform the master to make the way ready for our arrival."

"Yes, my lady." He bowed his head and raced away.

They rode a little farther, smiling and waving at the people gathered nearby. The road eventually opened at a wide intersection encompassed by a market.

The jade banners broke away from the others and turned left into a wide avenue, lined with rich gardens and neat buildings with tiny yards. At the far end of the avenue stood a tall palace that overlooked the city.

"This is where I leave you, sisters," Gilda said with a tear in her eye. "I wish you a safe journey and will think on you frequently."

Each of the other five bade farewell to the jade woman, holding her hand briefly before riding on.

"Set your garrison in place before you take rest, Gilda," Isabel told her. "You can never be too careful."

"Thank you, sister," she replied. "Remember to dress warmly in Wintermarsh. Even the name gives me chills."

Gilda then followed her bannermen towards the palace with her garrison marching closely behind her. She didn't wait to see the others continue on towards the port, knowing full-well that her responsibility was immediate.

Before the others had reached the ships, Gilda seated herself upon the throne in Dweagan palace. She posted her guards about the grounds and her garrison occupied the barracks.

All was going to plan.

Twenty-Two

His shoulders ached, a sharp pain shooting along his outstretched arms and down his spine. The clasps on his wrists were new and had never touched the flesh of a prisoner before. The chains attached to them were drawn so tightly that he feared his arms would be wrenched from their sockets.

The guards had removed all of his clothing, save his trousers, which were stained with grit and blood. His blood.

His bareback had scraped across the stone wall of his cell as they placed him in irons. The stinging sensation on his back informed him of fresh wounds. He was so numb in places that he couldn't tell if it was blood or sweat dribbling down his skin.

The sight of a small cot pushed against the wall to the side of the prison cell taunted him. He longed to have just a few moments to lie upon it. Instead, they bound him in such a way that his toes barely touched the ground beneath him.

His head lolled against his chest as he continued to weep. Tears and mucus had mixed upon his chest, creating a mess that trickled over his torso.

The sound of an iron gate opening drew his attention. He opened his eyes as best as he could, but both had swollen, and one remained closed tightly.

He hoped it was Alice coming to rescue him. He pictured her storming in with her flowing white hair trailing behind her, swinging her swords graciously and lopping the heads from the guards standing between her and where he was being held.

But he knew better.

The unmistakable sight of a damson cloak informed him of who it was that came to visit him.

"Arthur," the other started, waving his hand slightly. The door to the cell unlocked and opened with a long screech. "I have news for you. Would you like to hear it?"

Takmel moved close to his prisoner.

Arthur tried to keep his eye fixed upon his captor, but he was too weary. His head drooped and swayed.

A tight vice gripped him around the chin and lifted his face towards Takmel. Suddenly, Arthur's senses reactivated, and he saw, felt the other's hand tightening in his grasp. It felt as if Takmel's fingers were digging into Arthur's skin, penetrating through the bone.

A sharp pain pierced an area near his ear. Arthur's first thought was, *this must be what a broken jaw feels like.* His second thought was, *I'm not going to ever see my Alice again.*

"I asked you a question, Arthur," Takmel growled.

"Yehf," Arthur managed. His voice quivered timidly, fearfully. His face felt terribly numb. "Yehf."

"Yes?" The cloaked figure cocked his head slightly, as if he didn't hear the response. "Was that a *yes*?"

"Yehf," Arthur repeated.

"You would like to hear the news I have?"

"Yehf."

"Good." Takmel released his grasp. "Alice has returned home."

Arthur stared at the other in disbelief.

"It's true." Takmel looked pleased. "One of my spies saw her flying in on her pet. Isn't that wonderful?"

Arthur felt stunned and simply stared. A long strand of drool and blood spilt from his lips.

"Oh, go on and look at this, will you?" Takmel scowled. "You're making a mess of yourself, Arthur."

"Ah-iss," Arthur moaned. "Ah-iss."

"Yes, yes. Alice." The other nodded. "Alice is home. But that was the only good news. You see, there's some bad news that goes with it. She brought some of her dragon-riding friends with her."

Arthur's breathing turned to shallow gasps.

"I know what you're thinking," Takmel pointed to the chained boy playfully. "How is this bad news? She has more dragons.

"Let me tell you," he continued, reaching his right hand over and placing it on Arthur's left shoulder. The imprisoned lad felt the pressure pulling on his arm, increasing the already unbearable pain in his arm's socket. "First, I killed a lot of your friends and those lizard people. Men, women and children, all taken by my bowmen. I took you prisoner and brought you here.

"Then those two witches out there killed a bunch of my men. Fathers, husbands and sons. But I thought, that's only fair. I killed some. They killed some.

"We're even." Takmel slapped his hand against Arthur's skin. Arthur felt something pop. He screamed a little.

"What is it?" Takmel asked with false concern. "Did I hurt you? Poor Arthur. Where was I?"

Arthur groaned, wishing for all of this to go away.

"Right," Takmel smiled. "She then brings dragons into the glade, Arthur. Dragons."

The boy's head lolled again.

"Now, what am I to do? I can't just go out there and punish her. She'll order them to strike and I'll be a pile of ash before I realise. No. Arthur?"

He gripped the boy by the chin again and lifted his face to his.

"Pay attention," Takmel growled. "For this is truly the bad news. I intend to take it out on you, Arthur."

"Wha- yooh do?" Arthur gasped. A slight hint of a laugh resounded in his voice. "Wha- worhf than thihf?"

"What's worse?" Takmel placed his right index finger on Arthur's left shoulder. "This is worse."

A searing pain burnt into Arthur's limb.

Dark smoke engulfed the boy's upper arm. The vapour twisted and spun around and around, faster and faster. It raced over his shoulder, under his armpit, and back around. Again and again and again.

Something that felt like a thousand tiny biting pins ripped into Arthur's flesh as he screamed in agony. Tiny spatters of blood sprayed against the stone wall behind him and onto the floor beneath him. A harsh breeze swept over the boy's face as a wet crunching sound drowned out the ringing in his ears.

Suddenly, he felt another pop deep in the joint, followed closely by another and another. Something was breaking away with each sensation. His body dropped slightly on his left side with each snap. Lower and lower, until...

His left arm broke away from the socket.

Takmel stepped back to admire his work.

Arthur dropped, his knees almost smashing onto the stone floor. His back scraped open by the wall as he swung downward by the chain attached to his right wrist.

His eyes went directly to his left shoulder. A gaping wound trickled blood from where his arm once rested.

He continued to scream, not believing what had happened.

His eyes moved to the severed arm still hanging from the wall by the chains and clasp.

"Fetch the apothecary," Takmel commanded, calling through the iron bars of the cell.

"My lord," a voice acknowledged.

Takmel turned his attention to the boy.

"I don't see it, Arthur," he said, crouching a short distance away. "What is it about you that attracts her? You're not strong. You're not a warrior. You're not even the hunter or farmer that most women are drawn to. You read books and that's all. What good is that for a woman like her?"

"She's powerful. She's a fighter, and she is beautiful. She should be mine, Arthur. Not yours. How could she choose someone like you?"

Arthur moaned and wept.

The apothecary, an elderly man dressed in a clean, white outfit, moved into the cell carrying a large leather bag.

"I need to move him to that cot," he said. Takmel stared coldly at the boy. "If you wish for him to live, my lord."

"I'm not finished with him yet," the other replied. "He had better live."

"He will have a better chance of doing so if I move him," the apothecary informed him.

Takmel quickly weighed up his options.

"Fine." He signalled to the guards to unlock the clasp attached to Arthur's right hand. "But I want his feet in irons."

Within moments, the boy had been moved and dressing applied to his fresh wounds.

"He has passed out. The pain was too much I think. Do you intend on torturing this lad any further?" the apothecary asked.

"This *lad* is the enemy, dear doctor," the Maji answered coolly. "My intentions for him are my prerogative. Yours are to mend him to your best ability until I don't require you to do so any longer. Do you understand?"

"Yes, my lord." The apothecary bowed. "I merely meant that you may wish to keep me nea—"

"Leave," Takmel ordered, turning to face Arthur, who was lying asleep on the cot.

"Yes, my lord," the other replied, picking up his bag and leaving with the guards.

"I'm not finished with you, Arthur," he whispered. "I'll return when you are refreshed and feeling a little better. We'll continue our conversation then. If the rats don't get to you first."

***

"Arthur," gasped Alice. She sat on the grass by the charred, smouldering remains of the pyre. Tear streaks stained her cheeks.

"What is it?" Emily asked from her left.

"It's Arthur," Amicia informed the auburn woman. Both she and Ursula had taken up position on the girl's right. "He is in pain."

"Then we should get him," Emily insisted. "We should bring him home."

"Not yet," Alice replied, turning her head towards the piles of blackened ash. "Takmel wishes for a hasty retaliation. We need to organise and make a plan."

"You shouldn't leave again," the queen of Newholt said, playing with some strands of grass by her knee.

"I know," the girl said, peering at the charred shards of timber and finding tiny pieces of blackened clothing.

"We didn't feel as strong as we do when we're with you."

"You overpowered them," Alice stated. "Captain Thornton told me of how you opened the ground." She then looked at Ursula. "And how you threw lightning as if they were spears."

"We felt weak afterwards," Ursula explained. "We feel energy from you. It... It..."

"Revitalises us," Amicia interjected. "You are not only our prime, Alice. You're our strength. You shouldn't leave us again."

Alice sighed. "Next time I leave the glade," she sniffled, "we go together."

She turned slightly and moved her eyes slowly over the trees high above the caverns on the southern edge of the clearing. She stopped searching when she spied a small clearing amongst some pines high on the ridge.

"You see something," Ursula whispered.

"No," she answered. "But someone is hiding up there."

"One of those creatures?" the queen of Newholt queried.

"No." Alice got up. "There are men."

"Men?" Emily rose to her daughter's side.

"Spies for the Maji," the snowy-haired girl explained. "They are watching."

Alice started back towards the camp. The others quickly fell into step and followed.

They found Captain Thornton and his men seated about the hearth. There were cups of tea in their hands and empty, food-stained plates on the ground by their feet.

"Captain," Alice called.

Thornton turned instantly and got up. "My lady?"

"A word, please," she said, walking slowly towards her cabin.

Thornton placed his mug on the ground by his chair and followed the girl.

The other three women intended to follow, but Alice held a finger up to them, cautioning them to wait.

They watched in silence as the captain and the girl talked. They couldn't hear any words spoken by either of them. But, by the way Thornton nodded, they assumed she was giving him a long list of instructions.

When the discussion was complete, Thornton returned to his seat by the fire and Alice beckoned for the three ladies to re-join her.

"What was that about?" Emily asked.

"An arrangement," Alice answered. "Come. Let's go inside and try to eat something."

"Are you all right, Alice?" Ursula asked.

The girl raised her chin. "We need to keep our strength up for what is coming," she said as she entered the door.

David, Lor and Yuri sat around the table. At the head, in Alice's usual place, sat Gruloch. His bulbous yellow eyes moved from one host to another before sighting Alice in the doorway.

Behind them, Linet and Akasati fussed in the kitchen. Alice found it strange to see the Erilian warrior using a wooden spoon to stir a casserole. It seemed unnatural. Akasati was one who preferred a bow or blade in her hands and even appeared uncomfortable in her current location.

"I made stew," she said proudly, dishing some slop from the pot into a bowl. She then raised the bowl and offered it to Alice with a nod.

"Are they treating you well?" Alice asked Gruloch as she moved around the table to take the bowl from Akasati.

"We were just talking," the Haigok replied.

"Make sure you take some bread." Lor gave her an expressive look. Alice eyed him quizzically. He responded by gesturing to his bowl with his chin and offering a quick frown and shake of the head.

Alice looked back to Akasati, who hadn't noticed the exchange. Instead, the Erilian warrior continued to dish out more bowls of stew for the other three women.

"Talking about what?" Alice asked, sitting down beside her uncle and reaching for a chunk of bread.

"Why you thought bringing dragons to the glade was a good idea," David replied.

Alice took a deep breath.

"You don't want them here," Alice presumed.

"No," David told her. He then shook his head. "I don't know."

"Explain," she said as Emily took her place beside David. The other sorceresses found places around the table and tucked into their bowls. Amicia seemed to freeze upon placing a morsel in her mouth. She sat rigid with her spoon sticking from her lips.

Akasati looked at her, smiling and waiting for some recognition for her efforts.

"Mmmm." The queen smiled, reluctantly lowering her spoon into the bowl for a second time.

"Try the bread," Lor said, gesturing to the broken loaf in the centre of the table. Each of the three women quickly snatched up a handful of fluffy white bread.

"I'm sure you have grand plans for these beasts, Alice," David started. "And I will go along with whatever you decide to do. But dragons in Woodmyst?

"If Richard were here, he would be devastated. He saw first-hand, up close, what they can do. I was only a child, as was Lor, but I remember the days after the attack. They lay the entire city to ruin. The stones toppled on the ground were still too hot to touch after three days."

"I understand," Alice replied, melancholically.

"No, I don't think you do," Lor said gently. "Richard killed one of those creatures. But it was too late and all for naught. The one he killed was the one that burned all the village folk in the Great Hall. The Haigok were the ones who locked them in there for the dragon to do so."

"I have heard the story." Alice frowned.

"Then you also know that it was one dragon," Lor continued. "Just one that burnt the entire city to the ground. You have thirteen. What are your intentions here? I have a sister in that city. So do you."

Alice didn't realise that she had been holding onto her spoon the entire time. She placed it down beside the bowl of steaming stew and looked at each face around the table.

"I didn't ask to be your leader," she said calmly. "I didn't want to be Kayl'sro. But I am. All I wanted was to live out here with Arthur alone. But things have occurred and now you all turn to me.

"I understand, Uncle Lor," she continued, "that some of you, some within Woodmyst, would regard the Haigok as your enemy. Yes, they surrounded our city and slaughtered all within its walls, including my grandfather and grandmother."

"I am ashamed of that part of our history," Gruloch offered. "My father and I never really saw eye to eye. It was he that led that assault."

"Revenge for something that only a few did to your kind," David mumbled.

"Revenge." Gruloch acknowledged. "Yes. My kind has a way of holding onto past grievances to the point of insanity. After the destruction of Woodmyst, my people scattered once again. When my father perished in an attack from the Mirikin, I became Lord of the Haigok. I changed the way our people dealt with others. I tried to open trade with the nomads of the Core Lands and I sit here with you because I believe all peoples of these lands can live with one another. Revenge is a thing of the past for my people."

"Well, that's all fine and sweet," Lor put in. "But here you are with your twelve dragons ready for war."

"War and revenge are two very different things," Gruloch clarified.

"Try explaining that to those who fell on the battlefields when the White Witch attacked," David said. He then pointed to Alice seated across from him. "Tell that to her father, who died at the hands of that bitch. They did all of that because she sought revenge. Nothing more to it."

"There was more to it," Alice stated. "It was all for the ascension of the Maji. It was to place him exactly where he needed to be. If the White Witch had destroyed all of you at Woodmyst, she would have established her own kingdom there. She would have raised Takmel to become the very thing he has become. Instead, she died on the battle-field. She willingly handed over her ten-year-old son to be raised by those she sought revenge upon. Why?"

"Because she knew he would follow his nature," Emily whispered.

Alice nodded. "This was the prophecy," she explained. "He is the heir of darkness. The ruler of all."

"A false prophecy," David said, shaking his head. "Made up by the Sovereign."

"No," Amicia interrupted. "Not made up by Yasmeen Svoboda. Adopted by her, yes. But not created by her. The Mirikin were an ancient order, and they passed the prophecy down through the ages.

"Takmel is the Maji," she continued. "He is the only offspring from any of the Mistresses. The only one.

"Something dark chose Sumaiyya Tarkin to be the vessel that would bring him into the world. And now he lives in Woodmyst."

"Why Maji not wipe all out when he a boy?" Yuri growled.

"His age," Alice answered. "Some of us could use our abilities when we were younger, but we didn't come to our full potential until we reached a certain age."

"For women," Amicia added, "it's the age of womanhood. When we flower, so to speak."

"By the gods," Lor gasped. "I didn't need to know that."

"For boy?" Yuri queried.

Amicia shook her head.

"Takmel is the first," Alice told him.

"So, he could have always known what he was to become," Akasati added.

"I don't think so," Alice replied. "But I do think he knew before what happened on the bridge."

David locked eyes with her. He heard the horses running over the stones and saw his wives and baby daughter falling into the river all over again.

"I need to get my boy back," he said gloomily.

"We will," Alice told him. "But not yet. We have a more immediate concern to face. Spies have positioned themselves upon the southern ridge."

They exchanged looks around the table.

"We go get them," Yuri stood and started away from the table.

"No," Alice commanded. "I've already made arrangements."

The Agrodien turned and gave her a perplexed look.

"Arrangements?" he asked, not understanding the word.

"I've got it under control, Yuri," she said in his tongue. "Please, sit and take rest."

He hesitated momentarily before allowing his eyes to see the glint of the Iron Claws strung about the girl's neck.

"Yes, Kayl'sro." He bowed slightly and resumed his seat.

"The dragons," Alice explained, looking around the table to each of those about her, "will play a part in what is coming. But this threat has already expanded beyond the borders of Woodmyst."

"What do you mean?" Linet asked, still fussing in the kitchen. "Is there another out there who puts us in danger?"

"The Seven are on the move," Alice explained. "I could see it when I reunited with Amicia and Ursula."

"And your sister?" Emily queried.

"She is still in Woodmyst," Ursula answered.

"She doesn't concern me for the time being," Alice added.

"Doesn't concern you?" David asked, his brow furrowed. "She's your sister. She's by Takmel's side and she's dangerous."

"I'm more worried about the Seven," said Alice. "They are under the influence of the Maji and they move farther and farther away from him. Yet, it is as if they are right beside him."

"The bond is powerful," Amicia explained. "Usually, the more the distance, the weaker the connection."

"But not in this case?" Linet asked.

"No," Amicia replied. "It's as if the Mirikin have returned."

Twenty-Three

"Well," Joanne said, and sighed, sitting upright in her saddle. "There it is. Newholt."

She and Andris had ridden to the top of a smooth ridge that extended from the mountains, passing beneath the forest to their left and levelling out into a bare plateau several leagues to their right.

Her soldiers and cavalry waited in the dale behind them, out of the sight of the city by the sea.

The surrounding scenery might have appeared spectacular if night hadn't set in, preventing them from seeing much of the world surrounding Newholt. But the lights of the port were clear enough.

The masts of the frigates and battleships anchored so closely together that it made Andris think of picket fences. Salt in the air constantly reminded him of the ocean nearby. However, he couldn't see it, except for the sighting of ships and a glint of light reflecting from beside the dockyards.

The white palace on the hill in the centre of the metropolis drew their eyes from the shore and over the lamplit streets. Even from this distance, Andris could see people walking along the well-illuminated cobbled streets.

This sort of lighting made it difficult to try a stealthy attack.

Then there were the beacons.

Two pointed out to sea; one at the far northern edge of the city, the other closer to the south.

They spread four others along the southern edge of the community, lighting up the level ground between Newholt and their position.

Several others pointed into the forest just to the western edge of the municipality.

"They're ready for us," Andris informed her.

"No," she replied. "It isn't us they watch for. Do you see any of these lights to the north?"

"No," he answered. "There is too much glare. But I would assume they would cover that region as well."

"As do I." Joanne took a deep breath. "We have allies waiting for us to strike."

"Allies?"

"In the forest," she said, pointing to the edge of the city. "They wait to see our approach."

"We strike tonight?" he asked, puzzled.

"No. The ships are not here yet."

"Ships?"

"Were you not informed of the strategy that is to take place here?"

"They ordered me to protect you and lead this army north," he replied.

"And here you are." She smirked, peering down at the city. "Protecting me and leading this army." She pointed to the docks. "The ships will strike first and cause confusion. We will attack from this ridge and our allies will advance upon their western border at the same time."

"I see catapults." Andris pointed along the line of beacons to the leftmost edge of the city.

"Not enough for what we have in store," Joanne replied. "We will destroy Newholt. Queen Amicia will have nothing but rubble where her subjects once dwelt. We will take the palace and offer sanctuary to any who bow their knee to me. They, in turn, will offer their servitude and loyalty. And such will be the fate of Newholt, home to the Black Queen of Woodmyst."

***

The scarlet woman stood upon the poop deck of her designated galleon. It was the highest point on board the vessel, save the lookout posts high upon the masts.

The flag whipping about in the breeze above her head, jutting from a pole at the stern of the ship, bore her colour, trimmed with gold leaf upon black stitching. She admired it for a moment before turning her gaze to the vessel following them a short distance away.

A smaller ship, a frigate, laden with cannons and refurbished for war, it was flying the scarlet banner proudly, illuminated by lantern light.

A lump formed in her throat as she beheld the sight.

Beyond the frigate, moving away towards the west, eight more vessels bore the colours of their allegiance; olive, lilac, gold and white; two vessels for each of them; a galleon and frigate.

She felt a small sadness creep over her. She was leaving her sisters after such a long time. She was going to be on her own. They all were.

But it is for the better.

It is for the benefit of all people.

She shed a tear as she kept watch on the other ships vanishing into the night upon the Sea of Lunkhul.

When the last twinkling of their lanterns' orange glow disappeared, she turned back to face the route ahead. The sails, she could see, filled with air, pushing them southward over gentle waters.

Peering down to the sterncastle deck, she placed her hands on the guardrail and called out to the boy at the wheel. "Boy."

"Yes, my lady," he answered, smiling innocently as he turned his face up to meet her gaze.

He didn't look much older than nine or ten years old. His clothes were neat, appearing brand new. A scarlet waistband tied to the side sat above his dark trousers. A brown jacket with wooden toggles, left undone, covered a fresh white shirt. The breeze tossed his sandy blond hair, giving it an unkempt appearance, and his feet were bare.

"How far to the cape?" she asked.

"If this wind keeps, my lady," he replied, glancing to the sails, "we might round her on the morrow. Perhaps first light."

"And then?"

"Hard to say, my lady," he said back. "The wind acts differently on the other side of the cape. There's a good chance we will sail into the wind. But you can never tell until you get there."

"Very well," she said, looking away to the darkness beyond the bow. Her eyes drifted across the other decks. Several men moved about, rolling up ropes, working the rigging, keeping busy.

Most of the men, however, were below deck in their cots or milling about. Her own guards, apart from two standing on either side of the poop deck with her, were also in their makeshift barracks on board in the cargo hold.

They stored their horses and supplies there also, awaiting the time they arrived at their destination. But they didn't bring all that much in the way of building materials and tools.

The Maji had seen to that.

Other vessels had been moving to and from Dweagan, loading and carrying supplies to several locations around the land. Men had been relocated to establish some functionality to the facilities that his queens were to occupy.

Stone from Woodmyst's quarry; iron from Ironfields; wheat, barley and livestock from the southern farming towns such as Bellmore and Butteredge; had been in the shipping process for well over a year.

"Boy," Tricia called again.

"Yes, my lady?" He turned to her.

"How many trips is this for you?"

"To your destination?"

"Yes."

"I'm not sure..." He paused to think, scratching his fingers through his sandy hair. "Maybe nine."

"Nine?"

"Yes." He scrunched his nose a little. "I'm not sure. We moved stone and masons to the north some time ago. Then we took some large equipment on another trip. We also picked up cargo from Blackshore and took it all the way before returning to Dweagan."

"That's a great deal of travelling," Tricia offered, impressed by the boy's reply.

"We've been at it for a little over a year."

"A year?"

"Yes, my lady," the boy answered. "The Maji has been sending instructions for a long time."

"I see," she responded, gazing off into the distance. It would appear that Takmel had been actively preparing for this for much longer than he let on.

Not that it mattered.

After all, it was for the better.

She focussed upon the boy again.

"What do you know of the Maji?" she asked.

"Not all that much, my lady," he said, peering into the sails and the night sky beyond to get his bearings. "I know that the people of Dweagan believe they owe him their lives."

"How so?"

"Well," he began, "If I heard correctly. When the Mirikin attacked, the witches... Do I call them *witches?*"

"You can." Tricia smiled kindly.

"So, the witches wanted to slaughter everyone in the city," he continued. "But, the Maji stopped them. He ordered the soldiers left behind to touch none of the females, women and girls, or they would answer to him. He claimed them for himself."

"Claimed them?" This intrigued the scarlet woman.

"Yes, my lady. But they say that he never intended to follow through on such a claim. He did it to protect those who were still in the city.

"When the Mirikin were defeated in Woodmyst," he continued, "those who had fled Dweagan returned. Soldiers from the north came to liberate the city, but the Mirikin's forces that remained here had already set their allegiance to protecting and serving the people of Dweagan. With no more Mirikin to hold them, they were all free."

"And Dweagan kept their allegiance to the Maji," Tricia said.

"Yes, my lady."

"I see," she said. "You seem to know a lot for a boy of... How old are you?"

"Ten years, my lady," he informed her. "Soon to be eleven when the winter comes. And it's only what I hear others talk about, my lady. The other men on board and people at all the places I've been to. I don't know how much is true and made up. I've found the less exciting parts are usually the real things."

She looked at his bare feet. His toes kept curling and unfolding as he gripped the wheel in his hands.

"Suppose I give you boots for your birthday," she offered. "How would you receive them?"

"I'd thank you, my lady," he replied. "But the truth is, I do have a pair of boots stowed by my cot. I wear them when we go to land. I don't enjoy having them on when we set sail. It doesn't feel right."

She bit her lip as she watched the boy continue to perform his duty on the wheel. He peered into the sails again before looking at the sky. He adjusted his steering and gazed about the ship to each of the men on deck.

It was impressive, she believed, that such a young boy could be left to such responsibility.

"What's your name?" she called to him.

"Samuel Dimodan at your service, my lady." He turned and gave her a quick salute.

***

Many fireballs arced across the sky.

It was as if they had simply burst from the sea. Before anyone on land had time to react, the large, flaming balls of fodder and stone crashed into the warships moored at the Newholt wharves.

Fire engulfed the vessels as men raced to get away from the flames.

A bell clanged from the port, echoing across the city, apprising all personnel of the attack upon the harbour.

Shouting and running ensued as confusion set in.

Newholt wasn't ready for this.

Cannon fire opened up. The terrible thunder exploded over the waves and spewed countless chunks of iron into the ships and people fleeing along the wooden walkways of the pier.

Thick plumes of smoke rested upon the water several leagues away from the shore, masking the vessels from view.

Another barrage of cannon fire burst from the shadows of the sea, tearing into warehouses and smaller structures by the edge of the piers.

Sudden, enormous explosions lit up the night sky as the black powder on board the damaged warships caught alight.

One after another, rapidly and with ferocity, frigates and galleys splintered and burned.

Andris watched on in amazement by Joanne's side. They were still on top of the rise overlooking the city when the attack began.

The men accompanying the Black Queen saw the first fireballs that arced in the sky as their signal to advance. Now, as another barrage of the flaming projections filled the sky, they raced on horseback and on foot towards the southern beacon lights guarding Newholt.

Archers bearing black armbands aimed over their comrades and loosed their arrows towards the blinding lights hoping to hit any men standing near to them.

"Look!" Joanne pointed to the western edge of the city.

Andris followed her gesture and saw a swarm of black moving from the forest and into the light of the beacons. The sight reminded him of ants attacking an intruder to the nest.

"What is that?" he asked.

"Our allies," she answered with a grin. "It has begun.

Twenty-Four

Alice quickly looked at Amicia. They sat at the table, trying to pretend to enjoy Akasati's stew. The look on the queen's face bore deep concern.

"Amicia?" Alice questioned, moving her hand to her own stomach. A slight churning had started to annoy her.

"I'm fine," the other assured. "I just felt…"

"Newholt is under attack," Ursula informed the rest.

Eyes started darting to one another around the table.

"Attack?" Linet asked. "Are you certain? How can you know?"

"It is," Amicia assured her. "A darkness falls upon it as we speak."

"Should we send some riders?" Gruloch offered, tensing as if preparing to leave. "They could take flight within moments."

"It would take them half the night to get there," Alice told him. "By the time they arrived, the battle would be all but over. And by the time they returned, the Maji just may find another weakness to exploit back here on the glade. We can't risk it."

"Then what do we do?" Emily asked.

"Sit tight," the girl instructed them, wincing slightly and shifting her body to a more comfortable position.

"Alice?" Ursula lowered her brows, observing the girl's behaviour.

"Newholt attacked," David mumbled. "Dragons in the cave. Spies on the ridge. What's next?"

Alice was suddenly on her feet and bolting for the door with her hand over her mouth. Flinging it open so hard that it smacked loudly against the wall and shook the furniture, she barely stepped onto the porch before an eruption of vomit sprayed into the air and onto the grass outside.

"By the gods," David said, slipping out of his seat and racing after her. He was the first to her side, with Emily coming a close second. "Alice? Are you all right?"

He placed his arms on her shoulders as she gripped a support beam on the veranda to keep her balance. Her knees were bent slightly as she kept one hand on her belly.

"She's fine," Amicia said coolly as she approached from the open door.

"Was it my stew?" Akasati called from inside.

"No," Alice replied. "The stew is fine."

"Don't lie," whispered David. "Not at a time like this."

"It isn't the stew," Alice assured him, suddenly feeling the urge to throw up again but only bringing up air as a guttural burp.

David saw an opportunity.

"Tell her it was the stew," he pleaded. "We won't have to eat that slime ever again."

"She's with child," Amicia announced, beaming.

Emily's and David's eyes went wide with shock. They looked at the woman by the door, to Alice, and then at each other.

"No," David shook his head, not wanting to believe that his little boy and this little girl were about to become parents. "It must be the stew."

"It's not the stew," Alice straightened herself and took a deep breath. "Amicia is right. I've been fighting it for a few days. I am with child."

At that moment, a bunch of things occurred simultaneously.

Yuri clapped his hands with joy.

Ursula moved to Amicia's side, allowing a broad smile to form on her face.

Gruloch thudded his fist against the table and laughed.

Akasati knocked the pot of stew off the stove, spilling the remaining contents onto the floor.

Linet covered her mouth with her hands and stared at her husband.

Lor, in turn, watched the stew slowly spread over the floor.

"Well, there's some good news," he mumbled.

***

While Alice and the others gathered on the porch of the cabin, three men watched from the deep shadows of the pine trees from the ridge behind the caverns where the dragons dwelt. They were too far to identify each individual, but they recognised David by his form and Alice by her size. The others could have been anyone.

As they observed, others from the camp ran to the girl's location. Verbal exchanges were given and several of the men shook David's hand.

"What do you think is happening?" asked one man in a hoarse whisper.

"How should I know?" another answered with a shrug. "Perhaps it's his birthday."

"Isn't his birthday, you dumb git!" The third shook his head annoyingly. "The girl was just sick everywhere, wasn't she?"

The other two stared blankly at the scenery far below them.

"Yeah," one said and nodded slowly. "Yeah, you're right. So, what's that about then?"

"What's that abo—" The third glared at the other, dumbfounded. "The girl was sick, right?"

"Yeah," the other two replied.

"The big guy got his hand shaken, right?"

"Yeah," they chorused.

"He's the father of that little bugger they took back to Woodmyst."

"So?" one man asked, furrowing his brow.

"That little bloke is that girl's husband, isn't he?"

"Yeah," the same man answered, still wearing a confused face.

"I get it," the second man said excitedly and pointed to the gathering. "She's having a baby."

The third man threw his arms into the air. "Finally."

"A baby?" the other man gasped. "We need to report that. Don't we?"

The third man shook his head and signalled for the standing man to crouch back to cover in the shadows.

"Why I was put with you two, I will never know," the third man whispered. "Next time, I think I'll offer to clean the stables with my tongue. Gods know it would be less painfuh... Uh... Ackh..."

"What's wrong with you, then?" the second man asked, squinting to see into the darkness.

The glint of a blade tip protruding through the third man's mouth was all the answer he needed. Before he could warn the other, and lift his own knife from his belt, he felt a cold finger slide over his neck.

A warm sensation flowed over his chest, and the taste of blood laced the back of his tongue. His arms drooped to his sides as a hand from the shadows gripped his chin, pulling his head high to allow his veins to drain.

His eyes moved to the other man who was being held down by two others, one of which plunged a dagger into his companion's chest over and over and over again.

"You think that's all of them?" Lieutenant Brook asked, dropping his target onto the ground as he retrieved his sword from the back of the dead man's head.

"We should check along the ridge in both directions just to be sure," Thornton growled. "I'll take Sparrow, Bacon and Vawdrey with me back to the west. You take Cobham, Cheyne and Jendryng along that way. Keep to the tree line when you get to lower ground and move around the edge of the clearing. We'll meet up by the Agrodien huts on the other side."

"Aye, sir," hissed the Lieutenant before offering a quick salute.

With that, the troop split into two groups, each working their way around the glade in opposite directions.

"Keep your eyes peeled," Thornton grumbled as they crept through the pine forest.

"Do you think we'll find any more of them?" Sparrow asked.

"We'd better," Vawdrey replied. "Especially if they are hiding out here."

"Shut yer trap," Thornton snapped. "Speak only if you see something."

"Aye sir," said Vawdrey sheepishly.

***

"What have you done?" Catherine hollered, storming past the guards on either side of the assembly hall doors and along the aisle in the centre of the auditorium. They quickly came to their senses and pursued.

Takmel, seated in a high-backed chair on top of the platform at the front of the room, leant back, awaiting her verbal assault.

"You took his arm?" she continued. "Tore it right from his socket? I saw him. That boy is family. He's like a brother to you."

"You spoke to him?"

"He still sleeps."

"You have such boldness to come in here and point the finger at me for what I did," he snarled. "But you are hesitant to blame yourself for what *you* have done."

She stopped in her tracks, pausing roughly halfway along the aisle. The guards following her came within arm's reach.

Quickly, suddenly, she turned and thrust her hands in their direction. Both suddenly fell backwards, toppling over the stone floor.

"What I have done?" she raised an eyebrow. "Everything that I have done was only ever for you."

"You're one of hers," he hissed.

"What?"

"Your one of the four," he clarified. "She is your prime."

"I've not sworn allegiance to anyone," Catherine reminded him.

The guards slowly rose to their feet. One started towards her again. She turned and held a finger up to him, warning him off.

Takmel held up his hand, silently commanding the guard to retract.

"You've not even sworn your allegiance to me," Takmel said, returning his attention to his wife.

206 | ROBERT E KREIG

"I shouldn't have to," she told him. "My loyalty speaks for itself. Look at what I've done for you."

"Yes," he agreed. He rose from his chair and started down the steps from the platform towards the stone floor. "I remember. You killed that boy's mother. I remember that."

"I did that for you!" She jutted an angry finger in his direction.

"Careful." He held up his palms in mock surrender, gesturing to her finger with his chin. He reached the stone floor and moved along the aisle slowly. "We don't need to put each other's abilities to the test here."

"You promised," she said, crying.

"Promised?" He furrowed his brow and shook his head.

"You promised not to hurt him."

"No. No, I didn't make any such promise." He frowned. "I remember you warning me that if I hurt him, you would do something."

"You promised that no harm would come to him," she retorted. "Those were your words. No harm would come to him."

He stopped moving and shrugged casually.

"Perhaps you're right," he admitted. "I've much on my mind of late. I'd probably forget my boots if I didn't have another wife here who enjoys sharing my bed. A great woman that Lucy. Always looking after me."

She shook her head in disbelief.

"You're a pig," she spat.

"Now, now." Takmel gave her a stern glare. "No need to be uncivilised."

She balled her hands into fists as her fury built inside, hotter and hotter like a fiery furnace.

He saw her temper growing and decided to fuel her rage.

"I don't see why you are so concerned with the boy," he said. "He's nothing to you. Your sister's husband, yes. But what is she to you? They abandoned you here. They left you behind. You're nothing to them. You're a fleeting memory."

"No," she growled, gritting her teeth.

He stepped slowly towards her, knowing that he had touched upon a vulnerability that she harboured; her secret longing to be with her family.

"You're their enemy," he continued. "They hate you. They see you as my wife. Loyal to the Maji. In their hearts and minds, you may as well be dead."

"No," she repeated, trembling with anger.

"They are your enemies, Catherine. And your enemies are my enemies as well. Give in. Stand beside me. Use your gifts to help me destroy all my enemies, all your enemies. We can do this together. Just like that day upon the bridge."

He offered a loving smile and reached his hand out to her.

"No," she screamed, thrusting her fists in his direction.

A great wave of power extended from her, sending some of the neat rows of benches surrounding her scuttling across the floor in all directions. It was so powerful that the two guards standing far to the back of the room fell to the floor again.

But it wasn't powerful enough to take Takmel down.

Instead, he spun quickly on his feet and seemed to absorb, harness the energy as he rotated. He splayed his fingers and thrust his open hands back towards Catherine, hitting her squarely in the chest with the very power that she had thrown at him.

Her body arced through the air at tremendous speed and smacked high against the stone wall above the large doors to the hall. Her ears rang and stars filled her vision.

She then felt herself falling for such a long time before her face hit the hard, cold floor below. The taste of blood filled her mouth as she sluggishly opened her eyes to see Takmel approaching.

"Get her in chains," she heard him say to the guards. His voice sounded as though it came from the far end of a very long tunnel. "Lock her in the cells."

Her eyes closed again. She fought to keep them open, but could not.

Hands gripped her under her arms, and she felt herself being dragged away.

Gradually, she drifted into the darkness, leaving the echoes of consciousness behind.

Twenty-Five

Alice rested on the edge of the porch. The stench from what she had thrown up filled her senses and caused her to have further episodes. Thankfully, foul air was the only product of each outburst.

Gruloch had retired to the cavern where his men and dragons had set up camp. Yuri had remained to watch over Alice, concerned for her health and too excited to sleep after hearing the good news. Queen Amicia and Ursula sat inside, drinking tea with Linette while David and Lor talked with Yuri at the table and Akasati saw to cleaning up.

"You should try to eat some bread," Akasati told her, tipping the warm dishwater from a pail and onto the grass where Alice had ejected the contents of her stomach. "You need something to settle you."

"That doesn't always work," Emily offered, seated beside her daughter and stroking her white hair. "I remember when I carried your sister, there was nothing that could make it go away until it wanted to."

"Was it that way with me?" Alice asked, leaning into her mother.

"No," she replied. "You were different. I had quite a strange desire to eat a lot of pork and stale toast. I ate so much that I think that must be what you are made of. Pork and toast."

Alice chuckled quietly before a sudden, deep burp emanated from her lips.

"Sorry," she said as she covered her mouth.

Emily and Akasati both giggled.

"I think," Akasati stated, "that this coming season and the months ahead are a time when a lady like yourself can actually get away with behaving as unladylike as she wants."

"I'm not a lady?" Alice asked jovially.

"No, you are not." Akasati grinned, tipping the last of the pail's contents onto the grass.

Alice scrunched her nose up.

"I can still smell it," she said.

"I'll get another load of dishwater," the other replied. "There isn't much left, though."

"I think you'll be able to smell it long after us," Emily told her daughter. "Next time, try for a bucket. At least we can carry it away to the stream and dispose of it there."

The girl murmured agreement, then suddenly winced, bringing a hand to her chest.

"What is it?" Akasati asked, seeing the painful expression on Alice's face. "Are you about to do it again?"

She shook her head, baring her teeth and squinting her eyes tightly shut.

"Alice?" Emily turned her daughter face-up onto her lap. "What's the matter?"

Yuri suddenly stepped from the doorway of the cabin and onto the porch, pointing a finger back inside.

"Something wrong," he grunted.

Akasati stepped to the open door and peered inside, where she saw Linette cradling Ursula and David, holding Amicia as gently as he could. Both women were behaving as Alice was, wincing in pain.

"It hurts," Ursula groaned.

"What is happening?" the Erilian called from the door. "All three of you at once?"

Amicia opened her eyes and look up at David.

"It's the fourth," she managed. "She has been hurt."

Suddenly, her eyes closed and the three women went limp.

"The fourth?" David asked the woman in his arms, but there was no response. "Queen Amicia?"

"Help me," Emily called from outside.

Yuri moved to the auburn woman and lifted Alice carefully from her lap. Without being told to, he carried her inside, past the others and into the girl's bedroom.

"What is this?" Lor queried, his gaze following his niece before moving to the other women lying unconscious on the sofas in the sitting room.

"Put Ursula on my bed," Emily instructed Lor. "Then find Commander Brondt."

"What of this one?" David asked, standing to his feet with Amicia in his arms.

"Lay her on the sofa for now," the auburn woman replied.

"The sofa is not fit for a queen, Emily," Linet interjected.

"We've only two beds," the other said as she rearranged the cushions on the lounge. "It will have to do until Commander Brondt arrives."

David lowered the queen onto the sofa as Emily shifted a pillow into place under the sleeping woman's head.

"She said that the *fourth* has been hurt," David said, stepping back and out of the way as Emily fussed about.

"Fetch me a blanket." Emily pointed towards the bedroom. David followed the instruction, disappearing into the doorway of Alice's room.

"What do you think that means?" David asked. "The fourth has been hurt?"

"Shhh!" Yuri hissed, holding a finger to his lips before pointing to Alice sleeping on the bed.

"I think I'd rather have her awake right now," the big man told him. "There's nothing natural about this, and that can't be good."

"I try wake her?" the Agrodien offered.

"No." David shook his head as he rummaged through a cupboard, finding a neatly folded woollen blanket upon a top-shelf. "Not until we know what this is."

Carrying the blanket back into the sitting room, he looked at Emily for an answer.

"So?" he asked as he handed the blanket to her.

"So, what?" she queried as she unfurled the covering and laid it carefully over the queen.

"The fourth has been hurt?" he repeated.

"Catherine," she answered. She turned to face him, tears welling in her eyes. "Catherine has been hurt."

He felt stunned.

His jaw dropped, and he stared blankly at nothing in particular.

"So," Linet said, breaking the silence. "They feel her pain."

"It would seem so," Akasati replied. "Most covens feel a bond with their kindred. We did."

"We still do," Emily added.

"But our bonds are built on a different type of power," Akasati continued. "The Seven have another kind of connection. Different again. My guess is that the Mirikin, and any other sect, have their own way of linking. Who knows what these three are experiencing?"

"Four," Emily corrected her, moving to her daughter's bedroom door to peer inside.

"Four," Akasati acknowledged, taking a seat in a chair beside the sofa where the queen lay.

Emily watched her daughter's chest rise and fall slowly. Alice was in a deep sleep.

"They feel her pain," the auburn woman said. "They share it."

David looked at her, lowering his brows and trying to understand.

"What do you mean?"

"They have taken her pain," Emily continued, tears rolling down her cheeks. "Or she has given it to them. She must be hurt terribly."

The big man moved to her side and placed his hands on her arms gently. He felt helpless and did not know how to make this woman, the woman he loved, feel any kind of comfort.

"I'm sorry," he whispered into her ear before wrapping his enormous arms around her shoulders.

She broke down and cried.

"He must have done this," she blubbered. "He must have hurt my little girl."

"We'll get her back," David promised her. "We'll get her and my boy back."

Brondt burst in through the door, panic-stricken and peering around the room. His eyes immediately fell upon Amicia, who was in a deep sleep on the sofa.

"What happened?" he snapped. "Who did this?"

Emily wiped her eyes on her sleeve and moved away from the door, leaving David to keep his eye on Alice. Yuri moved by him and back into the sitting room to stand behind the girl's mother.

"Something has happened to all three of them," she explained. "We think it's because of the fourth of their kind. She must have been injured and has somehow shared her tragedy with them."

"For what purpose?" he asked, watching his wife.

"Perhaps for healing," Akasati offered. "It's the only thing that makes sense in my mind."

"None of this makes sense," he replied, shaking his head.

"No, it doesn't," Emily agreed. "What I know is that Alice, Amicia and Ursula are all sleeping. It also means that there is a level of vulnerability on the glade tonight."

Brondt locked eyes with her.

"You want me to set a guard?" he asked. "I've done that already. It didn't help us when they attacked before."

"I think you should set your men as if we are about to be attacked," she told him. "I think we shouldn't underestimate Takmel. He may already know the advantage he has and be moving into position as we speak."

Brondt thought about Emily's words for a moment and inclined his head.

"I'll prepare my men," he replied. "And I'll inform the dragon keepers."

"I get my warriors," Yuri offered. "We stand guard here."

Emily frowned as she placed her hand reassuringly upon the reptilian's arm.

"Do you want me to help you move Queen Amicia to her quarters?" Lor asked the commander.

"No," the other replied, shaking his head. "I can't think of a safer place than inside the house of the Kayl'sro, where twelve Agrodien warriors are about to stand watch. Could you?"

Lor shook his head, *no*.

***

Sub-Commander Landon Wake stood upon one of the palace's balconies, overlooking the city between his position and the docking yards. Fireballs filled the night sky like a hundred shooting stars drifting towards the blazing structures below.

He could see a few large patches of darkness where the flames hadn't already started their feasting. And now the new barrage of glowing missiles threatened them also.

Exploding puffs of smoke erupted several hundred yards offshore. A moment later, he heard the faint blast from the ships' cannons almost at the same time as he watched the terrible result of their call.

The warehouses by the water's edge splintered and started collapsing.

One structure must have been housing black powder, as a great plume of flame shot skywards through its roof, illuminating the buildings around for a moment.

"Have we nothing on the wharves that we can use to fight back?" he called to a young officer standing nearby.

"No, sir," he replied. "We moved all the catapults to protect us from those things in the forest."

Wake peered to the north, where he saw the outlines of horsemen charging through the line of defences. He raced back inside, rushing through the large sitting room which he had transformed into a command centre, and out onto the balcony facing towards the west. The officer was close on his heels.

The catapults were discharging payloads randomly into the shadows. The high-pitched squeals and screeches of the dark creatures informed him they were still causing some damage to the enemy, but closer observation, as he looked to the wide beam of light being cast from one beacon, showed him that the creatures were already at the line and crossing into the city.

One of the bright lights further to the north suddenly extinguished.

The distant screams of men followed.

"We're losing," he admitted. "Staying up here won't serve us very well."

"Sir?" the officer queried.

"I'm going down there," Wake said, pulling his sword from its sheath. "I'd rather die in battle than to wait for them to come and get me."

With that, he exited the room and started along the corridor that would lead him to the stairs down and outside.

"Bugger this," another senior officer from inside the command centre huffed. He strode around a large table where he previously wrote notes and messages to various posts and followed Wake out the door. Several other officers followed suit and hurried out of the room.

"What about the command centre?" The young officer gestured. "What if others need support? How will we notify them?"

"Bugger the command centre," another young officer put in, taking his sword out of its sheath and starting for the door. "Everyone needs support out there."

***

One by one, the beacon lights on the southern edge extinguished. The Black Queen's horsemen had broken the line of defences and quickly went about cleaning up the remaining men of Newholt who desperately tried to fight for their city and their lives.

The infantry was next to charge past the broken structures, noting the smoke and heat still billowing from the giant lanterns as they ran by. Although it hadn't been raining, their boots splattered in mud and filth, caused by the blood and carnage the cavalry and bowmen had inflicted.

Into the streets they ran, passing toppled buildings and houses and breaking into those that were still standing. Doors cracked and windows smashed before the black soldiers forced themselves inside to offer any occupiers a simple choice.

Surrender or die.

More skirmishes ensued as, now and then, a brave man or boy would rise to defend his family. The effort was always in vain. Outnumbered and overpowered, the courageous men or lads would end up being executed and their families forced into the streets through involuntary submission.

Street by street, building by building, the soldiers worked their way towards the centre of the city. The sound of iron violently meeting more iron resounded more and more frequently.

***

"Should we move in, my lady?" Andris suggested casually.

The two of them still sat upon their steeds at the top of the rise overlooking Newholt. The din of battle reverberated over the plain between them and the city.

"Not yet," Joanne answered coldly. "When the fighting has ceased, we will move."

Andris turned his gaze to the black creatures on the western border. The beacons there were slowly being extinguished, but the distant glint of steel told the commander that the defences were still holding.

He turned his face to the dockyards. Bright orange glares lit the region up momentarily as the flaming projectiles flew from the sea, over the waterfront, and into random areas throughout the city's eastern region.

More buildings toppled.

More people died.

Andris felt his heart sink as he watched on in sadness.

It was a strain for him to understand how the woman beside him could have changed so dramatically. This wasn't the Joanne he knew.

He wanted to say something. He even got as far as turning to her and opening his mouth.

Why are you doing this? You are not this person. Let's go home.

Her blank eyes and tiny grimace dissuaded him from following through.

This wasn't the girl he knew.

This wasn't Joanne.

She was a puppet and nothing more.

She was a slave to another's will.

This was the Maji.

***

The room rocked. Bottles and glasses rattled upon the shelves behind the bar. Several fell onto the floor and shattered.

"Now, that's a bloody waste," Nathaniel Monteacute slurred, sitting at a table near the middle of the room and lifting a mug of ale to his lips. He was one of the few occupants of the Upright Banker, and the only customer of the tavern. All others had left when the attack began, leaving Maud Eyre and her three young bar wenches to clean up.

"You could help, you know," Maud told him, moving the remaining bottles from the shelf and into a wooden box lined with straw.

"I'll get something to clean this up," Rose Heron offered, staring at the broken glass and spreading liquid. The aroma was sweet and sour at the same time.

"Don't bother," Maud replied. "We need to get into the cellar. Get some food from the larder instead."

"Yes, ma'am," Rose replied, turning to exit through a door behind the bar.

"Lots of it," the older woman called after her. "We don't know how long we'll be down there."

Another bright orange flare filled the windows, moving its beam through the room as the source of the light passed by to the north.

"Another one!" Monteacute lifted his mug in salute.

"Audrey," Maud called to the young, dark-haired lady who was packing bottles at the other end of the bar from her with another woman. "Go help Rose. See if you can find some candles while you're at it."

BOOM!

The room rattled again. Small puffs of dust erupted from the ceiling and floated down to the floor.

"I don't think the Upright Banker will be too upright after tonight," the drunk man at the table opined.

"You could at least shut yer trap, Monty," the third young lady snapped.

"Kateryn?" Maud locked eyes with the other. She could see tears welling in the young lady's eyes.

Monteacute stared dumbly at the girl. He watched quietly as a single tear fell from her eye, and his heart sank.

Another orange glow filled the room. Instead of raising his mug, he put it firmly on the table and rose to his feet. He staggered a little as he approached the bar, his frown deepening with each step.

"I'm sorry, love," he mumbled. "I didn't mean to upset you."

"We're going to die," she said pointedly, "and you're just sitting there drinking."

He thought about her words for a moment.

BOOM!

The room quaked again as the projectile smashed into the ground to the north.

"It actually makes sense," he said, and raised his eyebrows. "Why bother with all this packing when, as you said, we're going to die?"

"Monty," the older lady chided.

"No!" He held up a hand, using the other to balance against the bar. "You're right. How about this? I'll help you carry everything down to the cellar and then we all sit over there at that table and get blind drunk together?"

"Do you hear yerself?" Kateryn questioned. "You can't carry this down to the cellar."

"Why not?"

"You can barely walk on yer own," she answered.

"Can so," he argued, swaying slightly. "I'm as graceful as a bird in flight."

"Stupid fool," Maud growled, continuing to pack the box. "Stay up here, then. We're going to the cellar."

"Monty?" The young woman peered at the man. He noted the concern on her face. "I'll feel better if you're there with us."

"Of course, then I'll come with you," he said perceptively.

Maud offered a sigh of relief. Kateryn relaxed slightly and wiped her eyes.

"Can't stay up here, anyway." Monteacute gestured to the empty room with his outstretched arm as it filled with orange luminosity again. "You're taking all the grog."

***

Wake swung his blade in an arc, up from the ground and deep into the crotch of a shrieking black creature. It thrust its pointed claws in his direction, ripping through his sleeve, scratching him across the upper arm just below his shoulder.

He winced at the sharp sting as he forced the blade deeper into the being's body. Dark blood smacked against the cobblestones beneath its feet as it continued to scream.

The sub-commander looked past the form attached to his blade, spying movement in the shadows. A dimly lit narrow street lined with tightly packed houses lay beyond.

Scampering towards him, some on their hind legs, others on all fours, came many black creatures. Their long white teeth bared and the hissing panting of their breath grew louder and louder as they drew nearer and nearer.

"More approach," he hollered to the men behind him. "I need help."

Several officers charged by on either side of Wake, swords raised at the ready.

The creatures attacked from all angles.

Some bounded off the walls.

Some lunged from the ground.

Others stayed level with the armed men and ran to them at full speed.

More squeals ensued from the creatures as they struck some officers with their claws, drawing blood.

But not enough to deter the soldiers.

Their blades glinted in the dim light as the men hacked and chopped into the dark forms, releasing limbs from torsos and heads from necks.

Removing the body of the dead being from his blade, Wake joined his men. His next victim was unlucky enough to see the sub-commander's blade up close as it slid into the creature's left eye. Wake could feel some slight resistance as a loud crunch signalled the sword was cutting through the back of the dark being's skull and out the other side.

With a quick tug, he pulled the blade free. The creature fell lifelessly to the ground, allowing Wake to continue.

"How far to the defence line?" one officer called, referring to the catapults and beacons facing the west.

"I think this is the defence line," another hollered.

Wake glanced towards the western edge of the city, peering at the skyline.

"I don't see anything being hurled," he said.

"What?" asked a captain of the guard as he sliced the head off another beast.

"The catapults," Wake explained. "They aren't throwing."

"So?" The same officer turned up his hands. "Changes nothing. We keep fighting until we can't."

More creatures continued to attack.

The officers pushed on, thrusting and cutting into them. On and on.

A younger lieutenant took down the last of the beasts in the street. He thrust his blade through the creature's chest, but not before it gave a shrill cry into the night.

"Now what?" he asked.

"We move on and keep taking down as many of these things as we can," Wake told him. "As the captain said, *we keep fighting until we can't.*"

***

The orange fireballs eventually stopped their barrage, having destroyed the eastern sector of the city through their work. The ships retired their cannons and sat silently on the ebbing tide.

It was almost hauntingly beautiful, Andris thought, as he absorbed the view of Newholt before him.

A thin line of purple sat upon the horizon, giving the dark silhouettes of the thirteen ships anchored offshore a menacing appearance. Death upon the sea.

Smoke and flame lifted into the sky from countless sources dotting the landscape between the docks and the foot of the hill where the palace stood. The sounds of screaming, shouting and swords meeting still rang out from the region closest to where Andris and the Black Queen watched on. But it was growing dimmer and dimmer as time ran on.

"It won't be long now," Joanne told him, staring at the few beacon lights still ignited at the northern and western edges of the city.

Andris watched in silence as the area to the west of Newholt suddenly went dark. The beacons were taken.

"They won't kill everyone?" he asked. His voice sounded timid and afraid. "Will they?"

She shot him a perplexed glare and seemed to measure him with her eyes.

"What do you take me for, Andris?" she snapped. "I'm not a killer of women and children." She turned to face the city again.

He looked over the flattened and burned portion of the city near the docks and disagreed.

"All will have a chance to declare their loyalty to me. And, as a result, pledge their fidelity to the Maji."

"And if they don't?" he queried, wishing that he hadn't the very moment he had opened his mouth.

"They will receive... an education about such things." She grinned.

He didn't like the look on her face. It spoke of something sinister. Something disturbing.

***

Catherine opened her eyes slowly. They seemed to burn against the back of her eyelids and ache tremendously as she rolled them around in their sockets.

Her ribcage felt as if it was squeezing in on her as she sucked in air. A sharp twinge shot up and down her spine as she slowly moved, trying to sit upright and get her bearings.

She then wished she had waited, or at least tried to rise a little more slowly as her head started thudding in unison with her heartbeat. It was as if her skull was about to explode.

Gradually, her vision cleared. Instead of a dark blur, she saw a dark prison cell. Flickering light drew her attention to a lantern hung upon a stone wall outside of her cell, beyond the iron bars and out of reach.

She sat upon the edge of a cot; nothing more than a couple of planks of timber propped up on wooden legs. A bedroll rested on top of the boards and a hard pillow stuffed with straw sat at one end, strands of the dried grass poking through the material covering.

She was still wearing her dark cloak and boots. At least they allowed her some dignity.

The smell of sweat was strong, but the stench of urine was stronger. She wondered why until she heard the unmistakable sound of someone passing wind nearby.

She winced, peering past the glare of the lantern posted on the wall outside of her cell to see a tubby guard in a small alcove across the corridor from her. His trousers were down around his knees as he carefully aimed for a wooden pail on the floor. The thin stream of yellow made its target with ease.

"You must be an archer," she slurred, hearing a gravelly tone in her voice.

"What's that?" the guard asked, caught by surprise. He turned slightly and splashed a small puddle onto the floor. His eyes locked with Catherine's momentarily before a slight embarrassment swept over him. "Sorry," he blurted, turning away to hide his member from her sight.

"What's that, 'Arry?" another voice called.

Harry, the tubby guard, quickly finished, shook and lifted his pants.

"She's awake," he replied, hurrying into the corridor as he buttoned his trousers.

"She is?" the other said excitedly, moving into view. He was a smaller man in stature and frame. His face appeared strangely elongated and a few teeth missing from the upper row. "Well, hullo your ladyship."

"Hello yourself." Catherine held her hand to her right temple.

"Sorry 'bout the quarters, but his lordship commanded it and all."

"I understand," she said, trying to get to her feet. Her knees and thighs ached and a sharp pain seemed to stab her in the left portion of her groin. "Oh, dear."

"Are you all right, my lady?" the smaller guard offered. His demeanour changed from playful to concerned. "Can I help you?"

"The apothecary could be a good idea," she offered.

"He's been to see you already," he said. "He checked you and then he checked the boy again before he left."

"The boy?" she asked, her eyes still focusing on her surroundings.

"Yeah." Harry pointed into the cell next to hers. "Young Master Gyfford there."

Catherine moved her gaze into the cell next to hers, separated by thick iron bars and a portion of the stone wall jutting from the back of the cell. There, upon a cot placed against the rear wall, was Arthur. He had a fresh bandage wrapped around his upper body that covered the socket of his left. His face was swollen and bruised, almost to the point of unrecognisable grotesqueness.

Both of his eyes were closed tightly, puffed up from beating. His breathing was long and slow, signifying that he was in a deep sleep.

Her heart sank, and a pang of deep guilt swept over her.

She felt responsible for this.

She had sided with the monster that she had called her husband.

She had aided his ambitious exploits that had brought this punishment upon the boy.

"Water," she said, turning her attention back to the small guard. "Could you bring me some water, please?"

"There's water in the pail there," he pointed. "Beside your cot. Next to the privy pot."

She looked at the wooden bucket filled with water. A long-handled ladle rested against the side.

"It doesn't look fresh," she complained.

"It is," he argued. "Filled it myself."

"Couldn't I at least have a glass?" she pressed. "A mug. Something more fitting for a lady."

"I don't know…" The guard shook his head. "His lordship gave us strict instructions and all."

"Please?" She smiled alluringly. Her voice sounded almost melodic.

"Yeah." Harry looked at the other guard. "Come on. She's a lady and all. Who's going to know?"

"All right," the guard said, surrendering. "But you both keep yer traps shut about it." He jutted a finger at the tubby man beside him. "You unlock the pen and I'll fetch a clean mug. Right?"

"You're a good man." The large guard fished the keys from his pocket.

The smaller guard disappeared from view as the other tried several keys in the lock.

With a turn and a loud clink, the door swung wide with a gentle squeak.

"That's the one," he said happily. "Would you like more blankets or something?"

"You wouldn't have a different pillow, would you?" she asked.

He looked at the one she had and shook his head.

"Sorry," he replied. "They only offer ones filled with straw to the prisoners."

"We could make a request to the captain of the guard on your behalf for some better bedding, if you'd like," the small man offered as he returned with a mug of fresh water in his hand. "I don't like your chances though." He stepped into the cell and started across the small enclosure towards Catherine, extending the vessel towards her. "You are a prisoner, after all."

She reached out towards him with her left hand, giving him a friendly smile.

"I understand," she replied, sweeping her hand past the mug and gripping his wrist like a vice.

Before he understood what was happening, she pulled him towards her and clenched the fingers of her right hand around his throat.

The mug fell to the floor, smashing apart and spilling water.

"Absorb," she whispered.

The smaller guard cried and writhed in agony.

Harry reached for his sword and started into the cell. Suddenly, he stopped in his tracks when he saw thin twisting strands of pale light bursting from the other man, bending around his body and streaming into the girl's eyes like a fine mist.

"Bloody heck," he blurted, quickly backing out of the room and shutting the cell door behind him. "Bloody heck." He fumbled with the keys, trying them all unsuccessfully. He fixed his eyes upon the strange happening inside the pen.

The smaller guard's body quaked and trembled as Catherine pulled him onto the cot, straddling him like a lover. The pale cords of light-mist continued to be drawn from his body and into her eyes.

"Bloody heck," Harry called again, his hands shaking wildly.

The other guard's body seemed to transform. His skin turned an insipid grey, almost translucent. His cheeks became sunken and hollow. His eyes turned up in their sockets, displaying only white and lifeless orbs.

CLINK!

The door locked shut.

She lifted herself from the corpse of the smaller guard. Her head turned to face Harry just outside the bars of the cell, still within grasping reach. Her face appeared wickedly contented as she peered around the cell, stretching her neck and flexing her shoulders.

Her muscles had stopped aching.

Her head no longer throbbed.

Each breath was effortless.

There were no aches in her joints or back.

She felt no pain.

It was gone.

"Bloody heck," Harry said again, staring at the dead body on the cot and stepping backwards until he touched the wall under the flickering lantern.

She lifted the withered body from the cot with ease and flung it against the bars of the cell. It clanged before thudding onto the stone floor.

Reaching up with her arms, she stretched the muscles in her back and took a deep, rejuvenating breath.

She felt renewed.

She felt strong.

With a grin, she winked at the tubby guard and pulled her hood over her head.

Graciously, she sat back upon the edge of the cot, reached into the pail for the ladle and drew some water.

"Bloody heck," he said again as she sipped. Clumsily, he hurried from her sight.

She placed the ladle back in the pail and gazed at the broken and bruised boy in the cell next to hers. Her face turned suddenly from contentment to anger. She channelled her thoughts as she tried to make a connection.

She hoped the others were listening.

"Do you see this?" she asked in a soft whisper. "Do you see?"

Twenty-Six

"Arthur!" Alice cried suddenly. Her body flung upright into a seated position.

"Q'sharh," Nola'ee spat, pulling her sword from its sheath and instinctively jumping into a defensive position. Her tail coiled and her muscles tensed.

The covers fell from the girl's body.

The female warrior relaxed, sliding her blade back into place before moving to the girl's side.

"All is well, Kayl'sro," she said in her own tongue. "I've been watching over you."

Alice stared at the other for a long moment, coming to grips with where she was and what had just happened.

"Were you going to cut me up?" she asked with a cheeky grin.

"No, Kayl'sro," Nola'ee answered, crouching beside the bed. "It has been very quiet. You startled me."

Alice placed her hand over her bodyguard's leathery fingers and gave them a friendly, thankful squeeze.

"I must get up," she said, swinging her legs over the edge of the bed. "I must see the others."

"You must take care," the reptilian cautioned, touching her hand to the girl's stomach. "You are very young and carry a precious gift."

Alice nodded solemnly. "I know."

Still, she planted her feet on the floor and stood up. She staggered slightly, taking Nola'ee's hand to steady herself.

"Kayl'sro?"

"Don't tell anyone about that," Alice commanded, to which her bodyguard bent her head obediently.

The sitting room and kitchen were alive with activity. The sound of people fussing about with pots caused a slight twinge in Alice's head. She left the darkness of her bedroom and stepped delicately into the short corridor between the spaces in her cottage.

The door across from her bedroom opened. She was a little surprised when she saw Ursula and her aunt appear.

"You're awake?" Linet gasped. Her face softened, and she reached her hand across the corridor to touch her niece's cheek. "Thank the gods."

"I'm awake," Alice agreed before reaching a hand out to Ursula. "How do you feel?"

"My head aches a little," she admitted. "And my body feels stiff. Do you think she..."

"Alice," Emily's voice called from the sitting room.

She was on her feet and rushing towards the girl before Alice had time to respond. Motherly arms wrapped around her and tiny kisses exploded all over her forehead.

"I'm all right, Mama," the girl said. "Where is Amicia?"

"I'm here," she replied. Emily moved to the side, allowing Alice to see into the sitting room.

Queen Amicia sat on the sofa, elbows on her knees and hands on her forehead.

"I need to sit," Alice said, looking over her shoulder at Nola'ee.

"Then you should return to bed." Emily gestured to the bedroom door.

"No," she replied, shaking her head slowly. "There's no time."

She stepped towards the nearest cushioned chair, using her bodyguard's arm to help keep herself steady. Linet led Ursula to another chair positioned near the sofa where the queen was sitting.

"Should I get you some tea?" she offered.

"Thank you." Alice gestured to her aunt.

As Linet retreated to the kitchen, Nola'ee positioned herself next to her leader.

"Did you see?" Amicia asked, raising her eyes towards Alice in question.

Alice nodded sombrely, her eyes welling up.

"See what?" Emily asked, sinking into a chair near her daughter.

"We need to act quickly," Ursula proposed. "He won't last much longer if he is tortured further."

"I know." The girl frowned.

"Who?" Emily switched her confused gaze to each of the three women seated around the room. "Are you speaking of Arthur?"

"And he will be, Alice," Ursula continued. "Once he sees what she has just done, he will torture her by hurting him."

"Will someone tell me who you are speaking about?" Emily asked frantically.

"You already know, Mama," Alice replied, wiping her eyes on her sleeves. "They have hurt Arthur. Really hurt him. Catherine sits in a cell next to his. She has shared this with us."

"We need to bring them home," Amicia stated. "And we can't wait much longer."

Emily stared blankly at the queen for a moment.

"All right," she said eventually. "But I think we all need to know a few things before we race off blindly into Woodmyst to rescue your husband and my daughter."

"All right." Alice turned as Linet came back with a mug of tea. "But we don't have long." She sipped the steaming liquid slowly and swallowed, feeling it move down her throat and through her chest. "Good," she said, nodding to her aunt in gratitude.

"Why did the three of you pass out before?" Emily asked. "Why is it you woke at the same time? How do you know of Arthur's state? How do you know where your sister is?"

"As I said, Catherine showed us Arthur and shared this with us. We know where she is because we could see where she is. As for why we three passed out; Catherine was hurt. I don't know how it happened. But I know she was hurt terribly. She somehow tapped into our energy and used us to help herself recover, at least to the point where she could do the rest by her own efforts."

"But now, you're weary," Linet said, handing the other two women a mug each. "You will need to build your strength before you try for Woodmyst."

"It won't take long," Ursula told her. "I'm already feeling better."

"As am I," Amicia put in.

"Her own efforts?" Emily asked, her eyes trained on her daughter the whole time. "What does this mean?"

Alice frowned and looked into the hot liquid inside her mug. It swirled a little, forming tiny bubbles on the surface that spiralled towards the centre.

"Catherine took a life to replenish her own," the girl answered. "She has the ability to absorb life."

"And she did this?" Emily pressed. "She absorbed someone's life?"

"A guard's," replied the girl.

"And was this the first life that she absorbed?"

"No." Alice looked at Amicia and Ursula. "She has been practising this new skill of hers with small animals."

"But this is the first person she has killed?" Emily leaned forward.

Alice saw Amicia nod, urging her to answer truthfully.

"No." Alice quickly looked down to her cup, to her mother's eyes and back to her cup, ashamed for her sister.

"So," Emily wept. "She had a hand in what happened to David's family on the bridge. It wasn't Takmel forcing her against her will. She was a part of it."

"She did it for him," Alice answered truthfully. "They did it together."

Emily got up and started for the door. She was angry and wounded.

"She's not like that anymore, Mama," Alice tried to explain, her hand gesturing to Ursula, Amicia and herself. "She is one of us. We need to bring her home."

"She killed for fun, Alice," Emily snapped. "Little animals. A guard. Two women and a baby girl."

"She needed the guard to revive," Ursula put in.

"And just how did she get so close to this guard if she was in a cell?" Emily asked. "Do you know?"

Alice nodded slowly as she looked at the rug on the floor. "She asked him for water."

"My daughter is evil!" Emily gasped. She clasped a hand to her chest and shook her head. "If your father was alive to see this..."

Alice cried.

Amicia got up.

"This changes nothing," she said. "Arthur still needs to be rescued and your daughter still needs to come home."

"After what she has done?" Linet questioned. "How can you expect anyone to open arms for her after all of this becomes known?"

"You did it for me," the queen reminded them. "I was the Fuchsia Mistress, sworn servant of the Sovereign, fellow witch of the Mirikin. And I destroyed Oakbeach and every living soul within before I turned.

"Your daughter, Catherine, has murdered four people. Three were very close to all of you. But I killed hundreds. Perhaps thousands. Each of them was close to someone too, I suspect.

"I was a stranger. She is family. What gives me the right to be more easily accepted into your house over her?"

"She is evil," Emily blubbered.

"As was I." Amicia placed her hand on the auburn woman's shoulder. "We need to bring her home. She needs to be with us here. You can remind her of what it is to be loved by family. We can train her to focus her power for good."

Emily considered the queen's words. Her gaze fell to the floor as she wrestled with the idea of bringing Catherine back. She wondered how she would respond when she found Catherine. Would she place her arms around her lovingly, or try to strangle the life from her elder daughter? Anger and compassion were at war inside her. It seemed that both were not too far away from one another lately.

"I will speak to David," Emily said.

"He knows already," Alice told her.

Emily glared at Alice, angry because she felt as if she was the last to know.

"I will speak to David," she repeated. "If he does not want her returned to us, then so be it."

"No." Alice got up defiantly. "She is my sister, and she and I will be reunited. We go to take Woodmyst from the Maji; not to simply rescue Arthur and Catherine. If I decide to reclaim the city as my own, Catherine stays with me. If I decide to return here, Catherine comes too. It's not your decision. It's not David's decision. It's mine."

"How dare you speak to me in such a manner?" Emily stepped towards Alice with fire in her eyes.

Nola'ee quickly slid around the girl to block the woman's advance, her hand falling upon the hilt of her sword.

Emily stopped in her tracks, shocked.

The female warrior shook her head slowly, warning the other to back away.

"I'm her mother," Emily disputed.

"She is Kayl'sro," Nola'ee reminded her. "Agrodien commander. Leader of the glade."

The tension was thick.

Silence had filled the room.

Not a soul moved. Instead, they all silently watched the Agrodien and the auburn woman face off.

Alice was the first to act, gently guiding Nola'ee aside with a push of her hand.

"I love you, Mama," she breathed. "I always will. But I told you once before, I am leader here. I have made my decision. You don't need to agree with me. But you do need to respect my position. Catherine is coming home."

Emily shook her head and started to bawl.

"I'm sorry," she said, stretching her arms out to her daughter.

Alice stepped into her mother's embrace and held her tightly.

Twenty-Seven

The boards above their heads creaked and groaned as something slowly moved through the rooms of the tavern.

Maud covered her mouth with one hand and wrapped her other arm around Rose tightly. The younger lady stifled her tears and her instinct to cry out loud with every sound coming from above.

Clawing, scratching noises ensued as something dug at the flooring of the bar. They heard heavy sniffing and deep clicking, coming from several places.

Monteacute had his arms around each of the other two ladies. One had hold of his shirt so tightly, her fingernails had torn through the fabric and injured his chest ever so mildly. Still, he could feel the sting which only worsened with every bump or scrape made above their heads, causing her to dig her fingers in more and more.

It didn't bother him all that much as his focus was on whatever was up there, in the Upright Banker. He was suddenly sober and alert, hoping they didn't find the cellar door.

He had seen Maude place the beam of wood over the entrance as they clambered inside the dank space beneath the building. The problem, he knew straight away, was that the door would not appear locked from the outside. As soon as anyone tried to open it, they would know someone was hiding within, having secured it from inside.

A succession of thuds resounded, moving from one side of the room above to the other. Something had just scampered across the floor of the tavern.

Kateryn gasped.

The thudding stopped.

Silence.

Monteacute felt his heart racing in his throat.

Reptilian-like tapping, slow and methodical, made its way towards him. Claws tapped gently against the timber floor.

The boards creaked softly.

Something sniffed the floor, searching.

Closer.

Closer.

Rose let out a tiny noise, like a muffled squeak.

The thing above stopped.

Monteacute peered at Rose, who shot an apologetic look back at him. Her eyes were wide with fear.

He moved his gaze to each of the others, who shared Rose's terror.

A soft whimper reached his ear. Audrey, with her head buried into his neck, let out the tiniest whisper of a cry.

No one else in the cellar heard it but him.

His eyes flicked up to the support beams holding the tavern's floor in place.

He knew the thing up there had heard her.

A shrill cry, ear piercingly sharp, seemed to shake the very foundation of the Upright Banker.

Loud, quick scrapes scuffed against the timber.

It was trying to dig through to them.

Monteacute rose to his feet and pulled his sword from his belt.

"Monty," Kateryn called, wishing for him to stay beside her.

"Stay behind me," he said, peering up towards the source of the sound.

The thing screeched again, scratching and digging unrelentingly. The scraping noise deepened in pitch, signalling to Monteacute that it was having success.

Digging.

Digging.

Digging.

Monteacute felt sweat forming on his brow, dribbling down his back.

By the gods, I need to piss.

Suddenly, the scratching stopped, quickly replaced by heavy thudding.

Over and over.

The thing above was trying to break through using its weight.

THUD!

THUD!

A small crack formed on one board.

With each strike, it became larger. Splinters fell to the floor of the cellar as the boards bowed.

THUD!

THUD!

THUD!

A chunk of wood dropped a few inches from Monteacute's feet.

He tightened the grip on his sword as the gap in the floor grew.

He could see the smiling face of the black creature.

And it could see him.

It opened its mouth and cried out in frustration.

THUD!

THUD!

With a great crash, it fell to the floor, landing awkwardly on its back.

Still feeling the effects of his ale, Monteacute wasted no time and lunged at the creature. He stumbled slightly, but met the beast with his blade, slicing into its ribs.

Not enough to kill it.

The creature quickly shot to its feet and recoiled into the shadows of the cellar, darting behind a stack of boxes piled up by the stairs to the door.

"Bugger," the drunken man spat.

The creature screeched again.

The women screamed.

"Where is it?" Maud cried out.

"Over there." He pointed towards the door with his blade. "I think."

Something rattled to his right, causing him to spin around.

A smiling shadow raced past a small space of bare wall before disappearing behind more crates.

It was moving around the room, slinking through the darkness.

"It's moving," Monteacute said out loud, wishing he hadn't.

Audrey and Kateryn jumped to their feet and moved into the light coming through the broken floorboards above them. They shook and spun, waving their hands as if they had just accidentally walked through cobwebs for the first time.

I really need to piss.

Monteacute glared at the objects lining the wall. His eyes were unfocused thanks to the strange light emanating from above and the grog swirling in his head. He couldn't see how the creature could fit behind the crates stacked close to the wall.

Suddenly, it lunged.

From the corner of his right eye, it appeared from nowhere, just above Maud and Rose.

He swung his blade in vain, but he was too far away.

Its mouth opened wide.

Its sharp, white teeth seemed to stretch towards its victim.

With a loud wet crunch, they dug into Maud's flesh, engulfing the top half of her head.

A fine spray of blood spattered over Rose, who instinctively screamed in terror.

The creature shook its head viciously, tearing into the older woman's skin, muscle, and bone. Its claws pierced her shoulders and chest as it used all four limbs to grip her tightly.

Monteacute lunged, feeling warmth expanding in his trousers at the same time.

He brought his sword down in a long strike from over his back, intending to slice the creature through the head. Only, the blade struck a support beam of the floor above and stuck so.

The creature used its strength to tear Maud's skull open, swallowing what was in its mouth in one gulp.

Tugging on his sword, trying to release it from the timber's grasp, feeling the warmth running down the inside of his left leg, Monteacute observed the creature. His rapid heartbeat filled his ears. The screaming of the girls seemed distant.

Blood seemed to spill over the remains of Maud's face and onto her body forever.

The creature shovelled its face over the wound and feasted, as if oblivious to the others in the room.

A sudden release made him fall onto his rump. The sword was free.

Monteacute quickly got to his feet and lunged again. This time, he held the sword straight and true, stabbing the creature through the top of its head. He twisted the blade, just to be sure, before pulling it from the beast's skull.

Dark blood sprayed from the wound as the creature fell into a writhing fit on the floor.

When it finally stopped, Monteacute's heart sank. His breathing was rapid, and he leaned against his sword to help catch his breath. But his eyes locked upon the remains of one of his oldest friends, Maud Eyre.

Her lifeless body slumped against a potato sack with her hands in her lap. Her lower jaw and right ear the only recognisable elements of her face.

The three other women bawled, gripping onto each other for comfort. Monteacute would have allowed himself to cry also, if it wasn't for the shadow cast through the open floor above their heads.

He peered up to see another creature glaring down at the three girls.

His hand tightened around his sword again.

His legs prepared to lunge at the thing before it could reach anyone in the cellar.

"Get out of it, you shit," a voice growled from above.

A boot kicked the beast out of the way, sending it skulking with a yelp. Monteacute beckoned the three ladies over to him. They quickly moved behind him, still huddling together in fear.

"Hello," a voice called. A soldier's face came into view.

He was young and, for lack of a better word, handsome. At least, that was the best quality Monteacute could find for the time being.

He waved to the four survivors in a friendly manner.

"Stay back," Monteacute warned. "Or I'll gut you. I swear."

"Oh!" The soldier raised his brows. "I believe you, old man. But I don't want to hurt any of you. None of us do. I'm Lieutenant Atlee of the Black Queen's Cavalry."

"Don't give a shit who you are," Monteacute replied. "Your lot just attacked this city."

"Indeed, we did," the other said. "But that doesn't mean we want everyone to be killed. Hence, why I am here."

Monteacute shook his head in disbelief. *As if things couldn't get any stranger and lopsided.*

"If you'll kindly take the bar from the door, we can have you out of there in a flash." Atlee smiled. "Just one thing. I'll ask that you put your sword on the ground first. Thank you."

"And then what?" Monteacute asked. "You'll lock us up or feed us to those things."

"No," the lieutenant said, and shook his head. "Nothing of the sort. We've been establishing a refuge of sorts in the town square. There's food and water."

"I don't trust him," Audrey whispered. She frowned as she peered at the others through wet eyes. "We shouldn't go."

"I agree," Monteacute told them.

Rose nodded.

"Look," Atlee said, "you can stay here if you like. We need to move on to other locations to find more survivors. The problem is, these animals are getting hungry. They've apparently been out there watching in the woods for a long time. There is a good chance that another will find you and get to you. There is a better chance that a pack of them will attack before nightfall. They are making their way through the ruins, feasting upon the dead as we speak. Come with us and you will be protected. Stay here and you might perish. Not much of a choice, but there it is."

Monteacute looked at the girls.

"What do you say?" the soldier asked.

Each of the women looked to Monteacute. Their eyes were still afraid, but they wore the expression of surrender at the same time. Eventually, he dropped his sword to the ground.

"Good man," Atlee called before moving out of sight.

***

The soldiers led them through the rubble and devastation that was once Newholt. A small crowd marched towards the town square that was nestled at the foot of the hill where the palace stood.

Smoke billowed into the sky from countless locations, rising into the air in thick plumes only to be absorbed by clouds gathering in the sky above.

Monteacute looked up to the grand structure that overshadowed the city and saw black banners flying from the flagpoles and hanging from the balconies of the higher levels.

They had set a platform in the centre of the square with four thick iron poles at each corner.

The survivors of the assault were gathering to be an audience, seated in groups around the outside regions of the square where shade from awnings and structures offered solace from the threat of rain.

"Who are they, Monty?" Rose asked, looking at a row of men tethered to tall timber beams near the middle of the town square.

"The admirals of Newholt's navy," Atlee said from his horse. He was riding beside them as they approached the square, guiding them through the ruined city.

Several infantry soldiers started piling chocks of wood at the feet of the admirals. It became all too clear what their fate was to be.

"Is that what lies in store for all of us?" Monteacute asked.

"No," Atlee answered in apparent honesty. "It is as I said. There is food and water. Soon, shelter will be provided."

"Then what?"

"Then you will be in the service of the Black Queen."

"The Black Queen?" Monteacute repeated. "Who is she, then?"

"She is one of the nine wives of the Maji," Atlee replied. "Through her, he will rule Newholt."

"I see." The older man acknowledged, keeping his eyes fixed upon the admirals, with wood piling up around them.

***

It wasn't long before they were treated to some stale bread and mugs of water. Monteacute could smell the sour stench of his own piss-stained trousers as it dried in what light the morning sun offered.

"I wish I had a change of clothes," he mumbled.

"This is *food and water*." Audrey frowned, holding both in her hands. She shook her head; the image of Maude was still fresh in her mind. "I can't eat."

"You need to, sweetheart," Monteacute told her. "You'll feel sick if you don't."

She stared at it, giving a look of repulsion.

"I can't."

"Look." Kateryn pointed across the square.

Monteacute followed her gesture, thinking that she was pointing to one admiral tied to a post on the far side of the square.

"So?" he asked.

"It's that lieutenant from the wharf," she said, still pointing. "The one with the eyepatch."

Monteacute squinted and looked past the platform to a building just beyond. The structure had two levels, the top of which had a veranda that jutted out over the access below, creating a shelter of sorts. There, in the shadows and bound with some others, was the man from the wharf.

"Looks as if he's going to be treated to a similar fate to the admirals," Monteacute said, biting into his stale bread.

"Can't we do something?" Rose asked.

He shook his head, no.

At that moment, a masked man with a flaming torch arrived on the platform. Beside him stood a younger man with a rolled parchment in his hand.

The parchment unfurled, and the man read from it.

"Attention," he boomed. "All citizens of Newholt take heart that you are now under the protection of the Black Queen, Joanne Hamond. Submissions of fealty to her will ensure your safety and your place in the Kingdom of the one and only true ruler, the Maji. Failure to comply with this simple act will result in the shared fate of these traitors and conspirators, Amicia Elynbrigge's appointed military leaders. The flame will cleanse and purify them, ushering them into oblivion by the order of your queen."

"Not my queen," one admiral called. He was older than the others and his uniform was torn and stained with blood.

The speaker gave the hooded man a simple nod, to which the hooded man replied by touching the flame to the pile of timber at the outspoken admiral's feet.

"I am Vice-Admiral Trenton Morris and Queen Amicia Elynbrigge is my queen," he continued to call as the flames bit into the wood. "She will always be Queen of Newholt. This Black Queen bitch is nothing but an evil witch, seizing an opportunity in our real queen's absence. Fuck the Black Queen. I wipe my arse on her banners. Fuck her. Fuck the Maji. Fuh-ahh."

His screams filled the square and pierced the hearts and souls of those watching on. Silent tears were shed by those who lived and served in Newholt as they observed the murder of one officer, who had desperately tried to keep them safe and sound.

The masked man moved around the platform, igniting each wood-pile.

More screams ensued as each officer cooked alive.

Monteacute dropped his bread to the ground.

He crouched down into a ball and cried.

Twenty-Eight

The Scarlet Queen, Tricia, leant against the guardrail of the quarter-deck and viewed the rocky cliffs of Freymoor with the sun against her back. Sea birds, such as gulls and pelicans, visited the boat, perching upon the yards and spars from where the sails hung, in the hope to scavenge a quick feed as they usually did when visiting fishing vessels along the coast. Eventually, after waiting for some time and receiving no nourishment, the gulls and pelicans would fly away only to make room for others who came to see if any scraps were around for the taking.

A large rolling tide moved across the hull from the east, pushing the ship towards the coastline. Tricia watched as giant white sprays exploded against the dark, rocky cliffs at the edge of the sea. If the galleon was to be pushed farther in that direction, they would dash her and the others on board to pieces.

But she wasn't afraid.

The crewmember on the wheel watched his piloting carefully, steering the ship a little to starboard to counter the sea. With the wind pushing from the southwest, their passage was remarkably smooth and speedy. They had passed around the cape a little before dawn. She had not been awake to see it. The Freymoor pier was the first thing she noticed when she left her quarters and walked upon the deck. It was small, nothing more than a thin wooden path jutting from the coastal village to house small boats owned by fishermen. The land rose rather steeply to the north of the quaint town, transforming into tall, dark cliffs that Tricia now observed. Freymoor was far from view, and

Byview was the next township that they were to sail by. It was still a fair way to travel, the crewman on the wheel had told her.

"Perhaps we'll see her by mid-morning," he said. "Definitely before noon. I'm hoping to have passed Lindport by noon."

The Scarlet Queen knew that the distance from Byview to Lindport was a long way by land. She didn't know if it would be quicker by sea, but yielded to the seafarer's judgement. He seemed confident that they would get there rather speedily.

Perhaps, she thought, it might have something to do with the wind and a slight change in direction. After all, they were heading in a north-easterly course. Byview was on a point that jutted out slightly from the landmass. After passing the town, the ship would need to turn in a northerly direction. The wind would then be more at their backs and travelling, in her understanding, should be faster.

At least, she hoped so.

Travelling on the sea was not something she enjoyed, as she was finding out. Her stomach felt queasy as the vessel lolled over long rises and shallow falls. She figured she was receiving favour from Takmel, or the gods, as they avoided steep waves with high crests and deep troughs.

She peered to the south, spying dark clouds above the horizon. They were thick and black, carrying weather that she wished to avoid. She hoped the favour that she and the ship's crew were receiving would continue for the duration of their journey.

And it was a journey that was only just beginning.

"You're awake," she heard a small voice say from behind her. She turned and saw the sandy-haired boy who had held the wheel during the night before. "Did you see the cape?"

"No." She smiled at him. "I was sleeping. The crewman there said it was dark, anyway." She tilted her head towards the sterncastle deck where the wheel was located.

"No matter," he said, moving to her side and leaning against the guardrail. "We're heading north now. Well..." he pointed to the bow of the ship. "North-east."

She felt her smile grow as she watched the young boy relax and rest back on the rail.

"Did you sleep well, Samuel?" she asked.

"Yes, my lady." He grinned. He then took on a different demeanour, his jaw dropped, and he appeared upset. "I'm sorry, my lady. I should ask you that question. I am so stupid."

"No, you're not," she told him, her smile replaced by a concerned expression. "Never refer to yourself as such a thing again. I slept fine. It's not as comfortable as the bed I've slept in before now. But it was still satisfactory."

The boy had tears welling in his eyes.

"Please, don't tell the skipper that I didn't ask," he pleaded. "I don't want to get into trouble."

"All right," she assured. "It'll be our secret."

He leant against the rail, wiped his eyes and watched the sea birds circling near the cliffs as giant plumes of white spray erupted again.

The Scarlet Queen kept her eyes on the boy and felt something grab at her heart. She wanted to put her arm around him and tell him he was a good boy.

He is a good boy;; she thought. A wonderful boy.

***

Arthur's eyes were open ever so slightly. The room was a blurry mix of dark blobs and forms, with one flickering orange glare a short distance away. He couldn't tell how far.

Beneath the glow, a dark figure moved. He guessed it was a guard, or at worst, Takmel returning to perhaps take another piece of him away.

"Good morning, Arthur," the figure said jovially. It was Takmel.

"Dakmuh," Arthur grunted, trying to acknowledge the other as best he could. His tongue and lips were still swollen and his mouth and teeth didn't feel like his own. There was an incredible pain shooting through his jaw and into his ears.

"I trust you slept well?" the other asked.

"Mmmm," the boy, lying on his back, acknowledged. His neck was aching and his body was sore from head to toe. But it was his arm, or at least where his arm once was, that gave him the most grief. If someone was to have asked him how it felt, he didn't think there would be words to describe it.

There was throbbing, sharp stabbing, excruciating aching, and the list went on and on.

"Leave him be," a familiar voice called softly from the cell next to his. He wanted to turn and see, but his body urged him to stay still, and his eyes wouldn't have been able to discern who it was. The voice was enough.

"I'll do what I want with him," he said. "He's my plaything."

"She will destroy you for this, Takmel," she slurred, a hint of delight coming through.

"I think you should refer to me as Maji from now on," he told her. "You lost the privilege of using my name when you betrayed me."

Arthur's ears perked up.

Betrayed?

"You hurt me, Takmel," she hissed. Her boots scuffed gently against the floor as she moved towards him.

"Maji," he reminded her.

"I'm your wife," she said. "And you hurt me, then threw me in here. Don't you love me anymore, Takmel?"

"Stay back," he ordered. "I don't want you to touch me and suck out my life as you did to that guard."

She giggled.

"You're a fool, Takmel."

"Maji," he said again. "You will call me Maji."

"I don't need to touch you," she slurred. "I can do it from here."

There was a long silence.

Arthur strained to hear and picture in his head what might be happening.

"Stupid bitch," Takmel spat. His boots stomping away upon the stone were the next thing Arthur heard.

"He's gone," she said. "Probably back to his blonde slave girl."

"Bloh Lay Ghuh?"

"Lucy," she clarified. "She's the only one left."

He could hear her boots moving back across the cell and soft ruffling. She was on her cot.

"Cahphren?" he called softly.

"Yes, Arthur?"

"Whah habbehd here? Whah habbehd to yooh?"

"I've discovered some new power," she told him. "I've changed."

"Yohr hair?"

"Yes," she answered excitedly. "My hair is white in places."

"Ah-ice too." He tried to smile. "Awh her hair. Whiye. Liye snow. Ayn her eyes ahh blwooh." He cried. "I miph her so muhsh."

Catherine fell quiet for a moment.

"She will come for you, Arthur," she said eventually. "I know she will."

"Ayn yooh," Arthur added. "Yohr her sisdhuh."

"I've killed people, Arthur," she admitted. "I killed a guard right here, just so that I could be strong again. I lured him into my cell and took his life."

"Ihd's awhrigh," he assured her. "Yooh had dho."

There was a long silence. Arthur strained to hear, hoping that he hadn't passed out again.

She was crying.

"Cahphren?"

"I killed your mother," she sobbed. "I killed Martha and your sister."

Arthur felt incredibly numb.

He received her words as if someone spoke to him in a dream. He wasn't sure if what she said was real or something churned up in his head as his body tried to heal.

Have I passed out again?

Am I awake?

He felt his neck and cheeks growing hotter and hotter.

Anger was building inside, but there was no physical action that he could take, regardless of what he might want to do.

He pictured his hands around her throat.

Squeezing.

Squeezing.

"Whah?" he asked, wanting to be sure that he had heard her correctly.

"On the bridge," she said, her voice trembling. "Takmel and I freed the horses from the farms and caused them to charge over."

Tears ran from his eyes and towards his ears as he stared blankly at the ceiling of his cell.

"Why?" he murmured. "Why?"

A fresh pain swept over him that surpassed the physical. His heart felt as if a thousand blades had pierced it. A large lump formed in his throat as he cried.

"For Takmel," she admitted. She was sobbing. "For the Maji."

Arthur shook his head slowly.

"They wuhr good beobuhl," he whispered.

She heard his words clearly. *They were good people*, and each syllable cut deep.

"They wuhr good, Cahphren. My mama. Martha. They wuhr good dho yooh. They luhved yooh. Kadhrina..." He bawled noisily as his mind turned to his little sister, Katrina. He pictured her snuggled up and in Martha's arms, reaching out with her tiny hands and smiling as she always did. "Kadhrina was only a bayhbee. Whyeee?"

She didn't answer. She couldn't answer. The words wouldn't come.

Only tears.

He didn't hear her sobbing over his own loud cries.

Her stomach tightened as she listened to him.

She had just torn his entire world apart again, right when he was at his worst.

Lying on her side and curling upon her cot, she lifted her knees to her chest and wept.

***

Alice stood by the western edge of the clearing with a flaming torch in her hand. They had built a new pyre upon the ashes of the previous one. It was a smaller woodpile, built for one.

Wrapped in clean swaddling and laid delicately on top was the body of Oliver Weston, the last of the family. Alice considered this for a moment, that there were no more children to carry on his legacy. No one to prove that he was here, except in tales that would be shared by firelight.

The entire surviving population of the glade stood behind her as she lowered the flame to the timber. There were no words spoken. But there were tears to shed.

Alice stepped back to stand at her mother's side. She wrapped her arms around the woman's waist and held tightly.

Emily brought her own arm over the girl's shoulders and squeezed. "This has to end," she said. "There have been too many pyres of late."

Alice said firmly, "It ends tonight."

Twenty-Nine

By noon, a gathering had formed in the glade, near to the mouth of the large cavern. Horses were being saddled and supplies were being packed. Alice moved through the cluster, assessing and checking to see if anything was amiss. She was ready for battle. She strapped her swords to her hips and her leather armour was in place.

A tiny twinge of excitement built in her stomach. She hoped it wasn't more of the sickness that the child within had brought during the previous night. She hoped it was simply nervousness and antici-pation for what was to come.

She moved to the mouth of the cave where the Haigok had gathered. They, too, dressed for battle. Gruloch stood proudly before them and waited for the girl.

"Are they all well rested?" she asked.

"They are," he answered. "We won't saddle them until it is time to go. Otherwise, they get excited. But I think they know."

"I think they must," she agreed, peering into the dark recesses of the cave. Low rumblings and soft chirps echoed through the dark chambers within. "I can feel it."

***

"But I should come too, Papa," Alan Verney told his father, walk-ing alongside the man as he carried saddlebags loaded with food and two water pouches. "I'm the same age as Alice. And Arthur is my friend, too."

"I understand how much you want to do this," Lor replied, his hands laden with his saddle and his sword strapped to his waist. "But you're too young. I'll be thinking of you the entire time and not about the things I should keep my mind on."

"But Alice..."

"Alice is experienced in battle," Lor told him, lifting the saddle onto his horse's back. "She knows magic and rides a dragon. She is a special girl, Alan. She is her father's daughter, but you are *my* son. And I am ordering you to stay here with your mama."

"But I want to fight with you," the boy pressed.

"I know," Lor said, taking the saddlebags from his son. "But think about this. What if we lose? Who will care for your mama if I fall?"

"I will," Alan replied, lowering his eyes.

"That's my boy," Lor placed his hand on the lad's shoulder. "Now help me strap this saddle on this old girl."

***

Ruttger Harrow assisted Commander Brondt with his preparations. Food and water were gathered and saddlebags packed for the troop.

"Many of those men on the wall are my men," Ruttger said as he strapped a set of saddlebags to one steed. "Or, at least, they used to be. You would do me a service if you could spare as many as possible."

"You have my word," Brondt replied. "But I would feel much better if you were coming with us."

The old commander of the Lilac Mistress' forces sighed deeply. "My body just doesn't want to behave in the way it used to. I was old when we marched from the Western Sea. Besides..." he looked over to Courtney, his beloved wife. She was still young. How she stayed with him was something he couldn't comprehend. But there she was, helping the warrior women prepare for battle by strapping them into their armour and helping to pack their horses. "...I am needed here."

***

"Is my horse ready?" Ursula asked Thornton. He was standing beside his steed, petting its nose as she approached.

"This is your horse," he replied with a grin.

"No." She looked at him, puzzled. "This is *your* horse."

"It is my horse," he said, smiling. "And you will ride with me."

She wrapped her arms over his shoulders.

"You'll make me ride with you when Amicia gets her own horse and Alice gets to fly a dragon?" she questioned. "I am one of them. Should I not be treated with such respect also?"

"You're not a queen," he replied with a playful grin. "And you aren't the leader of some lizard people. You're the madam of a brothel with three whores to your name."

She laughed.

"And you owe me six gold coins, if I recall correctly."

"Five," he grunted.

"Five?" She furrowed her brow. "How do you figure?"

"Well..." He chuckled before he could get the words out. "I've been secretly charging you for every time you asked me to take my trousers off. I counted about twenty times since. So, I guess that's good for..."

"A quart of copper at best," she jumped in. She kissed him before he had time to object.

***

David and Emily rode alongside one another, with Jeremy Schoenbach and his wife Karlena behind them. They moved to the top of the rise, overlooking the meadow as they waited for the others to finish packing for the journey.

"Anyone would think we were leaving for good by the way they are fussing about," Schoenbach observed.

"Perhaps we are," David replied. He glanced down to Emily's hip, where he saw the curved Erilian blade the warrior women had gifted her. "Can you still use that?"

"I've been practising with Karlena," she replied.

David turned to Karlena. "Can she still use that?"

Emily reached over and smacked him on the arm.

"Better than ever," the Erilian said with satisfaction.

"Well, I'm ready," Akasati called. "Let's go."

She strapped her bow over her back and a full quiver of arrows was slung to the side of her saddle. Her sword was sheathed on her hip, worn just as the other two warrior women wore theirs. The three had donned their tanned leather breastplates and dark leggings. David was suddenly thrust back to the snowy plains by the Eastern Sea so many years ago when they ventured to Blackrock Haven. The Erilian women and Emily were a force to reckon with then, but they had lost three integral members of their pack. He wondered how they would fare so many years later.

***

Yuri pressed his snout lovingly against each of his children's. His long blade on his back and dagger on his thigh.

"Take care of each other," he told them.

"Yes, Papa," they replied.

He pressed his lips to his wife's forehead and hugged her tightly.

"I'll come home," he promised.

"I'll be here," she told him.

He mounted his steed in one leap and kept his eyes fixed on her as he pulled away with his twelve warriors in tow.

***

Alice waited for them all to be on horseback. She stood at the edge of the camp and moved her gaze to each. She counted forty-five on horseback.

Forty-five against the entire armed personnel of Woodmyst, a walled city that was well defended and well supplied.

"They outnumbered us," she said. "We are under-prepared. And we face a powerful enemy."

"Excellent speech," Porf called out. "I feel encouraged. How about all of you?"

"Shut it," Glaun rebuked.

"I think Porf has a good attitude towards this," Alice announced. "We may never return from this. We may all die and everything we do may be in vain. But if we do nothing," she continued, "then all will be lost, anyway. He will attack the glade again. He will eventually wipe us out and then the rest of the world.

"My purpose to go into Woodmyst is a selfish one. I want to bring my husband and my sister home. That's all.

"For you, it might be to help me. Or you might go to seek vengeance for what has been done here. Or maybe you just want to rid this land of tyranny before it takes hold. Whatever it may be, I simply ask that you try your best to come back when this is all over.

"Wait in the shadows," she ordered them. "Stay out of sight and keep silent. Advance when you see my signal and not before. Most importantly, be safe."

She signalled for them to ride.

The horses galloped across the open grassland and into the trees on the eastern edge of the clearing. Alice stood on top of the rise, watching until they had gone. She turned to Gruloch, who was standing in front of the cavern peering at her. He gave her a nod and tilted his head towards her cavern. She turned to see Becka standing on her porch, watching the eastern tree line with tears in her eyes.

Moments later, Alice sat beside the widow at the table in the kitchen, holding onto her hand as Linet poured fresh tea. Courtney and Ruttger Harrow had taken seats across from them. Becka was sobbing quietly, for obvious reasons. Richard wasn't with her anymore.

"He would have wanted to go," she said, looking at Linet and Alice as she spoke. "I would have had to remind him of his age and his inability to lace his own boots without my help."

"He was a stubborn old goat." Ruttger reflected. "I think I liked that about him most of all. He wouldn't tolerate being told what to do or what not to do. He would either do it or not."

"Unless I told him to or not." Becka smiled through the tears. "Then that stubborn old goat would have to do what I told him."

"I think he was the bravest man I ever knew," Linet said, placing mugs before the widow and the young girl. She returned to the kitchen and retrieved two more mugs for Ruttger and Courtney as she continued speaking. "I don't remember it all that well myself, but I know he faced the dragons. Every time I heard that story, hairs would stand up on the back of my neck. It wasn't until I first saw Alice's Liana that I genuinely appreciated what he did."

"He didn't *face* it," Becka corrected her. "He crept up behind it and stabbed it."

"Still..." Linet shrugged her shoulders slightly as she placed the other two mugs before Ruttger and his wife. "To do that, he must have had some courage."

"Well, that he had," she agreed, wiping her eyes on a kerchief that she found in a pocket on her dress. She giggled. "He had courage, and a lot of stupidity to support it."

"You need that," Ruttger offered after sipping at his tea. "One needs to be stupid enough to run into a battle or take on a dragon. There isn't much use for common sense in such a situation."

Alice remembered the first time she had lunged over the Rakmha Trench, when she had run the Kyhur Circuit. Most would pass the trench by climbing down a narrow, winding path to the bottom on one side before climbing back up on a mirroring path on the other.

But not Alice.

That took too long.

She had run at the wide gap as fast as she could and leapt over.

Not even a horse running at full pace could make that jump.

Once was stupid enough. Alice had made the jump twice.

The second time she leapt over the Rakmha trench was the very day she became Kayl'sro of the Agrodien. She did it to save her life.

Pursued by the Kayl'sro Greil and his loyal warriors, Alice had out-witted them and outmanoeuvre them to that very point on the circuit. Only Greil possessed the same amount of courage, or stupidity, as she did. He also opted to leap over the trench after Alice, except he was on horseback. Sadly, his horse perished, but he sprang from the steed and landed on solid ground. What ensued was a brief and bloody fight between a small girl and a large Agrodien.

Greil eventually lost when she tore his head from his body.

Alice was presented with the Iron Claws of Agrodia and given the title of Kayl'sro.

And now, here she sat with Aunt Linet, Becka and the Harrows, a leader of the Agrodien race and the people of the glade. All gratitude to courage and stupidity, she supposed.

"When will you leave?" Becka asked her.

Alice threw her train of thinking aside and returned her attention to the here and now.

"When it gets dark," she replied. "I want to use the element of surprise."

"So?" Courtney gave Alice a mystified look. "Why send everyone else now? It's not that far to Woodmyst."

"I know," she replied with a quick nod. "They won't be riding the whole way. They'll leave the horses some distance away from the sight of the towers. They will then go on foot and use the woods to the east of the city."

"That's some distance to cover between the woods and the wall," Linet said. "Why not use the forest to the west?"

"I think they must be watching it carefully," the girl replied. "It's much closer to the wall. And it makes sense to go there. But we tried that already when we sent Agrodien spies to watch Woodmyst. None of them returned. At least, not alive."

They still remembered Plo'shyk's head stuck on a pike near the edge of the clearing. They also remembered what had happened to Ivo Weston shortly afterwards.

Courtney shuddered at the memory.

"I ordered them to wait until dusk and use the farmhouses and structures as cover until they are close enough to Woodmyst to see my signal," Alice told them.

"And what will that be?" Becka asked.

"Something spectacular," she promised.

Thirty

A sudden knock at the door made the Scarlet Queen jump. She had been sitting in a chair by her bedside, reading something she had found in the quarters. *A History of the Realms Volume III.* She had seen the book before, or at least another copy of it, amongst Arthur Gyfford's collection back in Woodmyst. She had not bothered with reading anything that he was interested in, as she found it tedious and, hard to understand. She preferred tales of romance and intrigue over facts and realities. But she was bored, and there wasn't much for one to do onboard a ship, even a galleon with so many decks. So, she read the history book and had dozed off.

"Come," she called.

The door opened slowly.

"My lady," a man's voice called. "Sorry for the intrusion. May I come in?"

"Please," she said, gesturing to another chair as her guest stepped into the room.

He held a tricorn hat against his chest and wore a long, dark blue officer's coat with fancy gold epaulettes on his shoulders. He peered around and stroked his trimmed beard, clearly impressed by the state of the room.

"I see you have settled in," he said, looking at the neatly made bed and arrangement of cupboards and chairs. A dresser with a mirror rested against the wall beside the door and a light rug rested on the floor by the bed.

He took the seat she had offered near the dresser and placed his hat upon his thighs. "If there is anything you need, please don't hesitate to ask."

"Thank you, Captain," she said with a friendly grin.

"Skipper," he corrected her.

"Beg pardon?"

"I prefer the title Skipper," he explained. "Captain makes me sound like military. I am a captain, but I am not navy. I am just a merchant vessel skipper with a bunch of fancy clothes."

"I'm unfamiliar with the terminology and don't truly understand the difference," she apologised. "Would you like some tea?

She waved a hand to a table pressed up against the wall to the side of her quarters. There sat a small silver tray with a tea set on top. A small, thin line of steam extruded through the spout of the pot.

"Ah, no thank you," he replied. "I won't stay long. I just came to inform you we have passed Linport. There is also a storm on our heels. It will catch us before the day is out. Perhaps even overtake us. The weather will get rough, so I urge you to stay in your cabin for your safety."

"I understand."

His gaze fell to the book on her lap. "A History of the Realms," he said delightedly.

"Yours, I presume?"

"Yes." He gestured. "Isn't it wonderful?"

"Would you like it back?" She held it out to him. "I found it here before I moved in.

"No, no," he said, "please. Keep it. Enjoy it."

Enjoy it?

She smiled. "Thank you. But I'll leave it where I found it once I'm off the ship."

"No rush," he replied. "We've been ordered to harbour for a few days once we arrive."

She grinned and put the book on a bedside table.

"Cap... Skipper? What can you tell me about the boy on board your ship?"

He looked at her uncomprehendingly, and then his face cleared. "You mean Sam?"

"Yes. Sam. What can you tell me of him?"

"I don't know," he said, and scratched his head. "He's a good lad. Works hard."

"What of his parents?"

"Oh," the skipper said. "They died. They came from Barrowfield and were slaughtered by the Mirikin's army. A few of the younglings from the town escaped and hid in the woods and marshlands as they made their way towards the coast. Sam was one of them."

"He must have only been three or four at the time." Tricia frowned, imagining a toddler cowering beneath bushes and wading through muddy water, all the while scared out of his mind. "That poor boy."

"He wasn't alone," the skipper told her. "There were others, older and younger. By the time they reached Dweagan, the battle in Woodmyst was over and the Mirikin were defeated. A few of the older boys got some work on the docks, and Sam followed them like a lost pup. I took pity on them and hired most of the older lads, but Sam had to come along as part of the deal."

She wiped a tear from her eye and stared at the light-coloured rug on the floor, part of her trying to decide if it was the shade of a stale white or an off cream, another part of her thinking about the young sandy-haired boy.

"I want him reassigned to me," she ordered. Her eyes met the skipper's. He wore a puzzled expression. "He will be my cabin boy."

"Begging pardon, my lady," the other began, "but what are your intentions towards the lad? I took him under my wing and I consider him an integral part of my crew. And I consider my crew as my family."

"I understand your concern," she said. "But he is only a boy and I am considering a different life for him; a future where he will be taken care of and where every need he has will be met."

"You're going to take him into your care?" he asked.

"I haven't decided," she answered honestly. "But think about what I can offer him, and what future he has here."

"He's an innocent boy," he told her, almost pleading.

"I am giving you a direct order, Skipper." The Scarlet Queen got up. "Appoint him as my cabin boy."

He lifted himself from the chair and held his hat to his chest.

"Yes, my lady," he replied, his voice surpassing concern and filling with fear. "But, please don't hurt him."

"That will be all, Skipper," she said.

He bowed and turned, leaving the room and closing the door behind him.

She strode over to the table and carefully poured a cup of tea. Sitting back in her chair, she reached for the book, *A History of the Realms*, and opened it to where she had been reading.

She was bored, and there wasn't much else to do onboard a ship. Even one as big as a galleon.

Perhaps the boy might help to change that.

***

David slung his water skins over his shoulder as Emily started packing the contents of the saddlebags into a knapsack. Others around them were making similar preparations for the rest of the journey.

They removed the saddles and bridles from the horses and piled the equipment together near some thick underbrush, covering the heap with leaves and fallen branches. The big man peered into the sky and saw a thin layer of grey clouds sweeping over the sky above them.

"I think we may see some weather tonight," he said out loud.

"Good," Thornton growled, gesturing to Ursula with his thumb. "Have you seen what she can do with a little weather?"

"Aye." David turned to Amicia, who was lifting her knapsack onto her shoulders, preparing to carry her own and Brondt's supplies. "You ready for a long walk, Your Majesty?"

"Just lead the way, Mister Gyfford," she announced with confidence.

David looked at Yuri, who was talking with his warriors. Their eyes met and the big man signalled to the Agrodien by raising his eyebrows.

Ready?

Yuri nodded.

Yes.

"Keep in file," David instructed. "Two abreast at the most. Move slow and steady. Watch the sides for movement and be ready for anything. Remember why we are here and keep the talking to a minimum."

"Aye, aye, sir," Vawdrey called out with a salute.

"And stow that shit," Thornton grunted, giving the other a disapproving glare.

They started out through the woods, leaving the steeds to find their own way back to the glade, or to get lost amongst the trees. It didn't matter.

The mission was a priority.

Stepping quietly, keeping dried leaves and twigs in mind, the troop advanced through the thick growth. They turned their ears to the surroundings.

Bird chatter. The creaking limbs of the tall trees around them. The rustling of leaves as a gentle breeze swept by.

Even their own footsteps became a loud, noticeable intrusion to the silence they all desired.

David looked behind him now and then to make sure the crew was keeping up. They were.

Emily would give him a reassuring look as they made progress, but her eyes appeared sad and distant. He wanted to ask her if she was all right, but yielded to his better judgement and abstained. Besides, he already knew why she was harbouring grief. It was for the same reason he harboured grief. His son, her daughter, were both in that wretched city they used to call home. All he wanted to do right now, and he knew Emily felt the same, was to get them both out of there. But with only forty-five of them creeping through the southern reaches of the Forest of Khun, he wondered if they had any hope of success.

There is Alice, he reminded himself.

He had underestimated her before and she had always managed to overcome any obstacle placed before her. The Maji, he tried to tell himself, was simply that. An obstacle.

We will have success.

We will overcome.

We have Alice.

He chanted the words over and over in his head until he believed them.

He had to.

There was no alternative.

***

"I 'aven't ever seen anything like it, your lordship," the tubby guard said. He was standing at the feet of the stairs leading up to the platform in the assembly hall. At the top, upon a high-backed chair, sat the Maji. With his hood lowered and damson cloak draped around him, his appearance seemed regal. Standing beside him, Master Bookkeeper Lewis Drayton listened on with inquisitive interest.

"Strings of light?" the Maji asked.

"Yes," the guard replied.

"Dragged out of his body?" the robed figure queried. "You said 'dragged,' didn't you?"

"Yes, my lordship," the guard said. "Dragged out of him and into her eyes. I wouldn't have believed it if I hadn't seen it myself."

"Ridiculous," Drayton hissed.

"I believe you, Harry," Takmel said, offering a kind smile. "Why don't you return to your home and use the night to rest up?"

"I have duty tonight, Maji," the tubby guard said.

"No, you don't," replied Takmel. "Tonight, you rest. Those are my orders. I'll send word to your commander informing him of such."

He gestured to a sentry near the doors to take the message to the tubby guard's commander.

"Thank you, my lordship." Harry bowed.

"You are welcome," Takmel replied. "And your service is appreciated. That will be all."

Harry turned and started along the aisle, passing a few people who were rearranging the seating after the tussle between Catherine and Takmel during the previous night. Drayton watched the other leave and waited until he was out of earshot before speaking.

"You don't truly believe that twaddle, do you, my lord?"

"Of course I do," Takmel answered. "Did you see the body?"

"Well, yes," he replied.

"It looked as if it had been drained and squeezed out," the young man said, wringing his hands together. "A little like a water sack when you try to get that last drop out."

Drayton kept watching the tubby guard as he walked out through the doors of the hall.

"What will we do with her?" he asked.

"No one goes near those cells, except the duty guards," Takmel instructed. "They will deliver food and water as usual, but double the men on watch; particularly on her cell and Arthur's."

"Should we send someone in to assassinate her?"

"She's my wife, Lewis," Takmel reminded. "I can't just kill my wife. Not without a contingency plan."

"My lord?"

"I need nine," the Maji explained. "Until I find another to replace her with, she will remain alive."

"Nine?" Drayton furrowed his brow. "What's significant about the number nine?"

"Nothing," Takmel replied, moving his eyes to the master book-keeper. "Ten is the number that matters. Power has always been at its strongest with the grouping of ten. The Sovereign and her Mistresses. The entire linage of the Mirikin. Always ten. Their downfall occurred when they lost their leader. My mother tried to lead them, but they only numbered nine then. There were weaknesses in their fold, like chinks in their armour. Amicia betrayed them and the others were defeated all the way until the final battle on the fields outside of this city's walls.

"There must always be ten," he continued. "If one falls, there must be a replacement. I and my wives make ten. Even if this one doesn't wish to be a part of it, it is too late. She gave herself to me, just as the Mistresses gave themselves to the Sovereign. Just as the coven has always done. Therefore, she is mine."

"The coven?" the old man's eyes widened. "The Mirikin?"

A wicked grin spread upon Takmel's face.

"All the pieces are falling into place, my friend," the Maji replied. "The Mirikin have returned."

Thirty-One

Joanna leant against the rail of the balcony, overlooking the eastern portion of the city. There wasn't much left to see except smoke and flames still rising from the rubble and a few buildings left intact. Some patrols had set up camp in those, claiming them in her name. Now and then, she spied a gang of black creatures running through the ruins like a pack of wolves in search of food. A part of her hoped they found nothing, knowing full well that if they did, it would more than likely be people. Another part of her didn't care.

Peering out to the Eastern Sea, she counted the thirteen vessels that had sailed from Dweagan. Their cannons were silent, and the catapults installed upon their decks had ceased firing their payloads hours ago. They had spread out, forming a line just offshore that stretched the city's length.

"We have claimed the northern sector, my lady," Andris announced, walking into the makeshift command room that the Newholt officers had established. He turned his head to the left, then right in search of her, seeing her through wafting lace curtains that hung over the door to the eastern balcony.

"That's good," she replied. "I saw smoke coming from the town square."

"The first of the enemy's officers to be burnt, my lady," he answered coldly. His behaviour struck her as unusual. He stood rigidly, very soldier-like, with his hand upon his sword's hilt and his feet almost together at attention.

"The ships?" she asked, stepping into the room and gesturing to the sea with her hand.

"They sent word about an hour ago," he answered. "They are to remain anchored until the Scarlet Queen passes by. Their orders are to escort her the rest of the way."

"And then?" She moved closer to him. He didn't move. Not a muscle. His eyes were distant, staring at the wall to the side of the balcony door.

"They patrol the Eastern Sea, my lady."

She stood so close to him he could feel her breath against his neck. He could feel her eyes moving along his skin, following his jawline, along his cheeks and to his lips.

He steadied his breath and hid his nerves.

Her hand touched his breastplate.

"And you?" she queried.

"My lady?"

"How do you fare?"

"My men could use some food and fresh water," he replied. "But the survivors require it more so. With your permission, I'd like to raid the stores so we can prepare some fresh meals for the women, children and elderly."

"Always thinking of others." She stepped away disappointedly. "I'm right here, Andris. Don't you see? Don't you remember? You were meant to be mine. We can finally see this happen."

"You're the Black Queen of the Maji," he reminded her. "And I am a happily married man."

"You were my servant once," she sneered. "I have sent here you to be so again."

His eyes remained fixed upon the wall.

"Why won't you look at me?" she yelled.

He didn't comply, keeping his eyes steady, his countenance solid. To her, he appeared unmoving.

Inside, he wondered if what she said had any truth to it. Had Takmel merely sent him to be a servant to her, just as intended for him when the Sovereign assigned him to her when she was a twelve-year-old girl? It wouldn't surprise him if this was the case. Andris remembered all too well how the man-servants of Blackrock Haven were treated as nothing more than playthings for lustful pleasures. The Maji's plan could have easily taken this into account, sending each of his wives a companion to exploit in such a way. Perhaps, he thought, because there was a history between Joanne and his captain of the guard, he could rekindle that spark they had in the hope to keep his queen satisfied.

But Andris wouldn't have it.

No, not even a little.

He would admit, if anyone asked, that Joanne was indeed beautiful, even more so than his sweet Sevrina. But his heart belonged to one and one only. He had made vows to her, and he intended to keep them. Even, as the words he said to Sevrina promised, unto his last breath.

"Am I required to look at you, my lady?" he asked.

She glared at him, her eyes boring into him. Still, he didn't move.

"I could command you," she said.

"I would disobey." This time, he moved his gaze to her.

She trembled slightly, angry at his defiance. Her hands balled into fists as she desired to destroy him.

But for what?

For not sharing a bed with her?

To punish him would be a sign of weakness to the people of her new realm. A queen who couldn't sway a man, so she imposes a sentence or punishment as a result, as a sign of having little control of herself.

You were never like this before, a small voice whispered in her head. *Why do you intend to force yourself onto him? This isn't who you are.*

She pushed the thoughts away and continued to glower at Andris.

"Will there be anything else, my lady?" he asked.

She slowed her breathing in an attempt to compose herself.

"Go back to your duties, Commander," she replied. "Open the stores and feed the people after our men have had their fill."

"Yes, my lady." He bowed and returned through the door to the corridor beyond.

She found a chair and plonked into it, resting her elbow on the armrest and rubbing at her temple with her fingers.

This isn't who you are.

She winced, as if the words had brought pain with them.

***

The dragons spread out upon the glade, stretching their wings and legs after a long night in the cavern. They chirped as their Haigok riders petted them and spoke with them.

"How many are there?" Alice asked Gruloch.

"Dragons? In the world?" He looked at her. She inclined her head. "I am not entirely certain. Hundreds. Maybe thousands. Who can tell?"

"But yours is not the only Haigok village," she said. "And you are Lord of the Haigok."

"I am Lord of these Haigok..." he gestured to the riders, "and the Haigok of my village. There are more Lords of the Haigok out there who are Lords of their people. And yes, they have dragons too. They are scattered and hidden throughout the land. Some live high in the mountains near Kailibard, and others in the swamps to the north of the Sea of Solace. More are in the Core Lands and some have even ventured as far as the Frozen Waste."

"Do you keep contact with them?" she asked.

"Some," he said. "We have family amongst them and they have family amongst us. So yes, we keep in contact. We haven't heard from the clans in the Frozen Waste for some time. Many years." He looked to her as she watched the dragons and their riders. "You desire more? This is why you ask me these questions?"

"Yes. I believe we may be in for a much larger fight," she admitted. "I think this, what we do tonight, will only be the beginning. We may require a powerful hand, and I think this will only happen if we can ally ourselves with your people. All of your people."

"The last time the Haigok united resulted in Woodmyst being destroyed," he reminded her. "I don't know if the men that would follow you into battle are prepared for that kind of thing to happen again."

"It's not for revenge this time," Alice said. "It's to prevent evil from spreading over the land before it takes hold. Your people, the Agrodien, my people and every other race and tribe out there are threatened by the presence of the Maji. But I think his poison is already spreading.

"Seven of his nine queens are moving. Newholt falls and these dark creatures move about in all directions. We need more of us out there than we have. We all need to come together and organise our resources, conduct multiple attacks and keep each other informed at all times."

"And who will command?" he asked. "You?"

"I don't know." She shook her head. "Maybe Commander Brondt? You?"

"No. I will lead my people. I am not confident with coordinating multitudes of diverse tribes and groups." He placed his hand on her shoulder. "But you are becoming proficient at it. I think I will follow you."

She stared down at her abdomen, covered with armour, and placed her hands over it.

"It won't be long before my shape changes," she said sombrely. "I won't be able to ride Liana into battle, or wield my swords as I do. Command may not be an option."

A long, glittering line of moisture slid upon her cheek. Gruloch knew she was thinking of her husband.

"Let's not fret about such things," he said, peering into the lowering sun. "We should prepare for this battle and worry about the next when it comes. So, tell me again. Thirty towers?"

"Yes," she answered as she wiped her eyes. "Eight to the north and eight to the south. Seven more to the east and another seven to the west."

"All stone?"

"That's right," she replied. "But their floorings and ladders are not. They were the work of David's carpenters. Not the masons."

"I think this will work, Alice," he said. "I think this is a good plan."

***

Catherine sat upright on the cot, her back wedged into the corner of her cell and her knees tucked up to her chest, with both arms wrapped around her legs. She couldn't remember how she had got into such a position, but she didn't feel ready to get out of it either. Tears were still falling from her eyes and mucus she had wiped from her nose laced her sleeves. How her body could retain so much fluid was beyond her comprehension. She guessed Arthur would know the answer to that, but she dared not speak to him after what she had told him. After how he had responded.

Her forehead touched her knees as she felt another wave of guilt and sorrow flow over her. More tears followed.

"Enuhhf," his voice mumbled. "Yoohll mayhg yourselph sigg."

There wasn't any tone of anger. Not even a hint of hatred. She opened her eyes and deepened her frown. If it was her in the other cell, locked up next to the one who murdered her family, she would want to inflict so much terror and pain upon them.

But not Arthur.

Compassion and kindness filled his voice.

"I'm sorry," she blubbered.

"Stobb iddt," he told her.

She wiped her eyes on her cloak's sleeve, feeling the dampness soaking through the layers of clothing on her skin.

"Ahh yooh awll righd?"

His concern made her feel more condemnation for herself. She didn't deserve to be asked such a question. She didn't deserve his kindness.

"Yes," she told him. "You?"

"Nevah beddah," he answered. She heard him chuckle softly, then moan as the pain struck him again.

She wanted to be able to hold him and help him, but she couldn't because of the bars between them. She wouldn't because of the prison she had built for herself.

She had hurt those closest to her. Not just Arthur and his family, but her own as well. Her mother and sister were taken from her.

No. They were not taken.

You threw them away.

She wept again.

Through her actions, her own aunt had been led astray. And now she was far away, doing the Maji's bidding.

She had played a key role in destroying everything, good and pure, that her own father had fought to keep alive.

There was no way that they would take her back after what she had done. How could they?

But she hoped they would.

Arthur moaned again.

"They will come for you, Arthur," she said, clinging to a tiny amount of optimism that they were coming for her too.

Thirty-Two

Darkness fell upon the glade. A gathering of women and one man had formed outside of Alice's cabin. Agrodien females and younglings, the wives of the northern men, Ruttger and Courtney, Linet and Becka, all watched the dragon riders lift into the air and circle the clearing.

Alice directed Liana to the west. She intended to pass over the quarry before following the ridge of the mountains to the edge of the Lunkhul Forest. Gruloch and the other eleven riders were right behind her, forming into a single line.

Looking down to the left, she could see the tiny forms of the people by her cabin. Linet waved to her, possibly wishing her luck. Alice waved back and returned her attention to the sky ahead of her.

A dull and distant flash far to the south signalled approaching clouds. She guessed that the weather was right on Woodmyst's door.

This was a good thing.

With luck, the storm would break over the city before they arrived.

She pulled her cloak about her tightly, lifting the hood over her head, pulling her scarf over her mouth and nose.

Over the mountain tops, they flew and above the range. It wasn't long before she sighted the quarry. Quiet. Still. Desolate.

She had never enjoyed the sight of the place, believing they were doing nothing here but destroying the land upon which it sat. The forest had once thrived in this very spot, until someone had the brilliant idea of rebuilding the walls of Woodmyst.

They banked to the south and dived towards the surface.

Keeping as close as they could to the ground, the thirteen dragons skimmed over trees, glided by the edges of sheer rock faces, and raced through narrow canyons.

As they continued their flight, Alice felt her heart race with anticipation.

***

Crouching by a farmhouse, David put his hand on Emily's arm. They were both peering at the giant stone wall that bordered the western edge of their home. At least, it was their home not all that long ago.

The scaffolding to the northern end of the structure had been taken away. The stonework was complete and the torchlight on its top showed that it was well guarded.

The western gate had been drawn closed, and men occupied the towers on each side. David had to assume that all the other towers along this wall and the others, were manned similarly.

A flash of lightning to their south illuminated the area surrounding them. For a very brief moment, they were exposed. If anyone had noticed them, they didn't make it apparent.

He glanced around, noticing the others crouching by other huts, kneeling under carts and lying beside pens and animal troughs. The Agrodien lay in the tall grass in the open field. They remained still and silent. If it wasn't for another sudden flash of lightning, and the glint from Nola'ee's eyes, David would have missed them. They appeared like statues, lifeless and unmoving.

"Are you ready?" he whispered to the auburn woman.

She nodded, gripping the sword on her hip.

"We need to remember to find Sevrina," she told him. "I don't remember if we talked about her."

"Lor and I have," he replied. "You and I will go to the holding cells at the barracks with Jeremy and the Erilian women. Lor will take the northerners to get Sevrina. We're not leaving anyone behind. But if this all goes to plan, we won't have to leave at all."

"Right." She scanned the top of the wall.

Some men were moving slowly between towers. David could see by her form that she was nervous, even a little afraid.

"She'll be here soon," David assured her. "My guess is that we won't be needed all that much when she arrives."

"You may be right," Emily whispered.

***

The galleon swayed and rolled steeply as it climbed and fell over the enormous waves. The rain teemed down against the gallery window along the back wall of the Scarlet Queen's sleeping quarters. Loud creaks and groans filled the room as the ship's structure strained with each roll. The sharp whistle of the wind pushing the vessel, singing through the rigging far above the ceiling, reached her ears. It reminded her of wolves howling in the night.

"I've made more tea, my lady," the boy said calmly. His feet and legs instinctively moved and reacted to the motion of the ship. She, on the other hand, nervously sat upon the edge of the bed, gripping a pillow in her vice-like fingers. "Would you like a cup?"

She stared at him with scared eyes.

"Is it always like this?"

"This?" He gave her a puzzled look. "This is nothing, my lady. Just a spot of rain. You shouldn't worry about this."

"I'm afraid, Samuel," she admitted, smelling the salt as sea spray exploded over the window. The ship was climbing again.

"Let me pull the covers back on your bed," he said, walking over to her. "You can slide in and pull them over your head. Pretend you're in a tree swing or something."

"The last time I was on a ship and in a storm..." She shook as she spoke.

Samuel stopped in his tracks. "You were on a ship before?"

"It was the most terrifying experience," she admitted.

"It's just a bit of bad weather," he tried to comfort her, placing his hand on her shoulder.

She could smell the sour alcohol on the Sovereign's dirty commander. She felt his hands on her legs and breasts and suddenly she was back there in the iron pen, down in the dark cargo hold of the black ship.

"My lady?" Samuel sat beside her. "It's all right."

"Stay with me," she said timidly.

"I... I..." he stammered. "I don't think that would be wise, my lady."

"I'm scared, Samuel," she said, shaking, tears streaming down her face, almost jumping when a sudden flash of light filled the quarters. "Please?"

He nodded, secretly believing he was making a poor decision.

"You get into bed," he said, pulling the covers back for her. "I'll get the light and then return." She bent to unlace her boots. "Let me," he said, dropping to his knees immediately.

Within moments, she was out of her cloak and beneath the covers, wearing nothing more than her undergarments. Samuel had stripped himself to his braies before extinguishing the lanterns; one on the dresser by the door, the other on the table by the tea set.

There was another flash of light as the galleon dropped down a steep wave, suddenly rolling a little sideways before climbing again. He heard her gasp in the darkness.

"Samuel?" she called softly, her voice trembling.

"I'm here," he answered, climbing in next to her.

Her hands reached over to him, pulling him close to her body. He felt uncomfortable and out of place. No one had ever held him in bed. Not for as long as he could clearly remember. He slept alone in a thin cot beneath deck where the other crewmen slept.

She shuddered as the vessel rolled and banked again.

He nestled against her, feeling her warmth.

It was a long time before he closed his eyes. But it wasn't long afterwards that he drifted away.

He could feel her body relax as her breathing became more and more steady. He guessed she had fallen to sleep. And soon, he was sleeping too.

***

Four men stood atop the northwest tower. The rain pelted down upon the roof above them and obscured anything more than an arm's reach from their eyes.

"Got any cider?" one of them asked.

A rumble of distant thunder rolled the air above them.

"You drank the last of it," another answered. "We have water now."

"Water we got a plenty," the first said and gestured to the rain. "But I wish we had some cider. What do you reckon if I go over to the next tower and see if they have any?"

"I reckon you'll be in deep shit because your post is right here," another answered, peering into the dark gloom.

At that moment, a great sound, like thick fabric tearing, ripped through the sky. The roof over the tower shook violently, and a great gust of wind rushed through.

"What was that?" the fourth man asked, peering up at the rafters.

"Just the wind," the cider drinker told him. "Nothing."

It happened again and again.

Over and over.

If they had counted, they would have noted thirteen disturbances.

If they had seen, they would have noticed dragons rising into the night sky directly above Woodmyst, soaring into the clouds above.

***

Alice felt exhilaration as Liana passed through the top of the cloud cover. The moon was bright, casting a silver glow over the tops of a wonderland that the girl had never seen before. Fluffy vales and mountains stretched as far as her eye could see. She saw the other dragons breach the clouds, bursting through like fish jumping from a pond. How she wished she and Liana could explore it all.

Instead, Liana rolled backwards, somersaulting and turning her body back towards the land below.

Alice felt a little saddened because she was leaving this enchanted vision behind as they shot through the clouds and hurtled towards the ground. She steered Liana for the eastern gate, watching the tiny roof-tops rapidly grow larger and larger.

In the corner of her eyes, she saw the other dragons lining up with her, bearing down upon targets of their own.

The giant beasts knew their tasks well, opening their jaws and spewing jets of flame simultaneously.

The north, south and east gates, including the eastern river gate and all nine towers between them, instantly burst into flames.

As the screams of men burning alive echoed into the night, Alice and the Haigok riders steered their winged monsters back into the sky. They didn't return to the clouds. They simply turned their beasts around and made their way to the towers on the other side of the city.

***

"By the gods," David gasped.

"I believe that's our signal," Schoenbach hollered. "Look. The gate is down."

David saw the towers on either side of the entrance engulfed in fire. The gate lay crumpled and broken.

"What about the guards on the wall?" Lor called.

"They busy looking at dragons," Yuri replied. "We go now."

The big man saw that the reptilian was right. All the men on top of the wall that he could see had diverted their eyes, either to the dragons sweeping over Woodmyst or to the burning towers.

Without speaking, David started running across the open ground between the farmhouses and the toppled eastern gate. Emily fell into step behind him, drawing her blade from its sheath as she ran.

"Stay here," Brondt instructed Amicia and Ursula. "Wait until I signal you to come."

They both dipped their heads compliantly before he, too, was racing across the pasture. Soon enough, all the others were charging past the small huts outside the walls.

Lor silently pleaded for the guards on the wall to keep looking away. They were getting closer to the glow of the fire that had enveloped the towers on either side of the gate. It would only take one man a mere moment to look down and spot them all.

The terrifying, deep trumpeting sound of a dragon roaring from far across the city kept the guards transfixed. Not one of them noticed the advancing troop of men and Agrodien warriors below.

David reached the rubble of the gate first and clambered over the mess. Some stones were loose and difficult to climb upon.

"Watch that there," he pointed out as Emily followed him.

Thornton and his men moved through the gate and around to the right, towards the barracks, keeping as close to the wall as they could. Emily followed as David waited at the gate for all the others to make it through. Schoenbach crept by him with Karlena and Akasati. They moved after Emily, drawing their swords as they found cover in the shadows.

Lor was next, leading the four northern men around to the left, where the stable house stood. Brondt moved to David's side, signalling his regiment to follow Lor into the darkness.

"Meet you somewhere in the middle," the commander quipped before disappearing from view.

Without warning, Yuri leapt through the gap. David felt the breeze from the reptilian's wake as he flashed by. So too, the other Agrodien warriors bounded over the rubble and into the city. They didn't stop to wish the man luck. They simply tore off along the street at high speed. Their task was elsewhere, and they knew what part they had to play.

David watched in awe as he noticed the warriors using their forelimbs as animals would use their legs to run. Their tails whipped wildly as they sprinted away towards the centre of the city.

Turning towards the barracks, David moved after Akasati, who waited at the edge of a shadow cast by the barracks, formed by the light of a burning tower. Moving into the darkness, his eyes adjusted quickly and he saw two of Thornton's men silently climbing a ladder that built into the wall.

"Who's that?" David hissed.

"Cobham and Sparrow," Thornton replied softly.

"What are they doing?"

"What I fucking told them to," the captain answered. "Watch."

The two men crouched at the top of the wall, one facing north and the other south, eyeing the guards on the parapet. The dragons calling and the blazing towers on the far side of the city still held their attention.

Sparrow peered down to Thornton and held four fingers up before pointing to the south. Cobham signalled *three* and pointed north. The captain nodded and slid a finger over his throat.

With that, the men pulled their swords free and charged silently. There wasn't much of a skirmish. The guards on the wall did not know what had hit them.

The rain, combined with the spectacle of dragon fire, provided the right amount of coverage for the two soldiers to perform their ghastly deed. Seven men fell to the parapet with fatal wounds on their necks and chests.

Before long, the two men returned down the ladder and gave a quick report.

"Section cleared," Sparrow said.

"Yeah," Cobham affirmed, "but we can't get to the next section from up there. The tower separating this section of wall from that one is burning pretty hot. We'll need to climb the ladder."

"That means we would have to take each section of wall piece by piece," Lieutenant Brook said. "All the towers are on fire now. This could take all bloody night."

Thornton grimaced. "What about the tower guards?" he asked.

"There's nothing alive in there, sir," Cobham answered.

"Good." He leaned against the barracks wall and tilted his head to see past the tower to the next section of the wall. "Lieutenant, take Cobham and Sparrow to the next section. Clear that parapet. Our task is to clear the western wall so we can let the ladies in. We'll concern ourselves with the northern wall after we raid the barracks."

"Yessir," Brook replied, tapping the other two men on their shoulders before slinking away to fulfil their task.

"Now what?" Emily asked.

"We go in and rescue your daughter and your son," Thornton answered, moving his gaze to David.

Thirty-Three

Takmel came tearing out of the assembly hall and stood atop the stairs leading to the large doors of the building. Several guards followed him outside, forming a barrier to each of his sides. More guards, standing sentry along the exterior of the hall, joined them. Their swords were in their hands and their stance signified that they were ready to defend their leader.

But their eyes mirrored Takmel's.

He stared disbelievingly towards the southern wall far across the market square, over the river and along the long avenue to the south gate. All the towers were ablaze, and the gate was a flaming pile of debris.

His eyes moved along the wall to the west, where he saw a similar scene.

Fire and more fire.

A great tearing sound above him forced him to look away from the damage and to a winged monster in the sky.

A dragon.

Two.

He saw more zipping around and moving about in the air.

"She's attacking me?" he yelled as the rain spattered against his face, not believing his eyes. He stomped down the stairs and into the market square, watching the beasts swoop along the western wall. One of them flew along its length, igniting a section that stretched between two towers near the river gate. Takmel watched on, his anger rising like the flames bursting from the structure, as the men on the towers flailed and screamed with their bodies alight. Several fell from the wall, ending their lives abruptly when they hit the paved streets below.

"Surround the Maji," one guard called from behind him.

He turned to see twelve reptilian warriors moving into the market square. They walked tall and proudly, each with long swords in their hands and their eyes locked onto Tamel.

The guards moved into place, forming a circle around their leader as the Agrodien drew closer.

"Duga!" the eldest reptilian, pointed with his sword to the right. One warrior moved in that direction. He then pointed to the left. "Kyrjaa, Ska'klo, Rabor."

Three of the reptilians fanned around the circle of guards slowly, sizing up the men as they moved into position.

"Varssk," the Agrodien continued, directing the warrior to the right. "Draav, Kavnu, Mralner, Bein, Nakrah, Nola'ee." He pointed his blade to an area by his side.

The female moved into place, her tail coiled and her teeth bared.

"Yuri," he said, introducing himself, thudding his chest with a fist.

Takmel beamed.

"Maji," he replied. He suddenly splayed the fingers of his left hand and stretched his arm towards one reptilian who had moved behind him. His hand closed into a tight fist as he turned his head to glare at the warrior.

The young Agrodien, standing tall and impressively built, imploded into a ball of blood-drenched flesh. A tremendous crunching sound filled their ears and a cry of pain was suddenly silenced as the reptile was crushed to death.

Yuri watched on in horror as thick blood washed over the ground, seeping into the gaps between the stone paving and reaching the feet of the guards surrounding this boy. This monster.

He gave a terrifying roar of rage and charged at the nearest guard, bringing his blade over his head and slicing through the man's helmet and deep into his skull. He retrieved his sword from his victim with a hefty tug and turned his attention to the next man.

Nola'ee was next to act, swinging her sword across from her shoulders, aiming to strike the guard nearest her along his belly. But he was ready, blocking her with his own blade.

Takmel watched with eager interest as the skirmish unfolded. His men outnumbered them two to one. And he could ensure a victory by merely adding a few blows of his own.

He saw Yuri lop the head off one of his men, and then stab through the chest of another. If that continued, the odds would be in the Agrodien favour before long.

Takmel turned to see two of his guards fighting with one Agrodien. With a clap of his hands, the boy crushed the reptilian instantly, as if in a vice. The warrior's shoulders and ribs cracked into each other and his chest burst open.

Yuri cried out in rage and glared at Takmel as he pushed his blade into the belly of another man before sinking his teeth into the guard's face.

"So, you are nothing but a beast." The boy smirked. "No wonder she likes you."

***

Brondt moved back to the eastern gate and signalled for Amicia and Ursula to approach. His men had cleared the parapet from the gate to the river. He just hoped Thornton could do the same to the north of his position. If not, he might place his wife and the other women at risk.

The two women hurried over the open ground as quickly as they could. Brondt helped them climb over the rubble of the gate and back to the level ground on the other side.

"Where are Lor and the others?" Amicia asked, noticing only Brondt's men.

"They've gone to find his sister," he replied.

"We should assist," Amicia told him.

"We have our task to perform," he replied. "Lor can look after himself."

She nodded.

"How close do you need to be?" he asked.

"There's a bridge over that way." Amicia pointed it out. "Just along this street. That should be close enough for us to see what we're doing."

"All right." Brondt turned to his men. "Surround and guard the ladies. We move together."

The troop regrouped and started along the road, heading south. They passed by houses with darkened windows and doors. Some curtains moved as people hid their faces. Others stood upon their doorsteps, watching the beasts flying above the city.

"Back inside," Brondt told them. But they didn't listen. The display was simply too much to ignore.

One door swung open as they passed by the houses and out stepped a familiar figure. Amicia recognised the woman immediately.

"Lucy?" she called.

"Come on," Brondt urged his wife.

"Wait," she told him. "It's Lucy. She was Tomas' wife." She turned to face the woman and approached her. "Lucy? You should be inside. Where it is safe."

"What is happening?" The other stared into the rain, watching a dragon sweep through the sky above the city. She suddenly looked terrified. "Where is Takmel?"

"Lucy, we're here to help..."

"Did you kill him?" she asked, and her voice became angry.

"Lucy." Amicia reached out to her, trying to place a gentle hand on the other's shoulder.

Lucy recoiled as if disgusted by the gesture.

"Don't touch me, witch," she spat. She backed away and looked towards the city's centre. "I must find him. I must tell him you are here."

She fled along a cross street.

"Lucy?" the queen called after her, but the other wasn't listening. She was gone.

"Come on," Brondt said. "We're almost there."

The group moved on along the street and stopped at the edge of the bridge. From their position, they could see the eastern river gate with its towers still blazing. Across the river, between the plumes of fire and smoke of two more towers, several men stood atop the wall.

"This will do," Ursula told them.

"Now what?" Brondt asked.

The women stood side by side, Amicia on the left and Ursula on the right. They stretched their hands towards the wall.

"Break," said Amicia, curling her fingers.

The wall started cracking and crumbling instantly, taking one tower with it. Stone and dust exploded and tumbled, taking the guards down and crushing them in the wreckage.

At the same moment, Ursula faced towards the southern wall.

"Strike," she ordered.

A shaft of lightning, jagged and bright, fell from the sky and into her body. It instantly shot through her outstretched fingers and towards the southern wall. There, it branched out, hitting each of the men on top of their chests.

"By the gods!" Brondt gasped.

"Sir," one of his men called, pointing to a small piece of wall to the south. The commander followed the soldier's gesture and saw a few men scrambling down a ladder and off the wall. He watched them as they ran into the streets, vanishing from view.

"They're too far for us to reach by foot," Brondt said, looking at Amicia and Ursula.

"We risk destroying houses and innocent people if we blindly aim our abilities," Amicia told him.

He nodded.

"Then we should proceed," he said. "We move to the centre of the city."

***

Thornton wiped his bloodstained dagger on the sleeve of his victim. The young guard stared up at the ceiling with wide, lifeless eyes. The captain turned to see that his men had dispatched another four men, one of whom had the keys to the cells.

"Bloody heck!" he heard a voice gasp from the next room.

He walked through an open door to see David and Emily standing over a tubby man who was cowering in a cot. Turning about, he noticed Schoenbach and the two Erilian warriors spattered with blood and six cots with dead men lying in them. Another twelve cots contained more young men who were holding their hands up in surrender.

"Killed them in their sleep, did you?" Thornton asked.

"They were armed," Karlena answered, pointing to a dagger in one man's hands.

Thornton checked around the nearby cots and saw blades lying on the floor by those who had given up.

"Bloody heck!" the guard gasped again, peering at all the blood.

"Shut it," Thornton growled. He then turned to Vawdrey. "Find some cord and tie these bastards up."

"Yessir," the other replied, tapping Jendryng on the arm. The younger man followed him out of the room.

"We have the keys to the cells," Thornton told David and Emily. "It might be better if you two go in first. I think the girl might respond better at seeing a face she knows."

Emily nodded and left the room with David in tow.

"Bloody heck," the tubby guard said again.

"Gag this one," Thornton commanded to no one in particular.

**

Alice swooped high around the assembly hall, spying the Agrodien warriors surrounding Takmel and his men. It didn't look all that favourable for her friends, so she decided to try to get to them as quickly as she could.

Urging Liana to the north, she shot out of the city and past the northern wall. Leaning back, the dragon obeyed by climbing higher and higher until Alice leant sharply to the left.

Liana banked around and faced the city.

Alice moved her focus to the one target she needed to destroy before facing the Maji.

It was near to the western wall, surrounded by a large lawn and bordered by an iron fence.

The great oak.

"Go on, girl," Alice called to Liana.

The dragon dived for the city, directly towards the tree. Its giant outstretched limbs still bore many leaves of orange, red, and yellow. Autumn had not taken them all.

But fire would.

Liana opened her great jaws and spat a long, wide jet of flame at the oak.

As she did so, Alice unbuckled the leg straps holding her to the saddle on the dragon's back.

As Liana swooped low to the ground, passing over the flames that took hold of the tree, Alice leapt. She hit the grass a short distance from the tree and rolled to her feet.

The dragon continued into the sky, turning to the left as she reached the river, circling the girl at some distance. Waiting.

Alice turned to watch the tree.

She shed a tear as she considered what it meant to her. It was where her father's ashes had rested; a place where she felt close to him, which made her feel guilty for what she had just done. As if she was killing him all over again.

But it was also the meeting place where the Seven felt most powerful. She believed it was a source point of their strength and, if she could destroy it, perhaps its destruction would weaken their connection.

It burned slowly, not to her liking.

The remaining leaves still clinging to the outstretched branches blazed brightly, but the bulk of the tree had barely a spark upon it.

Alice wiped her eyes and looked to Liana, who was passing over the northern wall. With a wave, she beckoned the dragon towards her. She then pointed to the tree.

The magnificent beast adjusted its trajectory and spewed another barrage of flame over the branches and trunk of the great oak. Alice could feel the force of the dragon's breath, the heat blowing against her body like a wave, and saw steam forming in the falling rain around her.

Liana swept back into the sky to resume her circling of the girl.

Behind her, another dragon swept along the western wall, igniting the parapet. Most of the guards had taken the hint from the previous attack and had made it to ground level.

The tree was fully alight, crackling and burning away. One of the large, thick limbs reaching over the lawn buckled and bent. It groaned loudly before it snapped and splintered where it met the trunk of the tree and crashed heavily to the ground. Sparks and orange embers exploded into a cloud of stars.

Alice turned away and trotted along the path and out through the gate that surrounded the old ruins. There she turned left and started along the street towards the market square, a few blocks away.

Thirty-Four

The sound of the cage door unlocking startled Arthur. He had heard unfamiliar voices reverberating along the corridor, but wasn't able to determine who they belonged to.

"Mama," Catherine whimpered from the cell next to him. He turned his head to see, feeling a sharp pain in his spine. His eyes couldn't focus, seeing only the bright blurry flicker of the lantern on the wall outside of his prison cell, and dark, blob-like forms moving beneath.

"Catherine," a familiar voice replied. Although he couldn't see, he knew there were tears and smiles. Catherine's boots clicked against the stone floor as she raced to the pen door. The bars rattled as she gripped them.

"Arthur," she said.

"Where?" another familiar voice asked. His father.

"Baba," Arthur called out as loud as he could, trying to form the word with his swollen lips. "Baba, I'm here."

"Arthur?" David called to him, moving to the door of his cell just as the unmistakable clink of Catherine's door unlocking reached his ears.

He wasn't able to observe, but he knew there was embracing.

"Mama," she said, her voice muffled.

"I have you," Emily sobbed. "I have you."

The lock of his cell door snapped open and the soft screech of the hinges signalled it opening.

"Arthur!" David raced to his side and tried to lift him.

The boy cried in pain.

"Careful," Catherine called. "They hurt him badly."

"By the gods," David gasped. "What did they do to you?"

"Baba..." Arthur tried to speak.

"What have they done with your arm?"

"Baba, where is Alisss?" he asked.

"How can we move him?" David asked.

"I don't think we should," Emily replied, moving to the boy's side. "Baba?"

"I won't leave him here," David told her.

"Where is Alisss?" Arthur asked again. "Is she sayph?"

He heard boots clicking, walking away in rapid fashion.

"Caphrihn!" Arthur called as loudly as he could.

Emily turned to see that her daughter had vanished.

"Caphrihn," Arthur yelled again. Pain shot up and down his spine, through his ribs, into his head.

"Catherine," Emily cried as she took off down the corridor after her daughter.

"Shhh," David hissed. "Quiet, son. I won't leave you alone. But I don't think we can take you out of here right away. It's not safe yet."

"Alisss?" he asked again. "Dell me."

"She's attacking the city from the air," David informed his son. "She has brought the Haigok."

"Dragons," he said clearly; more clearly than anything else he could say.

"Many dragons," his father told him.

How he wished for his vision to return. How he wished he could see those magnificent beasts in the air.

＊

Catherine raced by Thornton and his men and out into the night. Emily gave chase, suddenly finding Akasati and Karlena running alongside.

"Catherine," the auburn woman called.

"Save your breath," Karlena told her. "She flees towards the market square."

Emily heeded the other's words and focused on the run. The market square was the intended meeting point for all of them. It was more than possible that Catherine was privy to this through her connection to Alice, Amicia and Ursula.

***

Lucy ran onto the edge of the market square where ten reptilian beings scuffling with twenty or so guards surrounding her husband. She started towards them, calling Takmel's name.

"Stay back, Lucy," he called to her, holding his hand up. "It's not safe here. You should return home."

"The witches are here," she hollered. "I saw them."

He looked to her for fleeting a moment, distracted. How was it he wasn't able to sense them? How could he not know that they would be here too?

Of course, they would come.

He suddenly felt self-condemnation for his own arrogance.

He thought he was safe.

He thought he was stronger.

He thought he understood them.

But here they were, working their way towards him.

Bein sliced down three of his opponents in an instant. Takmel quickly regained composure and turned to the warrior. He raised his hand and flicked his wrist as if brushing an ant from his sleeve.

The Agrodien warrior tumbled and rolled over the wet stones of the market square as if thrown by a significant force. He came to a stop by the side of the street bordering the north of the square.

And there she was.

Robed and hooded with her sword hilts protruding from under her cloak, she crouched beside the fallen reptilian and lowered her face to him. Bein lifted himself from the ground and bowed to her slightly.

Takmel watched on as she stood to her full height again and started towards him.

He felt his heart skip a beat as lightning lit up a cloud from the inside, revealing the silhouette of a dragon circling above.

"No," Lucy screamed with rage. She tore across the square towards the hooded girl with her hands stretched out like claws.

"Lucy, stop," Takmel called, but she continued. She screamed as she bolted towards the girl.

Nola'ee saw the threat and left the fray to intercept.

"No," Alice called, but the Agrodien female felt compelled to perform her duty and protect the Kayl'sro.

Her sword flashed and struck the woman in the chest.

Takmel cried out loudly, as if he was in pain.

Lucy fell to her knees, her jaw dropped and her hands clenched at the blood spilling from her sternum. She turned her head slowly to face him.

"Takmel?" she whimpered before falling lifelessly onto the wet stone.

He felt his anger grow hotter and hotter until the pressure built and an almighty cry escaped him. With a great lunge, he bounded over the heads of the Agrodien warriors, standing between himself and his fallen wife, almost as if he was flying. He knocked Nola'ee off her feet by smacking his heel into the side of her head. She dropped her sword with a clang and rolled over and onto her side, half-conscious and giddy.

Takmel bent and retrieved her sword from the ground. He lifted it above his head and prepared to bring it down across the female's neck.

Suddenly, he felt himself being knocked off his feet. He rolled across the stone pavers a few times before coming to a stop. Looking back, he could see Lucy's body a few yards away. Beside his fallen queen stood Alice with her swords held tightly in her hands.

He sprang up and raced towards her, screaming wildly, with Nola'ee's sword in his hands. She prepared herself. She let him come.

Takmel lifted the Agrodien blade over his head and brought it down. Alice blocked his blow and spun to her side, kicking with her right leg and sending him sprawling on the ground.

He responded by swiping his hand to the left, knocking her off her feet with an invisible arm.

Alice landed hard, quickly regained herself, and leapt to her feet. He was already running for her, sword in his hands again.

She pulled her dagger from her belt and threw it at him. It stuck hard in his thigh and caused him to topple over, hitting his chin on the stone pavers. His teeth clenched shut on the tip of his tongue and blood filled his mouth.

He howled in frustration and punched the ground with his bare knuckles, breaking the skin. Rising to his feet, Takmel plucked the knife from his leg and tossed it aside. He stretched his fingers towards the girl and closed them slowly.

Alice felt her body tighten. Her leather breastplate creaked and groaned as an immense amount of pressure pushed in on her from all sides. The pain was unbearable.

She tried to scream, but her lungs were emptying all of her air and her muscles wouldn't let her take any more gasps to save her life.

Dropping to her knees, she tried to counter his spell by lifting her own arms. An invisible bond drew them tightly to her sides.

Takmel laughed. His eyes, filled with rage and hatred, bore a sense of glee as his fingers tightened more and more.

Suddenly, the pavers split open around his feet, splintering into tiny shards. The shards lifted from the ground, moving as if tiny leaves caught in the wind. They circled him, moving faster and faster like a tiny vortex.

Faster and faster they spun.

Round and round.

His eyes widened as he considered this new occurrence.

A sharp sting across his brow and the feeling of warm blood flowing into his left eye caused him to lower his hold upon Alice and instinctively touch the wound.

Then came another bite across his cheek.

Another like a splinter of stone ripped his right ear lobe open.

He screamed.

Turning, he saw Queen Amicia reaching out towards him.

The spinning whirlwind of rock tightened in upon him, drawing more blood, tearing open more skin on his hands and face.

Mustering all the strength he could, he aimed his arms in her direction, knocking her off her feet, flinging her into the air before she smacked against the wall of a nearby building.

The small fragments of stone flittered to the ground around him.

Takmel spun on his heels, feeling blood trickling from countless places over his bare skin. His eyes landed upon Alice, who was on her knees, tried to get to her feet. He could see she was having difficulty breathing and planned to use her weakness to his advantage.

He stretched his arms towards her again and...

The world went as bright as it ever could.

He felt as if he was falling sideways. In fact, he was.

By the time his eyes refocused and he came to his senses, the ground was approaching rapidly. His head struck first. He rolled a few yards and crashed against the guardrail of the wide centre bridge of the city.

He peered across the market square to see another woman with lightning wriggling through her fingers. She lifted her hands again and thrust them towards him. Bolts of lightning shot out from her fingers and closed the distance at an incredible speed.

But he was faster.

He waved his hand and knocked her off her feet, causing her aim to be misplaced so that she struck the side of the bridge. Sparks and red hot chips of rock burst from the stonework.

"You bastard," Brondt bellowed, charging for the Maji at full pace, his men behind him.

Some of Takmel's guards saw the attack and broke from their skirmish with the Agrodien warriors, intending to intercept the commander's assault.

Takmel got up and scowled as he spat a mouthful of blood onto the ground.

"Enough!" His angry voice boomed like thunder.

A wave of invisible power emanated from his lips, spreading out and knocking all who were in the market square off their feet, including his own guards.

Now, he would destroy them.

Now, he would tear them apart.

Now, he would...

He felt her left hand upon his chest and her right on his forehead. She had him from behind.

"Why are you so upset, my love?" she hissed into his ear.

This was unexpected.

She kissed his neck and whispered into his ear one word.

"Absorb."

He felt his heart stop and his body became rigid.

His mind became a haze, as if drifting away to sleep.

His vision became blurry and the world around him seemed to cease entirely.

She was doing it.

She was stealing his life away from him.

Pale tendrils of vapour-like light started seeping from his skin.

The tiny wounds on his face opened wider.

Blood spilled over his cheeks and down his neck.

He felt weaker and weaker with each passing moment.

"No," he tried to scream, emitting nothing but a whisper.

He fought, trying to regain control.

Pushing past his weakening state, he saw only one way out. His body didn't matter now. He needed to gain control of his life force. He forced his mind to become clear again. His vision improved and his senses renewed.

He could see the gathering in the market square rising to their feet. All of their eyes fixed upon him.

Even his own guards seemed engrossed.

"No," he said louder, balling his hands into fists.

The pale vapours transformed into dark smoke. The alteration spread over him like a rushing wind. Inch by inch, piece by piece, solidity replaced with a black vaporous mass.

Her arms slipped through his form, almost causing her to stumble.

Seizing the opportunity, and feeling weakened by her touch, he did the only thing that he could.

He fled.

All eyes looked on, stunned and confused. They watched the streaming black cloud as it darted over the side of the bridge and westward along the river bank and out of view.

Alice crouched by Nola'ee. She was staring at her sister, who was still standing on the bridge.

"Yuri," she called. The Agrodien raced over to her and knelt beside the injured female. "Take care of her."

"Yes, Kayl'sro," he grunted as the girl rose to her feet.

Without taking her eyes from Catherine, she raced across the square, along the bridge, where she wrapped her arms around her sister. The older girl was taken aback, not expecting such treatment from her sister after all that had happened.

Alice was already in tears.

"I missed you," she blubbered.

That was it.

Catherine felt her knees weaken, and the corners of her mouth tighten. She put her arms around her little sister and cried. It wasn't long before the two of them felt another embrace them upon the bridge.

"Mama," Catherine whimpered as Emily tightened her hold.

Thirty-Five

Alice crouched beside Arthur, who still lay in the prison cell cot. She wore a few scratches on her face, but they were nothing to what they had done to him. She tried to kiss him on the lips, and he tried to allow her to do so, but he protested after the pain became unbearable.

"We should move him back to the house," she told David, who watched on from the cell door.

"It's too far," he replied. "Even with a wagon, the trip would be too far and rough."

"Not to the cabin," she said, shaking her head. "Here. To our house here."

He could almost smack himself up the side of the head for not thinking of it.

"I'll find a cart," he replied, dashing along the corridor.

Alice turned back to her husband. Arthur was trying to find her amongst the blobs and blurry objects.

"I have news," she whispered. "I'm with child."

His eyes opened wide, and a broad smile stretched upon his face.

"Yeah?" he asked.

"Yeah." She smiled back.

"Is ihd mine?"

She laughed.

A warmth came over her, starting in her chest, and there was a sudden need, a compelling urge to act.

"Hold still," she told him. She placed her right hand over his brow and her left over his chest. Closing her eyes, she controlled her breathing and whispered, "Heal."

She opened her eyes and peered down at him.

There was no difference in his appearance.

The bruises were still there, his lips still swollen, his arm still missing. She'd thought that maybe, just maybe, she could sustain and renew.

She was one of the four, after all. Each of them took on a quality of the gods. Amicia had the traits of Areang and could manipulate the earth. Ursula bore the merits of Haan with the ability to manipulate the sky. Even Catherine demonstrated the likeness of Grolle and wielded death like a tool.

But she couldn't bring renewing energy to her own injured husband. The assets of Gwendra, the goddess of life, seemed to manifest differently. She considered that and remembered the life growing inside of her. Perhaps that was her gift.

"I can see you," she heard him say with coherent speech. His eyes moved over the features of her face. "You're hurt."

"I'm fine." She beamed and moved his hand to her stomach. "We're fine."

***

After moving Arthur to a bed in the old Warde house, Alice returned to the market square. Ursula had reached into the sky, and with a wave of her hand, pushed the clouds away. The girl remembered doing something similar once, when she was in the glade. The dragons had gathered near the bottom of the steps leading up to the doors of the assembly hall.

The Agrodien warriors, along with Brondt and Thornton's men, had surrounded the guards of Woodmyst. More armed men were making their way to the square, where they handed over their weapons and joined their comrades, sitting in a group under the careful watch of Yuri and his reptilian fighters.

"Release them," Alice commanded.

"Kayl'sro?" Yuri objected.

"Set them free," she reiterated. "We have no reason to keep them prisoners."

Yuri shrugged and reluctantly signalled the other Agrodien to sheath their swords.

"You free," he growled at the guards of the city.

One of them gave the reptilian a puzzled look.

"But," he said. "We live here and have nowhere else to go."

Alice heard the soldier and turned to face him.

"I give you a choice," she said to all of them. "Serve me or serve the Maji. If you serve me, you will be welcome here. If you serve him, pack your belongings, collect what is yours and leave tonight. No one will stop you. But, if we see you on the battlefield again, and you are amongst those who oppose us, we will give you no clemency."

The captured soldiers sat on the wet ground, dumbfounded. They probably would have sat there all night until dawn if it wasn't for William Vawdrey.

"Go on, get," he hollered to them, like someone chasing off a stray dog. He even kicked the air in jest.

The captives hurriedly got to their feet and moved off into the city.

"Do you think that was wise?" Brondt asked her quietly.

"Most of them were under his spell," she explained. "Others were acting out of fear. Only a few of them are actually loyal. I think they will be the ones to flee back to their homelands in the west."

"I heard a name from some of those captured men," he told her. "Dakoth Risha. He supposedly came from Ironfields. The men told me he had a hand in what happened to Arthur."

"If we find here him," she replied, "I want him put in chains. If not, I'm sure we'll meet up with him again."

Amicia approached the two of them, eyeing the guards of Wood-myst as they dispersed into the night. She then looked up at the clock hanging high upon the assembly hall's façade.

"Still works," she noted with a tiny proud nod before turning her attention to Alice. "Several who were in close servitude to the Maji are waiting for you inside the hall. One is of particular interest. A master bookkeeper. He claims to have news of the Mirikin."

"The Mirikin are a thing of the past," Brondt growled. "He's simply trying to make a claim to earn favour with you."

"The Mirikin could have been renewed," the queen put in. "The Maji is a product of the Mirikin and therefore a continuation of it. Maybe he was re-establishing its hold. It may be worthwhile listening to what this bookkeeper has to say."

"And then we'll lop off his head," Thornton said from nearby, listening to the conversation.

Alice stifled a laugh as she peered back to the west. She could see the red glow of the great oak burning against the buildings and the city's wall.

"I have no doubt that's what Takmel was attempting," she told them, replying to Amicia. "But we will listen to what this man has to say. The four of us."

***

Four high-backed chairs rested upon the platform in the assembly hall. The sisters sat in the middle, Alice on the right and Catherine on the left. Ursula sat beside Alice and Amicia beside the elder sister.

Master Bookkeeper Lewis Drayton stood upon the stone floor at the base of the stairs leading up to the platform. Standing beside him were two Agrodien warriors holding long spears. One big male stood on his left and a tall female, with a bandage wrapped around her head, on his right. Drayton's body trembled with fear as he moved his attention to each of them in turn. Pausing on Catherine, seeing a familiar face, he smiled nervously.

"My lady," he said, acknowledging her with a slight bow.

"My sister doesn't share my patience, Master Bookkeeper," she warned. "Best speak your mind now."

"Of course." He bowed again. "I believe the Maji was attempting to bring the Mirikin back into power."

"They were never in power," Amicia snapped. "I know this for I was Mirikin."

"Ah, yes," he allowed. "Of course. But I think it was his plan to establish their power around the land. He has sent ships with his queens to port cities around the coastline. Just as the Mirikin were during the days of the Sovereign."

"You don't think that we are aware of this?" Catherine asked. "I was privy to this information, Bookkeeper."

"But did you know the number and its significance?"

"The number of witches?" Amicia queried.

"Yes," he answered.

"Ten," she told him. "It has always been ten."

"But not all are witches this time," he added.

Alice felt a cold shiver run up her spine.

"Lucy," she gasped.

"What?" Ursula asked quietly.

"Lucy wasn't a witch," Alice told her in a whisper.

"Explain," Catherine commanded the old man.

"He needs nine wives," the bookkeeper replied. "He told me so himself. It doesn't seem to matter if they possess abilities such as you do. He just needs the number."

Alice leant forward, and across her sister's lap to speak to Amicia.

"How does this work?" she asked. "How can a number be the source of his power?"

"I don't know," she replied. "But he could accomplish this much with eight wives who had abilities and one who did not. Imagine what he might have been capable of if all of his wives were to have been gifted in such a way."

"He intended for you to be one of his wives," Catherine whispered to her sister.

"What?" Alice sat up straight.

"Before he chose Lucy," she clarified. "He had you on his mind for a long time."

Alice tried to push that thought out of her head and returned her gaze to the old man at the base of the steps. He grinned at them with a prideful, arrogant gleam spreading over his face.

"Have you more to say?"

"I simply cannot believe how blind you all are," he chuckled. His eyes moved over each of their faces, pausing when he reached Queen Amicia. "You have no idea at all. Do you?"

Brondt, standing to the side of the raised platform, stepped forward.

"Be careful with your words when you address the queen, sir," the commander cautioned.

"What do you speak of?" Amicia asked the old man, lowering her brows as she locked her eyes to his.

"For years, he had you fooled," Drayton shook his head. "Even during the days of Chief Gyfford, you couldn't see."

"See what, bookkeeper?" Alice queried. There was a hint of anger in her voice.

Drayton sniggered. His voice crackled as soft hissing breaths escaped him, growing louder and louder.

"Talk," Nola'ee jabbed the old man softly with the tip of her spear.

"Right under your noses!" Drayton burst into loud laughter. His voice reverberated through the room, bouncing off the stone walls around them.

"You had best talk before I instruct my guards to run you through, old man," Alice commanded, growing impatient.

"We sent supplies and materials far and wide," he told them, trying to compose himself but still tittering. "We loaded ships in Dweagan and sent them to all corners of the land."

"Loaded with what exactly?" Ursula asked.

"Timber, stone, tools and food."

"For what purpose?" enquired Catherine.

"See?" Drayton pointed to her. "You were right there the whole time, and you were none the wiser. He did it all without you even knowing."

"Knowing what?" She got up angrily.

Alice reached to her, taking her hand and gently pulling her sister back into her seat.

"Knowing anything at all." Drayton snickered. "The palace in Dellmoor has been repaired. The wharves of Blackshore and Erimoor are restocked. Wintermarsh has been building an army for him while your good friends in Dweagan have obeyed his every command. But that is nothing compared to this piece of information. And I want you to listen very carefully."

He looked around and noticed all eyes upon him. The women were seated on the platform. The Agrodien guards to his left and right. The men to the sides of the room and by the large doors of the assembly hall.

All of them were paying careful attention to his words.

"Blackrock Haven has been reborn," he said malevolently. His smile had widened and his eyes glimmered in the torchlight.

"What do you mean, reborn?" Queen Amicia questioned.

"The palace is rebuilt, and the township repopulated with men loyal to him."

"He lies," Brondt interjected. He moved to look at his wife's face. "We would know if the lands to the north were occupied in such a way. After all, they are our lands. Our people are there. We've not heard any reports from them or any ships that have come to our harbour."

"The ships frequenting your ports know not who they work for," Drayton sniggered. "Papers can be forged. And they were. Usually by my hand."

"It matters not," Alice told them. She stared coldly at the old man. "I will deal with all of your friends soon. I have one more question for you."

"Ask me anything," the bookkeeper bowed again in mock fealty.

"Where do you think Takmel has gone, Master Bookkeeper?" she asked.

"I think the Maji," he began, stepping forward and placing the toe of his boot on the bottom stair casually.

Nola'ee was quick to respond, pressing her spear tip against his throat. "Back," she growled.

Drayton stepped away, his eyes fixed fearfully on the reptilian.

"Master Bookkeeper?" Alice called.

"The Maji would be most likely heading for his childhood home of Wintermarsh."

"Thank you," Alice said, leaning back in her seat. She then looked at Yuri. "Place the bookkeeper in the darkest, dirtiest, most rat-infested cell you can find."

"Kayl'sro," Yuri acknowledged her with a nod, and grabbed the old man aggressively by the scruff of the neck.

Drayton let out a pitiful cry of pain as the Agrodien yanked the book-keeper towards the aisle before leading him through the large doors.

"What now?" Amicia asked.

Alice took a deep breath.

"We need to plan," she said. "We need to take Newholt back. We need to gather what forces we can and cleanse the land from east to west of all the Maji's influence. We need to be rid of the Mirikin once and for all."

Thirty-Six

The storm had passed by and a new day had dawned.

They still had the wind in their sails and were rapidly approaching Newholt. The skipper estimated another two hours and they would be able to sight the city off the port bow.

Tricia kept one hand on the rail as she peered over the side of the sterncastle deck. Her other arm wrapped around the sandy-haired boy's shoulder. He, in turn, had both his arms around her waist and his head pressed against her body.

The skipper, manning the wheel, watched on with a twisted interest. Something was not right about the spectacle.

He knew they had shared a bed, and while that may give him reason to be alarmed, he also knew that nothing sinister took place between them. She had not molested the boy. He would have said so if she had.

No, it was something stranger.

He wasn't able to put his finger on it until she started speaking to him.

That's when he knew; she had manipulated the boy.

She had placed a seed into his head and made it grow somehow.

"Would you like to come and live with me, Samuel?" she asked him. "I can give you everything you need and anything you want."

The boy looked up at her with loving eyes.

Never in the whole time had he known the boy had he seen eyes like that.

"Yes," he replied. "I would like that very much, Mama."

Epilogue

It took many long days and sleepless, cold nights of crossing miles of open land. He passed through ruined cities, not touched since the days of the Mirikin, some not inhabited since the Realm Wars.

He navigated the edges of the Core Lands and slipped over the waters of the Sea of Solace. There he turned north and followed the mountains, over steep rock faces and through deep valleys until he came to Ironfields.

But he did not stop there.

Pressing on, keeping to his vaporous form, he moved northward still. It wasn't much farther, but it was still far.

His energy was all but spent.

He needed to rest.

He needed to recover.

But he pressed on.

He pressed on.

Enlightening jubilation swept over him when he saw the palace for the first time in a little over six years.

It didn't look any different to how he remembered it.

The white banner of the White Mistress still flew high from the flagpoles on the roof and on the grounds of the castle.

He raced through the city streets, frightening some children and spooking some beasts, but others looked on with mundane glances, familiar with the shape of the Gomatha; the shape he had stolen.

He passed through the gates and into the doors of the giant structure. Through the hall and into the throne room, white and clean, where he passed by guards near the door and some servants who were dusting and cleaning.

There, at the far end of the room, a great marble throne stood atop of marble stairs rising from the marble floor.

He collected himself on the throne and there he rested.

"You," a well-dressed male servant called. He held a rag in his hand that he had been using to polish a table by the side of the room. "You can't sit there. That is the throne of the White Mistress, not a place for a spectre like you to taint."

He reformed, bringing what was mist-like back to solid again.

"I am Takmel Hamond," he said. His arms and legs twisted and bent into shape. Strand by strand, his muscles and bones took form. His ribs and flesh reformed from swirling strings of dark smoke. His face and body emerged through the shadow. "Son of Sumaiyya Tarkin. And this throne belongs to me."

The colour of his skin, the fabrics covering his frame, materialised. His dark, damson cloak flowed over his body and his hood appeared on his head.

"Maji?" the servant gasped before falling to his knees. "Forgive me, my lord."

The other servants in the room had stopped and watched the occurrence, spellbound by the appearance of the man on the throne. They dropped to their knees one by one as they comprehended who it was that had arrived. The guards stood rigid and brought themselves to attention. Their armour clinked slightly as their nerves took hold.

Takmel peered around the room with satisfaction.

He felt a sense of warm comfort as his childhood memories came flooding back. The whitewashed walls with familiar paintings, landscapes, and historical scenes. The polished floor and steps that he had sat upon when he was much younger. The white stone throne with tainted streaks and stains ribboned over its façade and soft, white cushions filled with goose down.

He let out a deep and long sigh.

"I'm home."

About the Author

Robert E Kreig was born in Newcastle, Australia and grew up in its outer suburbs.

He has always had a love for books, particularly well-told stories involving action, adventure and fear.

Some of Robert's favourite authors as a young reader included J. R. R. Tolkien, Stephen King, Orson Scott Card, Ray Bradbury and Frank Herbert. As he grew into adulthood, the list continued to lengthen, adding more influential writers such as George R. R. Martin, Matthew Reilly, Nathan M. Farrugia, Dan Brown, James Patterson, Michael Connelly and Lee Child just to name a few.

Inspired by movies like Star Wars, King Kong, Jaws, Jason and the Argonauts and other great adventure pieces, Robert listened to the voices in his head and entertained the strange visions dancing through his mind to assist him with writing his fantasy series The Woodmyst Chronicles.

Robert has penned ten books for the series which follow the lives of many characters, particularly focussing upon a family who must face many trials before the epic conclusion. Clashing swords, strange creatures, flying dragons and sorcery inhabit the world surrounding Woodmyst.

Robert has also written a standalone book, Long Valley.

Robert currently lives in Canberra, Australia where he hopes to one day become a full-time writer.

Other Books By This Author

THE WOODMYST CHRONICLES

From a faraway land...
...comes a new adventure.
The Woodmyst Chronicles is the story of a small community that faces the hardest of trials in a world filled with darkness, violence and magic.

Books In This Series...
THE WALLS OF WOODMYST
THE SONS OF WOODMYST
THE HEIR OF WOODMYST
THE WARLORDS OF WOODMYST
THE HUNTRESS OF WOODMYST
THE SHADOW OF WOODMYST
THE BRIDES OF WOODMYST
THE GODS OF WOODMYST
THE WEAPONS OF WOODMYST
A FAREWELL TO WOODMYST

LONG VALLEY

In the small community of Long Valley, nestled comfortably beneath snow-capped mountains, people quietly go about their business. Everybody knows everybody and there are no worries to give mind to.

But something has awakened.

A tragic accident near the valley's army base sparks a number of terrifying events, placing the local civilians in mortal danger.

A contagion is subsequently released into Long Valley, infecting pets, livestock, wildlife and people.

It's up to the local law enforcement and a small band of citizens to try to keep the town safe.

In the end, it becomes a struggle for survival as the people of Long Valley are overcome by the urge to feed.

THE CALM VOICE

No one in the remote town of Edwards Hill could have known that she was capable of such carnage.

Least of all her parents, the first to die.

Driven by the gentle words of The Calm Voice, she inflicts a barrage of carnage and death, leaving a trail of blood in her wake.

Her goal is to bring death to all who have hurt her.

All she needs to do is listen to The Calm Voice.

All she needs to do is just focus...

Just focus...

Focus...

The Calm Voice is a dark psychological novel surrounding the actions of one girl on a fateful morning in April, 2017. Kristin Matthews is fed up with her life, her oppressive parents, and her bullying schoolmates. She is compelled by a soothing voice thrumming in her head to seek revenge on those who have wronged her. At the top of her list is a trio of girls who have taunted her to breaking point. After careful planning, she embarks on a deadly rampage through Edwards Hill State High School, bent on destroying all her pain one final time. What follows is a haunting description of the day's events, culminating in an ending no one will expect.

www.robertekreig.com

www.whitekeepbooks.com